THE BOOK OF REVELATIONS

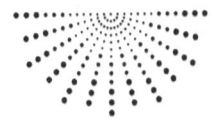

IDELLE KURSMAN

ISBN: 978-0-9965922-3-9 (print)

ISBN: 978-0-9965922-4-6 (ebook)

Cover design by Claire Brown Design

PROLOGUE

BRIGHTON, MASSACHUSETTS

Ozzy kicked a stone on the gravel road. He was so mad he wanted to kick it at somebody, anybody.

The principal of Brighton High School had to cancel their meeting because a mother needed to speak to him immediately.

Ozzy worked as a correspondent for a local paper, writing a monthly column for thirty-five dollars a pop, while collecting unemployment. It had been six months with no potential job prospects.

He threw his notebook, pen, and recorder in the passenger seat of his dilapidated car, cursing to himself but yearning to hurl them at the world so everyone would hear his frustrations.

Upon slamming the car door, he heard a ball dribbling. Then the sound of young guys talking and laughing. High school boys had gathered to play basketball.

Ozzy glanced over at them, turned away, and then did a double take. One of the boys caught his eye.

He had written the celebrity column for the *Boston Herald* for a few months before getting fired for embellishing a story. Ozzy fumed just thinking about it. How else was he supposed to get promoted if he wrote the same tired articles: this celebrity bought this house, that celebrity was engaged, another one signed on for this movie? His editor told him he wanted more heavyweight articles if Ozzy expected to move up, but he couldn't sniff out any meatier news. So he exaggerated a little. He was desperate.

Ozzy walked over and approached the fence surrounding the court. Putting his hands in his pockets, he tried to look like he was casually observing. That one boy had an uncanny resemblance to a famous actor. A teenage version with his blue eyes and tall, lanky build. If there was one thing Ozzy had spent time studying, it was the celebrities.

Another man came over to the fence to watch. Ozzy nodded to him, and in the most offhand manner, he pointed to the boy and said, "That kid looks so familiar. He must be my friend's son. I've got a son his age. He's going to this school in the fall, and I'd like to introduce them if that's who I think he is."

"That's Tim Goldberg. Nice kid," the man said to him. "Do you live here in Brighton, or are you moving in?"

"Oh, we're moving in. In fact, I'm going to call this friend tonight and arrange an introduction. My James would feel better if he already knew someone at the school," Ozzy lied.

"Yeah. My son's graduating this spring. I've got nothing but good things to say about this school," the man added. "The teachers and programs helped my son tremendously. He's got to decide which college he wants to attend." He pointed to the school building. "This school did him a lot of good."

"Yeah, you don't say? Well, hopefully James will have that

experience too," Ozzy said, shaking the man's hand before leaving.

Ozzy glanced back as he made his way to his car. If that kid was the son of the Hollywood actor, coming to this high school today would change his life for the better.

CHAPTER ONE

HOLLYWOOD HILLS

It was 8:00 a.m. when Ryan woke up and reached for his blue silk robe. Momentarily startled by the sound of a light snore, he turned and surveyed the gorgeous brunette sleeping in his bed. He had forgotten she was still there.

He had invited her to his sprawling Hollywood Hills estate after the party at the Point, the swankiest club in the entire city of Los Angeles. She barely looked twenty and had the makings of a supermodel – tall and leggy. The faint smell of the musk she wore permeated the sheets. Musk was his favorite scent – his first love always wore it. The woman lay flat on her back, her hands resting on her chest. Her mouth curled into a smile even while asleep. He noticed her makeup was still intact, and her hair appeared neat and combed even after a night of continuous lovemaking. Dead drunk last night, Ryan couldn't recall what her hair felt like. He fought the urge to touch it and find out if it was stiff from hair spray or gel.

After drinking and socializing until four in the morning

with little sleep, he needed time to himself. He intended to get her name and phone number. Forgetting he was in a relationship with Megan, Ryan thought about taking her out on his new sailboat for an entire day, chatting about her life and goals to get a feel whether this would be a long-term relationship or if she was only using him for media attention to advance her own career. Yes, a day-long trip was always his testing ground for a new relationship.

As Ryan stepped into the shower, he welcomed the quiet and isolation that allowed him to think. As he grabbed the shampoo to massage his scalp, his thoughts drifted to the two movie offers he was seriously considering. His fingertips gently rubbing his scalp allowed him to go into a meditative state to focus on each offer both more objectively and instinctually. One was the lead role in a Frank Sinatra biopic, working with a seasoned director; the other was an indie production, playing a southern slave owner helping finance the Civil War. Which had a better plot? Which would potentially generate more sales and advance his standing in Hollywood? Was either one Oscar material? He personally preferred the edgier, more challenging roles, and his body pulsed with excitement whenever he thought about winning an Academy Award, thereby cementing his reputation as a serious actor.

After a while, Ryan's thoughts shifted back to last night. His head still felt the buzz of the crowd at the Point. There he had met tons of hot women, and the champagne was the finest he ever tasted. He was so distracted he kept forgetting to ask the name of it.

Ryan never knew what he did to deserve such a lucky life. He never took time to contemplate it but simply enjoyed it. His acting career began when he was spotted by a talent agent while playing basketball with his buddies the summer before his sophomore year of high school. The man gave him the creeps the way he studied him, staring right at him as he moved around the court. During a water break, he was about to ask his friends how to get rid of this guy when the man came over and introduced himself as a talent scout. He gave Ryan his card, and his parents checked him out to make sure he was legitimate before calling. Since then, Ryan had taken one role after another, starting out with bit parts on television before landing small parts in movies. Most of the projects were successful and, in nearly all of them, his work received excellent reviews. He was now considered one of Hollywood's best and brightest, and he heard critics praising his latest role as a man who rescues runaways from a human trafficking ring, calling it "Oscar worthy." If he won, this would be his first Academy Award. But it was only October, and other actors had given stellar performances that could eclipse his before the February awards ceremony.

Ryan put a towel around his waist and used another to dry his hair as he sauntered back into his bedroom. The brunette moved slightly, and her eyelids flickered. His eyes hungry with desire, Ryan sat at the edge of the bed as she stretched her arms. When she opened her eyes, she stared around, seemingly struggling to orient herself to where she was. But once she caught sight of him, she relaxed and smiled. Overtaken by her big, beautiful eyes and sensual lips, Ryan inched himself closer beside her and prepared to taste her with his kisses.

"Morn', handsome," she said as she reached out to kiss his lips.

Their lips locked in what should have been a glorious reuniting of their bodies the morning after. Instead, their fairy-tale encounter evaporated. Her stale morning breath repulsed him.

"Mornin'," he mumbled, turning his head away as fast as

he could so she wouldn't see how her breath offended him. "Gotta get dressed and get going."

Glancing back at her, he saw she was observing him with her mouth turned downward in a frown.

"I didn't want to wake you," he said soothingly, attempting to grin in an effort to hide his disappointment. "How did you sleep?"

"Wonderfully." She smiled widely as she wrapped her hands under her head.

Ryan couldn't help noticing the nicotine stains on her teeth.

The woman scrutinized him for a moment and then sat up on her elbow in a sexy pose that would normally turn him on. But Ryan looked away and got up to open his walk-in closet. While choosing a pair of jeans and a white T-shirt, he dug into the recesses of his mind, trying to remember the woman's name. Turning around to study her again, he noticed the blood-red polish on her fingernails was chipped. Biting nails was a habit he found most unbecoming.

When he remained silent, she spoke. "I'm thinking of auditioning for the Gem Modeling Agency. You know, the man you were talking to last night signs models there?" She pushed back a strand of hair and gently tucked it behind her ear. "He said he's looking for models." She gazed steadily at him with a sexy smile. "So what do you think? Will you put in a good word for me?"

Ryan hung his head to hide his disappointment. *Either they want a commitment or they use you to get ahead,* he thought. *Another one using me to further her own career. Couldn't she be a little more subtle than that?*

But he lifted his head and faced her again. "Sure thing," he told her, and then ducked into his enormous closet to change.

"When can I see you again?"

"Ah, wait a sec," he called from inside the closed closet, pretending not to hear.

Instead of admiring her beauty, now he couldn't wait to get rid of her.

I'll just tell her I have a very important appointment first thing this morning, and I gotta leave right away. I'll take down her name and number and pretend I'll refer her to that modeling agency. What was her name anyway? Was it Becky or Angie or something?

He decided to refer to her as merely BB. Bad breath.

Ryan walked out of his closet ready to put the finishing touches on his appearance.

She was sitting up in the bed when he walked out of the closet. She must have been rubbing her eyes as she waited for him to come out because her mascara had gotten smudged, and the dark lines underneath her eyes reminded him of a football player. Her hair was no longer perfectly coiffed but rather sticking out near both her ears. "I'm going to take a quick shower," she announced as she sprang up out of the bed.

"Oh actually, I've gotta leave now for a meeting." He grabbed his Rolex from the nightstand. "The cleaning people are coming, and the whole place has to be vacant. Sorry, but I've gotta rush you out."

Ryan spoke softly and gently, but even he couldn't muster up a genuine appearance of regret.

BB's eyes narrowed. "Is there time for me to use the restroom at least?"

"Sure," he said, turning away to hide his discomfort.

He looked down in shame as BB slammed the bathroom door. He winced, hoping she hadn't damaged the hinges. Ryan reached for his phone and quickly called an Uber driver friend of his to discreetly pick her up outside the security gate of his home. This friend had done it many times before and knew how to keep things under wraps from the media, for which Ryan paid him handsomely.

In two minutes, she opened the door and marched out of the bathroom wearing the little black dress with spaghetti straps that she had on last night. She brushed past him to the front door without glancing his way. He could almost see her nostrils flaring as she stood by the door with her arms folded, waiting for him to escort her out. Fortunately, his friend had already texted him that he was on his way.

"I paid for an Uber to bring you home, or any place you want to go." Ryan smiled widely, hoping she would be touched by his generosity.

She grunted.

He opened the door, and she stomped to the gate, neither saying good-bye nor turning back. Ryan gave a signal to the security guard as she departed. His friend pulled up in his car.

He shrugged. *At least I didn't have to bother getting her name and number,* he thought. *Whatever her name is.*

Ryan headed for his Maserati. He knew he was very lucky to have plenty of money at his disposal for these occasional trysts. Sighing, he felt justified in his actions because the two serious relationships in his life had both ended badly. The first, which he considered the love of his life, ended abruptly and he never found out why. Kim was the second relationship. It was so promising until he found out she was using him to advance her career. She turned vengeful when she realized he didn't have the clout back then to help her. At a red light, Ryan bowed his head, remembering how she had lied to directors, claiming they were engaged and that he wanted them to star in a movie together. This was after he won acclaim as a supporting actor in a major movie and was even nominated for an Oscar. By the time he broke up with her, she actually tried to blackmail him by threatening to write a tell-all about their relationship.

Fortunately, Ryan wasn't a big enough star at the time to entice any publisher. Kim eventually moved on.

The blasting horn behind him alerted Ryan the light had turned green. He stepped on the gas. *Oh, well,* he thought. *I have to be content with occasional dates like BB. And Megan, of course.*

Megan was his semisteady girlfriend, though he had explained to her that he couldn't commit to an exclusive relationship. It was not in him. He convinced himself that she would understand that he would sleep with other women from time to time. Past girlfriends were shocked when they found out he had strayed, and Ryan couldn't understand why – he thought he made his intentions clear that he could never commit.

He shook his head, wondering what was wrong with them.

Hopefully, Megan gets it. She's a smart girl, he reasoned.

CHAPTER TWO

BRIGHTON

"You're sure you don't want me to come with you? I could call my boss now, and I bet she'd understand," Christine said, staring intently at her husband, hoping he would change his mind.

Daniel put down his coffee cup on the hallway table. "Listen, honey, if something comes up, I promise I'll give you a call. Now stop worrying and have a good day."

Christine Goldberg shook her head. "All right, then," she said as she walked out the front door.

Her heels clicked on the cement pavement as she hurried to her Honda Accord. Her new briefcase was a bit bigger and more stylish than the old one. She did not want to admit, even to herself, that it was getting too heavy for her to carry. Her boss kept giving her more portfolios to read through, and Christine would never complain about her aching back. Watching her struggle upon leaving the house, her husband gently suggested she buy a bag on wheels.

Christine put one hand on her hip and said, "You're making me feel old and weak."

"I'm just thinking about making your life easier," said Daniel. He was grinning, his palms up in the air in a show of innocence.

Christine shook her head again and trudged with her briefcase to the passenger side.

Tim and Trudy, their seventeen-year-old twins, followed her out the door with their backpacks strapped to their backs.

"Bye, Mom."

"See you later, Mom."

They waved as they walked to their bus stop.

"Have a good day, kids! Love you," Christine called after them.

As her children stood at a distance waiting with the other high schoolers for their bus, Christine wrestled the briefcase into the passenger seat before settling into the driver's seat. She relaxed her shoulders as she watched her husband wave and blow her a kiss. She winked and waved back at him as she backed out her car down the driveway. Her husband was a sweetheart, and she was lucky to have him. She only wished he would let her accompany him to the doctor. Medical tests were frightening, and there was no reason he had to play Mr. Brave and go alone.

On her way out of the neighborhood, she spotted Bob, the retired man who was widely known as "the gardener." He was planting more flowers in front of his house. He was all wrinkled and stooped over, but the wide, beige, floppy hat he wore every day made him endearing. Christine waved, but he was too busy tending to his flowers to notice.

Brighton, a section of Boston that felt more suburban than other parts of the city, was home to mostly middle-class people in their thirties and forties. They were upwardly mobile yet still struggled to pay their bills.

Christine forced herself to smile. Her husband was vice president of a start-up marketing company, and she was proud his bosses quickly noticed the improvements he had implemented in attracting new clients.

Daniel. At a red light, she closed her eyes and breathed in deeply. His tests at the doctor would show there was nothing seriously wrong. She kept repeating that to herself. Her loving, supportive husband was going to check out fine.

A shiver went through Christine's body just thinking about medical tests. She remembered her own pregnancy, how she had to go in and out of the hospital because she had early contractions with the twins for months. She had never been in such pain in her entire life. Her gynecologist reassured her that if she were carrying a single baby, it would have been a normal pregnancy. She remembered being forced to take a leave of absence from her job as a receptionist at the modeling agency because the twins were born premature and too fragile to go into day care.

After her harrowing experience, Christine was not at all shattered when she married Daniel and found out he was unable to have children. Still, she often wondered what a single pregnancy would have been like. Would it have been much less painful and more pleasant carrying just one baby? Would she have had the opportunity to continue working up to the time she gave birth? Christine had accepted housing from relatives and relied on food stamps during the first few years as a single mother. She was thankful when she was eventually promoted to her current position and her boss was understanding when she had to take time off to care for the twins. But she remembered others she worked with getting promoted through the years. Did she miss more promotions because she had to take so much time off? Were her coworkers actually more deserving? Was she overestimating her own talents? She would never know.

The Boston traffic interrupted her thoughts. Christine would have to fully concentrate as she navigated her way into the congested city filled with cars, trolleys, buses, and pedestrians. Christine parked her car in the parking garage of the modeling agency and then walked into the building, her shoulder-length blond hair bouncing as she smiled warmly and greeted employees who passed her in the hallway. Men stopped and attempted to make conversation with her, but she told them she was running late. Christine was still striking enough to turn the heads of men of all ages. At almost forty years old, she maintained her slim figure by working out during her lunch break. As she approached her department, her mind reflected on the family trip to Fenway Park to root for the Boston Red Sox in the 2004 World Series. They hugged and did high fives every time the Red Sox scored. It was such a fun, exciting time that she wished it could have lasted forever.

She had a solid family life.

Daniel was going to check out just fine at the doctor's today. She ignored the nervous flutters in her stomach that attempted to refute her struggling optimism.

They would grow old together and enjoy many more happy memories.

CHAPTER THREE

BEVERLY HILLS

Ryan parked his car in his parents' circular driveway. He checked his phone. Megan had texted. She wanted to get together tonight.

Maybe, maybe not, he thought. *It all depends if I can make a decision I can live with about these movie offers.*

Then again, a romp in the sheets might help settle my mind. I'll see.

As Ryan got out of his car and walked toward the front door, he passed the kitchen window and saw his mother, Sara, pouring herself a cup of coffee. Her eyes brightened upon seeing him, and they waved to each other.

"Finally!" she exclaimed as she opened the front door and planted a kiss on his cheek.

"What finally?" her husband called from another room.

"Ryan's here," Sara called back.

Even though they had allowed their son to buy them a swanky Beverly Hills home, they refused his pleas to provide them with a full-time cook and a maid.

"I don't share my kitchen," Sara would always respond, guarding it as if it was her sacred sanctuary.

The most they would agree to was cleaning help once a week.

"Your mother could use help with the cleaning," his father conceded to Ryan. "But I don't want people staring at us all day. We need our privacy," he insisted.

Ryan had rolled his eyes. Their home was spacious enough; he did not feel privacy was an issue but knew better than to argue.

"Come in, come in, dear." His mother ushered him in.

"Hi, Mom." Searching for his father, he found him in the next room lounging on his massive reclining chair in the living room. He was wearing his glasses on the bridge of his nose. His father peered up from reading the *Los Angeles Times*.

"Hi, Dad."

"Hi, son. Come on in. Mother just put up a fresh pot of coffee. She went to the bakery and bought you croissants," Jerry told him, his face lighting up like a candle. "How's the movie business going?"

Ryan was about to reply when his mother interrupted.

"And how's Krystal?" she inquired, raising her eyebrows.

Ryan's shoulders slumped. "Mom, Krystal and I broke up a month and a half ago."

"Krystal, Megan, Tori, Danielle! I don't care who it is! Just give me grandchildren already!" Sara shocked the two men with her wail, holding up her hands and looking up toward the heavens.

"Now, Sara, you're being ridiculous! He can't just go out and impregnate any woman so you can have grandchildren."

Ryan felt weary even though it was only nine o'clock in the morning. He toyed with the idea of telling them he had

17

forgotten about a very important meeting and making his escape.

His father seemed to read his thoughts. "Sara, if you're going to keep hounding him about grandchildren, he's not going to want to come here anymore. Stop this already."

Sara bowed her head and tightened her lips, capitulating.

"Anyway, with all his fame and money, women are just going to use him to move up and get attention for themselves. I don't have to remind you about Kim," he continued gently but firmly. "How many times do we have to go through this?"

"All right! All right!" She shrugged her shoulders and gently put her hand on her son's arm. "Come, have some coffee and something to eat."

Ryan bowed his head but let his mother lead him into the kitchen. He was one of the most sought-after actors in Hollywood. He made sure his parents lived like royalty and had nothing to worry about. Why couldn't that be enough? After having the two serious relationships in his life fizzle, he remained reluctant to venture onto that road again. He opted for casual relationships rather than screw up another serious one, figuring that would make his life easier.

Ryan trudged toward the kitchen with his mother. His father joined them. They were a close-knit family, and despite their little squabbles, most of the time they enjoyed each other's company. He began discussing with them his two script options while enjoying his favorite croissants.

"I always loved Frank Sinatra," Sara told her son.

"You playing a slave owner? I can't even imagine that," Jerry chimed in.

"That's what makes him such a great actor, Jerry. He can take on a totally new personality."

Ryan bit into his croissant, enjoying his parents discussing the roles. Then he glanced up at the clock.

"Oh, I've got to get to my meeting with Phil," he said, rising from his chair.

"We'll see you on Sunday for breakfast. That's always a more relaxing day for you," his mother said.

After kissing his mother and patting his father on the back, he headed to his Maserati.

* * *

LOS ANGELES

As soon as Ryan stepped into his agent's office, Phil jumped out of his chair with a wide smile and declared, "I got you the role of a lifetime, baby! It's got Oscar written all over it."

His agent's enthusiasm was contagious. Ryan quickly forgot about all his other cares as he took a seat. "Why don't you tell me all about it? I'm still debating between those two offers you told me about."

Phil made a face and waved his hand. "Those two don't hold a candle to this one. Just listen to this: a compulsive womanizer becomes a hero, saving a woman in jeopardy. She's got two small kids, and he rescues them from all sorts of henchmen, blackmailers, the mob, and even her crazy ex-husband. Women will be falling at his feet as they watch this cad make good and learn responsibility after years of spending his time on women, drink, and drugs. Men will love the action scenes. There's something in it for everyone. It's a story of redemption by fire and edgy as hell!"

Ryan raised his eyebrows, intrigued. "Let's go over it. I don't want anything full of stereotypes with a sappy ending."

Phil shook his small bald head vigorously. "No, no! I studied the script all night. Look at this." He held up his large cup of Nitro Cold Brew. "This is Starbucks' strongest stuff.

My instincts say, 'Yes, yes, yes.' Read it over and see what you think."

Ryan gingerly took the script his agent handed him. "OK, I'll look at it, but I'm not making any promises. I have to listen to my own instincts."

"Of course. Take your time and read it over. You know I never push you to take on a role you don't feel good about. But I must say, I haven't felt this confident about a script since I saw *Beguiled*."

That touched a nerve. His role in *Beguiled* had launched him from strong supporting gigs into starring roles.

"You want coffee?" Phil asked.

Ryan shook his head as he settled into Phil's plush couch and began reading.

As he read, he realized the character would be a tantalizing challenge. Beginning with a drugged-out, dissolute lifestyle, the character appeared hopeless and headed for an early grave, neither to be mourned nor missed but rather ridding the world of a destructive human being before his heroic transformation.

Ryan nodded and rubbed his chin. "I definitely want to keep reading. Thanks, Phil. I'll let you know. It does sound like it has more potential than those other two roles."

He got up and shook his agent's hand.

"Be in touch. I'm always on the lookout for you," Phil assured him as he came around his desk in short, jerky movements and gripped Ryan's hand warmly.

As he left the building, Ryan felt in his bones this could be another hit for him. His performance in *The Hunted* three years before was highly praised and a big box office draw, but other actors had even stronger roles and ended up nabbing the Oscar nominations. Ryan's last role, in *The Rescuer*, earned him a nomination, but other movies were coming out, promising to be blockbusters with critical acclaim. An Oscar would be a dream come true; it would firmly establish him as one of the great legends in Hollywood. He couldn't wait to tell his parents.

CHAPTER FOUR

BOSTON

Christine arrived at the office and warmly greeted her assistant, Linda Page. Christine's winning smile gave her a warm glow that instantly made others feel comfortable and accepted.

"How was your weekend, Linda?"

"Most of the time I was busy chaperoning my kids here and there. Can't wait until Rory gets her driver's license and lends me a hand. She's taking her driver's test next week. Keeping my fingers crossed." Linda brushed back her dark hair and then placed a few strands behind her ears, showing a flash of grey streaks coming in at the roots. "Did you convince the twins to apply to other colleges?"

"Nope. We had a long conversation with them this weekend, but they have their hearts set on Boston College. We're lucky they applied to a state school, but we want them to try another one too."

Linda nodded her head knowingly. "It's always good to have a Plan B."

"And a Plan C and D too," Christine said, her mouth a tight smile.

"Don't worry. Things tend to work out the way they're supposed to."

Christine raised her eyebrows and nodded as she went over her mail. She never felt comfortable keeping her employees at a cool distance; on the other hand, she never confided anything too personal because she feared she would inadvertently reveal certain details of her past that would make them lose respect for her.

After tossing advertisements in the trash, Christine headed into her office and, as always, viewed the Boston skyline outside. Her shoulders relaxed, and she found herself smiling: it might not be New York City, but having her own office in Boston with the Prudential Center looming above all the other buildings gave her the feeling she had made it to a certain degree. Christine reflected that she was not the luckiest in many areas of her life: she was never able to graduate college, her modeling career never took off, and she realized she would never rise higher than being one of the modeling agency's many representatives. She was good at what she did but not exceptional enough to move further up. Besides having a loving family, she had a career, albeit not a top-paying one. No small feat, considering she had to drop out of college and spend a few years struggling as a single mother.

Just as she sat down in the ocher leather chair at her desk, the phone rang. Upon seeing it was Daniel, she picked it up immediately.

"Hi, honey. How're you doing? What did the doctor say?"

For a moment, all she heard was silence on the other end.

"Oh, good, good," he reassured her. "The doctor wants me to come in again on Tuesday next week to go over the tests I had last week, but otherwise, he said I should just continue my life as usual."

Christine didn't believe him. She knew by the sound of his voice that something was not right.

"So the doctor said there's nothing to worry about?" she asked tentatively, reaching for a pen. Scribbling always calmed her nerves.

"No, nothing to be concerned about," Daniel said, trying to sound more cheerful. "But my parents called me before I had a chance to call you. They want the whole family to get together Sunday night for Rachel's birthday."

Christine slumped in her chair.

It seemed every time her in-laws were mentioned, she felt a headache coming on.

"Can't just you and the twins go?"

"Why don't you want to go?"

"You know the reason just as well as I do."

"Christine, don't you think after all these years they've finally accepted you? They really do consider you part of the family."

"It's more like they've resigned themselves to the reality that you didn't marry a Jewish woman like they hoped you would."

"Anyway," Daniel said, "I've got to go to work now. We can discuss it later, sweetie. Just please keep in mind that my parents really do like you."

Christine rolled her eyes. *You're talking like you're in la-la land again.*

But she refused to say it aloud. He had been through enough this morning with all the medical testing to make sure he didn't have cancer.

"All right," she answered, thinking, *I'll try to think of an excuse to get out of it by Sunday.* Aloud, she said, "Have a good day, sweetie. Love you. Hope these awful medical tests come to an end real soon."

"Believe me, I couldn't agree with you more. Love you."

She stared down at her messages and schedule. She had to begin the process of matching models with recently arrived job opportunities.

Time to quit worrying and get to work, she reprimanded herself.

CHAPTER FIVE

Los Angeles

Upon exiting his agent's office, Ryan gazed up at the sky. It was the first time he had taken a moment to appreciate the clear sunny day. No sign of clouds. With his role dilemma likely resolved, he felt a flood of relief, calming his rushing heartbeat. The city of Los Angeles was buzzing with traffic and pedestrians. Wearing his Ray-Ban sunglasses and his Lakers cap pulled low, Ryan wanted to make the most of the day before he read over the whole script.

He headed down the stairs and hurried to the parking garage while pulling up Megan's number on his phone. He had been wanting to try that new Italian restaurant everyone was raving about, and what better time than now?

"Hello?"

Ryan could barely hear her over the noise in the background. He had forgotten she was at a trade show soliciting clients for her insurance company.

"Hi, it's Ryan. Looks like I caught you at a hectic time," he apologized. "Wondering if you'd like to have dinner tonight, but we can go into details later."

"It is very hectic, and the answer is yes. Call me back in a few hours."

"Sure thing, hon."

* * *

Watching Megan come out of her apartment wearing her black leather miniskirt, Ryan was aroused by her perfectly shaped legs.

Her thick blond mane was neatly coiffed in a chignon. Her clear, oval-shaped blue eyes were her most striking feature. And that tall, slim body – she would look great even if she were wearing rags.

Ryan, leaning on his Maserati, surveyed her as she came over and kissed him.

"How are you?" he asked, staring into her luminous eyes. He didn't know what perfume she was wearing, but the strawberry-infused scent made him want to wrap his arms around her and consume her mouth.

She sighed and blew a strand of hair hanging on her forehead. "Another busy day at the office."

"You'd never know it by looking at you. Fresh and beautiful, as always."

Megan smiled as she took his arm. "I'm anxious to try this new restaurant."

"I've heard great reviews. I only hope you won't be disappointed."

She stared up into his eyes and said, "I'm never disappointed when I'm with you."

Ryan opened the passenger door for her. "I want this to be extra special. I know your birthday's coming up, and I don't know if I'll be in town to celebrate with you."

Her smile disappeared. "But I wanted you there at the party. I need you there. This is a traumatic birthday for me."

"Because you're turning twenty-five?" he asked.

Megan nodded. "Just think. In another twenty-five years, I'll be fifty. How scary is that?"

"But I'm closer to that age than you are."

He didn't wait for her to answer but gently closed her door. As he swung around to the driver's side, a dark mood overcame him. Would he still maintain his box-office appeal at fifty? Each time he went to get his hair colored, he noticed more grey hairs. He often studied himself in the bathroom mirror. What about those wrinkles under his eyes? His agent kept reassuring him makeup would conceal them. But how deep would those wrinkles get?

Ryan used to poke fun of people who kept getting plastic surgery. But what if he needed it and the media noticed a change in his appearance? Would he then be the subject of jokes on late-night TV?

He'd heard plastic surgery was addictive. He was afraid he would end up like Michael Jackson, a distorted caricature of his former self.

By the time he opened the driver's side and plopped down, he felt disheartened by these future prospects and had forgotten Megan brought up the subject.

"But it's a lot easier for men than it is for women," she commented. He turned to her and was at a loss as to what she was talking about. He didn't want to appear disinterested, so he asked her, "Why?"

"Sometimes, men look more handsome as they age, sexier and more sophisticated, but men just notice the wrinkles, extra fat, and grey hair on women. They're no longer considered desirable."

"Honey, I bet that won't happen to you. Look at Paulina Porizkova."

"And would you consider dating her?"

Ryan took a breath and said, "She's married and has kids. Even if she was single, what would we talk about?"

With that, he turned up the stereo and focused all his concentration on pulling out into the main road.

Megan began to speak, but Ryan cut her off.

"So I hear the pasta carbonara is particularly good there. So's their Caesar salad. I know you'll appreciate that after a hard day at work."

Ryan turned up the music a little louder.

"So where is the location of this movie you're starring in?" Megan had to shout over the music.

Glad they were off the subject of aging, Ryan relaxed his shoulders and his body loosened up.

"Actually, Phil showed me a script about another movie. I think it takes place in some big city in the East."

"How long will you be there?"

She spoke in such a low tone that Ryan had to turn toward her. He noticed her eyes moistening.

"What did you say, honey?"

"How long will you be there?"

"Oh, I don't know. If I take it, I'll have to go there for research for a few months. But don't worry," he said as he smoothed her cheek, "I'll be back and forth, and you can come and visit me."

When Ryan looked over, Megan was rubbing her hands on her knees. "I already used up all my vacation time for the year. We spent one week in Europe and one week in the Bahamas."

"Then I'll come back here every chance I get," he promised.

"I know you will. Your parents are here," she replied, turning to gaze out the passenger window.

They drove in silence the rest of the way to the restaurant.

CHAPTER SIX

BRIGHTON

By Sunday, Christine found herself out of time and excuses as she sat in the passenger seat of the car, staring straight ahead as she braced herself for another dinner at her in-laws'. Tim and Trudy chatted happily in the back seat, excited to see their cousins. Daniel glanced over at his wife.

"So do you have a busy week coming up at work?" He smiled.

"Same schedule as last week," was all she said, staring straight ahead without looking in his direction.

"Do you have to interview some more models?"

"A few," Christine replied sullenly and turned to look out the passenger window.

Observing their mother, the twins ceased their conversation.

"Mom, Grandma and Grandpa want to see you too," Trudy said to her mother.

"They love you," Daniel added, grateful he had support.

Christine closed her eyes. "You remember that comment your mother made the last time we had dinner together? She told us about her friend who was hysterical because her son was engaged to a shiksa."

"Honey, you know she didn't mean it as an attack on you. That young man was thinking about becoming a rabbi at one time. Her friend had been hoping he would end up going to rabbinical school. Besides," he added, "I took my mother aside and told her that was an inappropriate topic of conversation in front of you."

"Dad, you took Grandma in the kitchen, but everyone heard you," Trudy said.

"Yeah, you tend to talk loud when you're upset," Tim said with a grin. "You might as well as have said it in front of everyone."

"My mother did apologize."

"To you privately. I don't recall her saying anything to me."

"She was too embarrassed," Daniel said.

"But Grandpa told you he was sorry," Trudy added.

"He wasn't the one who said it."

"That's immaterial. He knew it was wrong, and he said it for my mother."

"Grandpa said he'll take us to visit BC," Tim chimed in. "He even offered to drive us for a tour of the campus if you and Dad are too busy that day."

They were all relieved when Christine relaxed her shoulders and her frown disappeared.

The kids were always a great help whenever they visited Daniel's family. Daniel's parents were good to the twins, whom Daniel had adopted after their marriage. In fact, his whole family embraced the children as soon as they came into their lives. Christine knew Daniel was as cognizant as she was of his family's shock and disappointment when he announced their engagement eleven years ago. She knew they still had reservations about her, but through the years, the twins and her dedication as a wife and mother had softened their initial outrage. The tightness in Christine's stomach loosened, and she was finally able to relax.

* * *

"Grandma, here they come – Uncle Daniel, Tim and Trudy, and the shiksa." Michael, ten years old, grinned mischievously, looking out the window.

"The shiksa's coming! The shiksa's coming!" Charlie jumped up and down and stared out the window. Even though he was only three years old, he wanted to be part of the action.

"Shhh! Don't say that! One of these days she's going to hear you, and then we'll all be in big trouble," their grandmother, Judy, reprimanded them.

Rachel, the boys' fifteen-year-old sister, rolled her eyes as she put away her magazine. "Yeah, you guys got to control yourselves. We don't want any fights or speeches. You remember the tongue-lashing from Uncle Daniel the last time."

The mention of their uncle was enough to silence their banter.

"Is that Daniel and the shiksa?" Harry, their grandfather, boomed as he trudged down the stairs.

"Umm, we agreed not to call her that," Judy said, glaring at him. "Harry, will you run a comb through your hair? You want to look a little presentable."

Harry headed for the downstairs bathroom, mumbling, "I'm an old man. Aren't I entitled to take a nap during the day? I spent forty years looking my best for my job. Can't I take it easy at this stage in my life?"

"Not when we're having company—" Judy began.

"Company, hmpf! My own kids and grandkids. Should I put on a shirt and tie too?" he growled as he headed toward the bathroom.

"Harry, just do it, please," Judy told him with a clenched jaw.

Harry rolled his eyes and obediently took a comb out of his pocket to go through his grey, fuzzy hair.

Judy was looking out the window. "And here are your parents," she said to Rachel and the boys. "I hope they enjoyed their night out alone last night... oh, I see Uncle Daniel's car up the road."

* * *

The brothers and their families entered the living room and began chatting.

"Hi! How's everyone?" Seth, Daniel's younger brother, shook hands with his brother and his nephew and kissed Christine and Trudy on the cheek. "Getting ready for college?" he asked the twins.

"We're still waiting to hear whether we're accepted or not," Trudy responded, biting her lip.

"Don't worry," said Seth's wife, Heather, approaching Trudy for a kiss. "It'll all be good."

After Heather greeted everyone, she exclaimed, "It was such a relaxing night without the kids. Christine, I'm so glad I took your advice and had them stay over at their grandparents'."

"Every couple needs a break," Christine agreed. "It did wonders for Daniel and me when the twins were little."

"And they let us do whatever we wanted. We drank

coffee, ate lots of ice cream, and stayed up late," Trudy chimed in.

"Yeah, it was actually a bummer when you picked us up," Tim added.

"I'll bet," Daniel replied in mock anger, but his wife had to swallow her objections. She never allowed the twins to drink coffee and was always strict about their bedtime when they were little. To this day, she encouraged healthy habits.

Grandparents are grandparents, she thought with a smile. Her own parents had listened to her instructions more carefully when they used to babysit, but you couldn't have everything.

Heather reached for Christine's arm and showed her the new pumps she was wearing.

"Very nice." Christine smiled approvingly.

"This is the style all the models are wearing, isn't it?"

Christine nodded.

"I got them on sale. Otherwise, they'd cost a fortune. With you, I feel like I have a fashion consultant."

Christine chuckled. Her sister-in-law considered her a fashion guru.

Daniel and Seth's mother came out of the kitchen, carrying a bib for Charlie.

Before any greetings, she put her hand over her chest and announced, "They were wonderful, but Dad and I aren't as young as we used to be."

"We know, but thanks, Mom. I think in a year Rachel will be able to take over the job," Seth said as he kissed his mother.

"I hope you had a good time last night."

"Oh, Judy! The break did us wonders!" Heather exclaimed. "We now feel refreshed and energized."

"Then it was all worth it." Judy smiled and turned to

Daniel. "Daniel, how are you, honey?" His mother studied his face. "The doctor said the tests were fine, right?"

"That's right, Mom." He kissed her and turned away so he would not have to lock eyes with her.

Tim and Trudy kissed their grandma and promptly went over to their cousins. Trudy put Charlie on her lap and soon got into a discussion with Rachel about hair and makeup while Michael begged Tim to arm wrestle with him.

Judy finally turned to her other daughter-in-law; she opened her arms to hug her but then settled on patting her shoulder awkwardly. "How are you doing, Christine?"

"I'm fine. And you?"

Harry emerged from the bathroom with his hair well groomed. He shook his sons' hands and kissed both daughters-in-law. The twins stopped what they were doing and greeted him.

As much as Harry was opposed to the marriage, Christine noticed he wore a wide smile when he came over to kiss her. She reasoned he knew she must have appeared uneasy when she was with her in-laws, but she couldn't help concluding he relished kissing her. Harry was a dedicated family man but appreciated other women from a distance.

"Come on, let's all gather around the table while the food's warm." Judy gestured to her family.

Everyone took a seat except Michael. He hesitated pulling out his chair.

"Michael, what's wrong? Have a seat," Judy told him.

Michael wore a serious expression that stopped all conversation. "Grandma, these Sunday dinners aren't going to work for me. I'm going to start baseball next month."

"Me too!" chimed in Charlie.

Everyone smiled. "Charlie, let's put your bib on," Heather coaxed her son while tousling his hair.

"Oh!" Grandma Judy put a serving fork on the chicken

tray. Her relaxed expression vanished. She turned to Harry. "Then let's start having Friday night Shabbos meals instead."

Harry nodded in agreement, and Seth said, "Oh, I love your Friday night meals, Mom! Chicken soup, gefilte fish, brisket…"

"I love those Shabbos meals," Heather enthused.

Everyone turned to Daniel and Christine.

"Friday night meals are fine with me," he said, and then turned to his wife.

All eyes fell on Christine. She felt as if the word "shiksa" was emblazoned on her forehead. It had taken Christine a long time to get acquainted with all these Jewish holidays and customs. Everyone waited for her response.

"S- sometimes I have to work late on Friday nights," she said.

"But we can make the dinner at eight or eight thirty, can't we, Mom?" Daniel asked.

Judy nodded.

Christine noticed Harry shifting around in his chair. He always went to bed no later than ten.

Her face red, she said weakly, "Sometimes I work later than that if we have a big project. If I have to be late, you can always start without me."

Everyone gazed down. Judy coughed.

Finally, Daniel broke the silence. "Why don't we take it one week at a time?"

"Now that sounds good, Daniel. I may even have to work late a few Friday nights myself," Seth said, with a glance at Christine.

"Judy, you've got to make this Italian chicken again, and not just when the family's over," Harry said, anxious to change the topic.

"Mom, it's great! Better than anything you could get in a restaurant," Daniel said.

Yet Christine noticed he was moving his food around his plate more than he was actually eating.

Deep in her gut, she worried Daniel wasn't being entirely truthful about his health. Try as she might, she couldn't get the whole story out of him. She felt Daniel was protecting her, but from what? She was his wife, not a child whom he needed to shield from the sadness of the world. Her shoulders drooped. At least he had told her more than he had told his own family. Christine closed her eyes and resolved that she would accompany him to his next doctor's appointment. No more vagueness or sidestepping answers.

"Christine, are they showing the latest fashions at the office?" Heather asked.Christine was so immersed in her own thoughts that she didn't even hear her sister-in-law's question.

Daniel touched her hand. "Honey, Heather asked you a question."

"Oh, I'm sorry. What did you say?" Christine forced herself to focus.

"Are you seeing the latest fashions at your office?"

"I should be seeing them next week when they begin auditioning more models," Christine answered. "I'll let you know what's in style this year."

"I've got to make a business trip to Philadelphia in two weeks," Seth said.

"For how long?" Harry asked.

Seth sat back, already looking haggard. "One week."

Seeing Heather's distressed look, Judy reached over and patted her hand. "Don't worry. Help is on the way. Besides, Rachel is a great help, isn't she?"

"When she isn't with her boyfriend," Heather said, her eyes directed toward her daughter.

Rachel shot her mother a glance. "Mom, that's personal!"

"So who is everyone here, a bunch of strangers?" Seth admonished her. "Mom's going to need your help with Charlie. If that boyfriend of yours is worth any weight, he'll understand."

Seth, Heather, and Rachel glared at one another. Tension quieted the room.

Judy turned to Trudy. "Trudy," she asked rubbing her hands against her skirt, "do… do you have a boyfriend?"

Trudy's expression clouded. She traced the flowers on the white tablecloth with her finger. "It's hard to have a boyfriend when your mother gets so worried you might come home late."

"Trudy," Christine said after clearing her throat, "I've told you there may be drunk drivers on the road late at night on weekends."

"But you do the same thing on weekdays."

"Yes, I do because they're school nights." Christine held up her shoulders in a defensive gesture.

"We're just looking out for you, as you well know, Trudy," Daniel interjected.

Trudy said nothing.

"Who's ready for the birthday cake?" Harry asked, impatient to end the argument. His wife rushed into the kitchen.

Christine welcomed another subject. She didn't want to talk or think about the twins dating.

Judy returned, her eyes sparkling like the candles on the birthday cake she held. Fifteen candles lined the edges of the chocolate cake, and one was planted in the middle for good luck.

Harry broke into the happy birthday song, and the others followed his lead. Rachel grinned from ear to ear, forgetting about her open spat with her parents.

As the cake was being served, Christine thought about the constant reminders to Tim about not drinking too much when he goes out on a date. She knew he confided to his friends that his mom was more than a little nuts.

I certainly don't want the kids to make the same mistakes I did. It's better they hold off with serious dating than to risk something happening to cause all their plans to fall through, she thought as she sampled a small piece of cake.

CHAPTER SEVEN

Los Angeles

Ryan returned back to Phil's office first thing on Monday morning. His step was light and his eyes were sparkling.

"Phil, I like the role. I like it a lot. You have a nose for finding the right scripts for me," he declared as he sat down in his agent's office.

Phil smiled in satisfaction. "I was a little hesitant afterward because they're not sure yet where to shoot this film. In some major city somewhere."

Ryan waved a hand. "You know I never hesitate to travel for a film. When can I start negotiations and researching the role?"

"I have to check with them. I'm sure they'll be delighted you've agreed to sign on. Tell is the hottest director in Hollywood, and he thinks this role is perfect for you. I'll get in touch with him and text you his reply." Phil rubbed his chin. "I'm taking my wife to Colorado this afternoon for a few days for our anniversary. We're going skiing. But don't worry, I always stay in touch with my contacts."

"I know you do, Phil. How many years have you been married? Thirty?"

"Twenty-five," he said. "And are you still seeing Megan?"

"On and off," Ryan replied. "Not steady."

Phil hesitated before saying, "Not all women are like Kim, you know."

"I know, but it never seems to work out. I'd rather keep it casual than get in too deep and take months to get over it."

"You can't let Kim put a stain on all your relationships."

Ryan shrugged. "There was another serious one I had earlier that ended abruptly. It was a sign I can't commit." He rose. "But I'm going to go on as I'm going, and I'm doing fine. I'm looking forward to getting all the research material I need and head to wherever they send me. See you soon and happy anniversary."

"Thank you. Sounds like a plan. We'll be in touch."

Ryan was glad Phil got off that subject. The men shook hands.

Upon leaving the office, Ryan tried to force his mind not to travel back to eighteen years ago, when his girlfriend cut him out of her life. He never wanted to relive those moments, and he squeezed his eyes shut to block out the memories.

"Mr. Monti! Ryan, wait!"

He snapped out of his reminiscing when Phil's assistant called him. "Oh, Ryan. Sorry, I forgot to give you this when you came in." She rushed outside and handed him an enve-lope. It was marked same-day express, but there was no return address. He barely noticed his name was in extra-large print on the envelope.

"Hmm, I wonder what this is."

"You've gotten letters like this before. They're usually a

request from a budding screenwriter wanting your help getting their foot in the door."

"Thanks." Ryan took it and put it in his inside jacket pocket, thinking, *I simply don't have time to help every aspiring screenwriter or author advance their career. If only they knew how little leisure time I have.*

He was tempted to toss it in the trash but then thought better of it.

I'll look at it later and have one of my representatives send out a nice letter stating I only accept scripts through my agent. If I'm told it's a friend's relative looking for a break, they'll change the wording a little to make it look like I've actually given it some consideration, he thought. *No sweat. No added pressure.*

Ryan checked his watch. He now had to go tape an interview for a talk show, discussing his latest movie. Right after a quick lunch, he had another interview, this one for *Esquire* magazine. Ryan sighed. This was the critical time to promote his latest movie, and he had to make plenty of public appearances.

By the end of the day, when he finally completed those appointments, Ryan was looking forward to getting home. Checking his phone, he saw Megan had texted. Other occasional girlfriends had also left messages. Sex wasn't what he needed tonight: Reaching for his cell phone to call his cook to warm up dinner and take out the wine of his choice was enough of an effort.

Mercifully, the drive home only took twenty minutes. He waved to the security guard and sluggishly took the steps up to his front door. Ryan collapsed on a plush chair in his dining room, which was decorated with Cassoni furniture imported from Italy. The cook promptly brought him his dinner. He relished the shrimp fettucine alfredo and the chardonnay. In fact, Ryan felt so energized that he considered calling Megan, but when he rose from his chair, the envelope fell out of his jacket pocket.

Oh well, I'll look at this crap and tell my assistant tomorrow to send a polite rejection letter.

He opened it as he rested on his leather recliner in front of the giant TV screen. His favorite team, the Lakers, were playing against the Boston Celtics. A commercial he must have seen dozens of times appeared on the screen, so he decided to open and peruse the letter. Ryan read it from start to finish. His jaw dropped. He read it a few more times, making sure his eyes were not deceiving him.

Secret's out, Mr. Monti. I saw your son. In high school in Boston. Spitting image of you. You have a choice: give me two million dollars or I'll pass this information to the media and they will descend upon your kid and your wonderful image will be ruined. YOUR CHOICE. More details to follow.

Ryan's immediate reaction was to stand straight up, but he was leaning too far back on his recliner. *What? A son? What's he talking about? Is this some crazy joke?*

After he read it a third time, his eyes bulged as its implications dawned on him. At first, he thought the letter's writer must be deranged. He began to wonder how many people were involved in concocting this wild scheme and who was possibly going to believe it. How could he have a son? As if in answer to his question, the image of his first love came to mind. He jerked up. Could she have had his child without telling him? Why would she have done that? Imagining all the possibilities, fearing this was the beginning of a grand blackmail scheme, he placed his hand on his heart. Was he too young to get a heart attack? No, he had heard of others in their forties all of a sudden dropping dead.

The Lakers were back on TV, but he forgot all about them. He finally grabbed the remote and turned it off, closing his eyes tightly, hoping upon opening them, this letter would disappear from his reality. But no such luck. Closing his eyes again, his mind drifted as if he were in a trance, going back years ago and recalling events that he hadn't thought about in two decades. Memories flashed before him as a young man in Lowell, Massachusetts, starting out in the movie business and wooing his first love. Her shoulder-length blond mane swaying whenever she turned her head. Her long, toned legs and her tall, thin frame. He remembered the warm smile that was always fixed on her face as the eyes of men of all ages darted in her direction wherever she went. Yet she was oblivious to their stares. She was raised a strict Roman Catholic, and her parents instilled in her, their only child, traditional values and morals. He remembered she was convinced she and Ryan were soul mates. He, Ryan Monti, a struggling actor, of all people. She was determined to tame his all-night partying ways; she gave him perspective when people in Hollywood were tempting him with drugs and heavy drinking. Ryan even admitted to her that he would most likely have self-destructed without her level-headedness in his life.

Could he possibly have impregnated her?

Ryan's cook knocked on the open door. "Do you need anything else, sir? Was everything satisfactory?"

Ryan didn't even hear him.

"Sir... Mr. Monti, are you all right?"

It took great effort to move from his paralyzed state to nod and wave. Ryan breathed in relief upon hearing the cook depart.

Ryan remained in his recliner as still as a corpse for the rest of the evening.

CHAPTER EIGHT

BRIGHTON

As Christine drove home from work on Monday afternoon, she marveled that her job was relaxing compared to the Sunday night dinner at Daniel's parents' house.

That's what a dinner with the in-laws does to me, she mused. *But I made it through. The shiksa made it through.*

Daniel had gotten a call from his doctor early in the morning, and he swore up and down, backward and forward, that his tests were fine – she had nothing to worry about. Having never been married before, Christine pondered if this was the usual behavior of husbands when they are undergoing crucial medical tests and don't want their wives to worry. Were they all pretty much like this, or was Daniel some kind of saint? Christine smiled to herself – maybe she should stop at the Jewish bookstore in Brookline and buy a Torah, so that he could put his right hand on it and swear that everything went well with his tests.

Christine continued to feel exhilarated, as if she were

floating in the clouds. She smiled as she drove through the harrowing Boston traffic: she could not believe she had gotten lucky enough to find Daniel. She recalled informing him on their first date that she had twins. Christine was so certain that would be their last time together. Instead, he asked to see pictures.

Upon reaching home, she waved to Bob the gardener, who was inspecting his flowers. He waved and smiled a large, toothless grin. Her neighborhood friends joked he had a crush on her and would observe her comings and goings whenever he was outside pruning his garden. Christine would only laugh but admitted to herself that it felt good to be admired even though she was no longer twenty-five. She exercised and followed a strict diet regimen to maintain her svelte figure, determined to look as good as she could.

Daniel's car was already parked in their driveway.

"Hi, honey. How was your day?" she said, walking into the kitchen.

As usual, Daniel was getting all the ingredients ready to help prepare dinner. The twins had not arrived home yet. Tim was at basketball practice, and Trudy was training with her cheerleading squad.

"It was fine. How was yours?" Daniel said as he kept his focus on tossing the salad.

Christine couldn't help noticing the worry lines on his forehead. The upbeat tone in his voice seemed forced.

"How have you been feeling? Are you still tired?" she asked as she kissed him.

"No, I'm feeling all right." He seemed to be taking great care tossing the vegetables, as if he wanted to put them all in perfect balance.

"Is everything OK on the job?"

"Oh, we're courting a fussy client. Making all kinds of

demands. Nothing's quite right. I wish I could pay him to take his work elsewhere."

"Hmm, I know just what you mean. I've had my share of prima donnas at the modeling agency. And then there are the young women who plead with me to believe they're the next Heidi Klum."

Daniel nodded in acknowledgement and stopped tossing the salad. He sighed. "After dinner, I'll answer some emails, and then I could use a good movie. I'll have to find out what's on tonight."

Christine ruffled his thick, dark-brown hair and leaned toward him. "At least your tests came out fine. It's great to have something less to worry about."

Daniel turned and stared into her blue-green eyes.

"What?" she asked, shaking her head. "You swore to me everything was fine." She giggled nervously. "I've even thought about buying a Torah so you'd swear on it these tests were over."

"There is still one more test I didn't get the results on. The one that checks if I have the proper white cell blood count," Daniel said. "Then I should get a clean bill of health."

As soon as the words came out of his mouth, Christine couldn't help noticing he looked thinner. She took her husband's arms to stop him from tossing the salad again and said in a whisper, "Daniel, what aren't you telling me? And have you lost more weight?"

Daniel closed his eyes and shook his head. "I just want to be sure there's something to tell you. I don't want to scare you unless there's really something to worry about. Lately I've been feeling fine, so there's no reason to think otherwise."

Christine felt so pained and depleted that she had to plop down on a kitchen chair. She sincerely believed they had turned a corner. Earlier, the thought that the mysterious illness was nothing had planted seeds of joy in her existence. That vanished; now the specter of dark clouds was hovering over them, like a sunny day turning to rain and gloom.

They said nothing for a while. Her head drooped down and she covered her face with her hand. Finally, she faced him and said, "When are you going to tell me exactly what's going on? When are you going to tell your family?"

"Listen, I feel better, and I remain optimistic that everything's fine. I'm not worried, and you shouldn't be either."

"Daniel, I'm not a child. Husbands and wives are supposed to confide in each other," she pleaded with him.

When he made no reply, she lowered her head and said, "Let's order a pizza. I don't feel like cooking tonight."

* * *

No one spoke much as the family ate pizza and salad.

"Man, my teachers keep telling me high school is easy compared to college. I've taken all the AP courses I can. What more do they expect me to do to prepare?" Tim shook his head, attempting conversation.

"College is structured differently, and the students have to take on more personal responsibility," Daniel commented as he bit into a slice.

"Dad, did you have trouble adjusting to college when you started Tufts?" Trudy asked.

"I had difficulties at first, but I learned to be more disciplined," Daniel replied.

"How?" Trudy pressed.

When Daniel shrugged his shoulders and didn't say anything further, Tim and Trudy glanced at each other.

"I hope I can be more disciplined when I'm in college like you did, Dad. I want to finish in four years like you did and get on with my life," Trudy declared.

Daniel stopped chewing and bowed his head.

"What's wrong, Dad?"

Daniel lifted his head and continued chewing until he'd swallowed the last of the slice. He planted a smile on his face that didn't reach his eyes. "Nothing, Trudy. I actually had to take a semester off for personal reasons."

Trudy sat up, waiting for the reason, but Daniel did not elaborate.

"What about you, Mom?" Tim asked, attempting to change the subject.

Trudy was about to bite into a slice when she put it down. "How can you ask such a question, Tim? Mom couldn't finish because she couldn't afford to stay in school after she had us and our good-for-nothing father took off." She glared at her brother.

"I'm not asking about graduating, Trudy. I'm just asking about how she managed college while she was there." Tim glared back at her.

Christine didn't answer. She was listening to the conversation but kept getting distracted by the fear her husband was withholding a grim prognosis from her.

Tim decided to try again. "Mom, did you have a tough time managing in college at first?" he asked.

Christine didn't reply. Images swirled around in her head of preparing for her husband's funeral, leaving her and her children alone again. She put down her slice and stared out the window. That fear came back to her every now and again. Daniel did nothing to get her attention but simply took more salad and examined the vegetables, tossing them around with his fork like he was deciding which to eat first.

Christine broke from her own thoughts. "Oh, what is it, honey? I didn't catch your question."

"Did you have a tough time managing in college at first?" Tim repeated.

"Not really. I lived at home and set aside time every day to do schoolwork, just like I did in high school."

Tim looked at Trudy and shrugged his shoulders, signaling to her that they should forget bothering to make conversation.

When the family was finished, Tim and Trudy trudged upstairs to do their homework while Daniel and Christine cleaned up.

When they were done, Daniel wiped his hands on the dishtowel and said, "We have to talk."

Christine shook her head, her blond locks swaying back and forth. She didn't even look at him when she said, "OK, I hope you're going to come clean as to what's going on with your health."

Daniel turned away and combed his hair with his hands. After pacing a moment, he faced her. "I have a particular philosophy in life. I don't believe in upsetting people until I know for certain there's something wrong." He stared at her, his face flushed. "Am I a terrible person for believing this?"

Christine tossed her dishtowel on the chair and said, "Of course not, but when a couple is married, they love and depend on each other. If there's something wrong, you're supposed to share it with your spouse. If not, who the hell are you supposed to share it with?"

Daniel looked away and sighed. Then he pulled out a chair at the kitchen table and said, "Come sit. We have to talk."

Christine sank down into the chair, waiting with her arms folded.

He covered his eyes with his hands and began. "I haven't faced such a problem as this in over twenty years, and I don't want to alarm you. I hate alarming the people I love and want to be certain there's really something to be alarmed about."

Christine leaned forward, intrigued. "Wh- what happened over twenty years ago?"

Daniel paused and studied his hands. "I have long dreaded the day I would have to tell you about this…"

Christine put her elbow on the table and her hand under her chin. "Tell me what?"

Daniel sighed as he raised his head to face his wife. "It was actually a case of mistaken identity."

"Huh?" Christine narrowed her eyes and turned to look at him. "Can you explain?"

Daniel cleared his throat and readjusted himself in his chair. "You see, I was always kind of nerdy. In my senior year of college, I just studied. I belonged to the debating society and the business club, but basically, I studied most of the time.

"One day, a friend of mine who belonged to a fraternity invited me to a party on a Saturday night. 'Come on, Daniel, you gotta live a little. Loosen up. I'll bet you'll love it,' he told me. Well, I was burned out from continual studying, and since I already had a few job interviews that went lousy, I thought, 'Why not? Maybe I'm strung too tight, and I should just loosen up and relax.'"

"That makes sense," Christine interjected, "but what does it have to do with you not telling me what's going on with the doctor?"

Daniel held up a hand. "Wait. I haven't finished yet."

Christine shut her eyes for a moment and nodded. "OK, I'm listening. So what's the connection? You're not the type to get dead drunk." She opened her eyes and slowly faced her husband, putting her hands on her lap and leaning forward. "Don't tell me you got drunk and out of hand at the party?"

Daniel blinked hard.

His wife jerked her head up and peered into his eyes. "Daniel, is that what happened?"

"No, no," Daniel said, not even acknowledging her concern. "I danced with a few women, but none of them were my type." He shook his head at the memory. "One got so drunk I had to rush her to the bathroom before she vomited all over the place."

Christine said, "Sounds like a typical frat party to me."

"Sure, but at this particular party, a college senior raped a freshman in one of the rooms of the fraternity house. None of us realized this at the time. Maybe the music was too loud. There were a lot of people dancing and talking."

"That's horrible! What happened to the poor girl? Was the boy punished?"

"Yes, the boy was caught, expelled from school, and served jail time for his crime."

"Well, that's a relief! Justice was done... but what about the girl? And for God's sakes, what does all this have to do with you?"

Daniel's shoulders tensed up once again, and there was panic in his eyes.

"The... the girl left the school... I heard she took a year off and then ended up at another school. One close to home so she could commute."

His wife stared at him, nodding, encouraging him to continue.

"You have to understand, everyone, including her, was drunk. She had trouble recollecting the guy who raped her. He was my height and had similar skin coloring, and his hair was thick and wavy like mine – I mean, the way it used to be." Daniel flushed.

"Oh, honey, it still looks great." Christine reached out to tousle the hair on the crown of his head. "So the girl initially thought it might have been you who raped her? But then she realized she had made a mistake, and they found the right person. You can't let that traumatize you for the rest of your life."

"Unfortunately, she didn't realize her mistake all that fast. The police arrested and fingerprinted me." He glanced down. "You sometimes read about people mistakenly found guilty and ending up in jail with their reputations ruined. Well, I was really scared this was going to happen to me."

"Surely, your friends vouched for you."

"Oh, they did. But the girl was so hysterical. Understandably so. She swore it was me. It took her a while to clear her head – she must have come to her senses and realized I was not the one who raped her. It took several weeks until the investigators had enough evidence to arrest someone else. The girl eventually recalled a birthmark her rapist had that I did not." Daniel lifted his eyes toward the heavens and said, "Thank God, the real rapist's arrest finally brought a conclusion to that nightmare."

Daniel then stared at the floor, appearing as if he were studying the patterns of the tiles. "During that time, my mother came perilously close to having a nervous breakdown. She believed I was innocent, of course, but the stress and the stares she got from people were too much for her," he said, shaking his head at the memory. "In fact, one of her so-called friends told her she did not want to be associated with a woman whose son was a rapist."

Christine's eyes widened. "Oh my God! I can't believe I would ever say this, but I actually feel sorry for your mother." She shook her head. "So she's had worse moments in her life than when you married a shiksa."

"Christine, please. This is no time for joking around." He turned away from her, his eyes tired.

"You're right. I'm sorry." Christine looked down, penitent.

"Anyway," Daniel continued, facing her again, "my father was so upset and distracted during that time that he actually asked for a demotion in his company because he couldn't handle all the responsibilities and the stress. Instead of bringing home paperwork, he started seeing a psychiatrist and comforting my mother." He sat back. "This ordeal took about six weeks, but it took years off my parents' lives. My brother had to keep coming home to make sure they were all right. Needless to say, I had to take the semester off because I couldn't concentrate in school and my grades were plummeting. I thought I'd never be hired by anyone and would live the rest of my life in disgrace."

Christine said nothing. She just stared at him with a stricken expression.

"The point I'm trying to make is from then on, I vowed I would never ever do anything to make the people I love suffer needlessly."

His wife was about to speak, but he cut her off.

"Until the doctors are positive something's wrong, I'd feel a lot better and more at peace with myself if I waited until I knew for sure something was wrong. Then I'll have to tell my family."

"But don't you realize, all this secrecy is taking a toll on me," she said softly, her eyes pleading. "Daniel, please, I need to know what's going on. I love you so much, and this is all I think about."

"The doctors need the results of one more test to check out if everything's OK, but they remain optimistic."

"What do they think it could be?"

Daniel put his head down and said, "They're concerned about abnormal white blood cells. The tests are not yet conclusive."

"Then it could be cancer! Right?" Christine shot up, her face turning bloodlessly pale. She clutched the table.

Daniel reached for her hand, but Tim unexpectedly walked into the kitchen, his face crunched up in intensity.

"Dad, you've gotta help me with this calculus. Nothing's coming out right, and I've got this damn test tomorrow."

Daniel shielded his face so his son wouldn't see his anguish. By the time he took his hand away, his expression was normal again.

"Sure, Tim. Let's go upstairs to your room so we won't disturb Mom."

When they left the kitchen, Christine didn't move for some time.

CHAPTER NINE

LOS ANGELES

Buddy Catalano relished his job, learning all the dirty secrets of his celebrity clients, who put their trust in him and his discretion. Indeed, he would never tell a soul about what he uncovered, but sometimes clients decided to divulge details to the press. Whenever dirty laundry did reach the media, Buddy couldn't help reading with glee that he was the one who'd uncovered the truth. Being known as a bit of a character also enhanced his reputation: people did not know what actions he would take, but they almost always proved correct. Whenever he attended a celebrity event, which he often did for purposes of gathering information for a client, he fought to contain his enthusiasm as he observed people stare at him with a mixture of awe and fear.

He was an important guy, and he knew it.

His notoriety allowed him to own a grand home in Bel Air and a condo in the Tribeca neighborhood of New York. It also afforded him the opportunity to have a couple subtle plastic surgeries: one to gently smooth out the wrinkles in his skin, and another to erase the deepening lines beneath his eyes. Buddy had had his stomach stapled, and he worked out with a personal trainer twice a week. He had even considered more plastic surgery, but his wife cautioned she would not stay married to another Michael Jackson. That put an end to speculation about more surgery.

But lately his calendar was encountering a dry patch. The celebrities, sports superstars, and CEOs seemed to be behaving themselves lately. The phones had not rung with calls from frantic notables requiring Buddy's skills to maintain or salvage their reputations.

So when A-lister Ryan Monti called for an appointment that morning, telling him he canceled all of his other appointments this morning to set aside the time, Buddy sat up in his chair with raised eyebrows and a wide smile. Ryan Monti! He couldn't believe his good fortune. Buddy had been getting nervous about paying the mortgage on his Tribeca condo. His wife had been listening to him ranting that they might have to sell it if things stayed slow. He even had wild musings about concocting a scandal himself. But now he could breathe a sigh of relief. Ryan sounded heart-stricken on the phone. He needed to see Buddy right away. Even though he was a lapsed Catholic, it was moments like these when Buddy wanted to go down on his knees and thank the good Lord for rescuing him.

Buddy stepped into his private restroom; after washing his hands and brushing his teeth, he gargled with mouthwash for a full two minutes. He then styled his hair with the gel that his wife said boosted his professional demeanor. While putting the finishing touches on his personal grooming and practicing his power posture in the bathroom mirror, Buddy heard his phone ring.

"Mr. Catalano, your client's here," his assistant said breathlessly.

Buddy could imagine her awe that Ryan Monti was in the office.

"Send him in, Shana," Buddy instructed.

"Oh, OK," she answered softly. He detected a tone of reluctance that the handsome actor was leaving her presence.

Despite his eyes being wide open as if he were in shock, Ryan still made his presence felt with his extraordinary baby blue eyes and dirty blond hair. Buddy was heterosexual, but standing before him was the most handsome man he had ever seen. He had no trouble understanding Ryan's popularity, given his beautiful face and exceptional acting ability.

"Good to see you!" Buddy said, shaking his hand. "I believe the last time we met was during that Screen Actors Guild party in Miami."

Ryan merely nodded; Buddy knew he didn't remember.

"Have a seat." He ushered him into one of his brown leather chairs. "Would you like anything to drink? We have just about everything here," he said proudly.

Ryan shook his head as he sat down. Clearly, he wanted to get down to business.

"Of course, it's always a pleasure to see you, sir, but what brings you here this morning?" Buddy said as he sat upright, shoulders straight, his hands folded on his desk. He was putting his best professional face on, the one reserved for his highest-paying power clients.

Ryan looked around the room. Finally, he said, "This is all strictly confidential? I trust there'll be no press leaks?"

"We maintain the strictest confidentiality here. Nothing said in this room goes anywhere without your consent. If you know any of my previous clients, whose names I would never divulge, you can rest assured that discretion is the key to my success. In fact," he said, picking up a contract on his desk, "you can read through my contract. Even if you decide not to hire me, you are entitled to sue me if anything you tell me ever comes out of this office."

Thinking about writing a check for those lapsed payments on his condo, Buddy had to quell his shaking knees in anticipation as Ryan took his time reading the contract.

After reading it through, Ryan signed it. He then glanced around for a minute before taking out the mysterious letter.

"It's a copy," Ryan told him as he handed it to Buddy. Apparently unable to sit still, he cleared his throat and asked, "Excuse me, is there a restroom I can use?"

"Of course," Buddy said. He pointed toward his private one. Ryan shot up and entered it like an awkward, restless teenager.

After Ryan closed the door, Buddy put on his reading glasses and read over the typed note several times before pondering its contents.

Ryan a father? Well, I'll be! He's had tons of girlfriends over the years, but who could have sent this letter? Whoa, and they're asking a hefty amount too. Could this be nothing more than a crazy prank? No wonder he looks like he's afraid of his own shadow.

When Ryan returned, Buddy had his hands folded on top of his desk and smiled as if the problem were solved.

"Let's give it a few days. Don't act so fast. It's most likely a prank," he told Ryan, who was blinking his eyes and putting a hand on his knee to control it from shaking. "Do you have suspicions about who this may have come from?"

Ryan shook his head wordlessly.

Buddy put on his glasses again. "It states that the child is in high school." He looked over his glasses at Ryan. "Do you recall the women you were going out with at that time, approximately fifteen to eighteen years ago?"

Ryan sat as still as a statue. His eyes diverted to his hands.

Buddy wondered if he would even answer the question. Finally Ryan's eyes met his, and he answered, "Yes."

Buddy knew he had to tread lightly. In a quiet voice, he asked, "So do you think this may have actually happened?"

Buddy feared Ryan would take a long time to answer, but he quickly replied, "I don't know."

Ryan, did you sleep with girls back then or not? Buddy yearned to ask. "You mean you did not have any physical relationships at that time, or you don't remember?" He used a gentle, patient tone.

Ryan stood up and turned his back. Rubbing his hand on his forehead, he faced Buddy again and said, "No, I really don't know if anything happened. I've always been careful to use protection – except maybe once. I'm sure she would have told me if she got pregnant."

Buddy jerked his head up with a start, not sure what to make of this evasive answer, tempted to ask, *What the hell does that mean?* Knowing very well he couldn't ask that, he picked up a pen and asked, "What was this woman's name?"

Ryan bowed his head and closed his eyes, as if the memory still haunted him. "Christine Zarzycki. We were both living in Lowell, Massachusetts."

"Spell the last name, please."

Buddy noticed Ryan's whole body jerked as he recited the letters.

Buddy sought to placate his client into trusting him by sitting back in his reclining chair and smiling. Staring at the middle-aged actor, he added, "Believe me, I deal with these paternity claims all the time. The vast majority of the accusations are false, and the press never even gets wind of them."

Ryan nodded, trying to duplicate Buddy's relaxed demeanor by returning to his chair.

"Did you have another girlfriend soon after?"

"Yes, but like I said, I've always been careful after that. I traveled in the same circles with many of these other ex-girl-friends, and they never got pregnant until they got married or years afterward."

"Did you try to contact Christine after the two of you broke up?"

Ryan stared at his hands. "After our last meeting, she wouldn't see me again. I tried to contact her many times. I even went to her house, but her father told me never to try to contact her or go there again. It was all very strange."

"Hmm, I think so too. And no one ever told you she got pregnant?"

Ryan shook his head.

Buddy rubbed the tip of his fingers on his chin. "It sounds like a hoax to me. The kid could just resemble you, that's all." He sat up. "I'm going to put some feelers out for this woman, but I suggest you go out tonight and forget all about this."

"I can't imagine Christine had my baby and never told me. Some jerk is trying to get money out of me." Ryan sighed. "Someone always wants something."

Buddy tapped his desk. "Exactly. You know yourself everyone is on the make. I'll let you know what I find out as soon as I do. But I wouldn't sweat it. Sounds a little far-fetched to me. Go out. Have a relaxing dinner and put this all out of your head for now. It's most likely nothing but a crazy get-rich-quick scheme."

The men rose and shook hands. "I'm going to do exactly that. Chalk it up to one of the pitfalls of fame," Ryan said.

Buddy walked Ryan to the door, Shana practically drooling as the actor departed. Buddy watched him leave and lifted his eyebrows toward his assistant.

"He's hot, right?"

Shana blushed and tried to look busy.

Buddy chuckled on the way back to his office. His expression changed from lighthearted to serious when alone. An uneasy feeling nagged at him. This was a most unusual blackmail letter – the kid was already a teenager. Why'd they wait so long? College, of course, he thought, answering his own question, but what about all those intervening years? Why hold back until now?

* * *

Departing Buddy's office, memories of the past clamped down on Ryan's mind and refused to release him – memories he had worked to suppress for years but which crept up into his mind every time he considered getting serious with a woman. Now they were unleashed, and he was helpless to drive them away.

He remembered Kim waiting for him when he opened the door of their Los Angeles apartment.

"I didn't get the part!" she had wailed with tears in her eyes. She was gripping a folded sheet and carrying it like a torch.

"What part?" he'd asked her, taken aback. Ryan had never seen her so out of control before.

"What part? *What part?* The part playing your girl-friend in that movie where you're a cocaine addict!" she yelled.

"Kim, calm down." He put up his hands in a defensive gesture. "I didn't know they had already chosen another actress. What can I do?"

"Talk to them! They promised you I was going to get the part!" Kim's mascara was running down her cheeks from crying.

Ryan had to hold back a laugh. "First of all, they never promised me. I recommended you to the director. I'm just one of the many supporting cast members. They don't owe me anything."

"But the director gushed on TV about how happy he was you joined the cast," Kim said, rubbing her eyes.

"The part was supposed to go to another actor, but he dropped out at the last minute for a bigger role. Kim, I can't guarantee you get roles. I don't have that much clout. I thought we already discussed this."

In response, Kim walked over to the closet and took out her coat.

"Where are you going?"

"I need to get away and think. Ryan, my career is very, very important to me."

"I know. We can talk about it."

She moved past him, put her hand on the doorknob, and turned to face him. "Critics are always praising your work, saying you show a lot of promise. I was hoping we could move up together."

"We still might be able to. Let's have a quiet dinner, cuddle under the covers, and forget about this," he said with a twinkle in his eye.

Kim shook her head. "Ryan, your star is on the rise, and you have to help me get roles."

"I always recommend you," he said gently. Then he stared hard at her. "Are you saying that's all I'm good for?"

"I just don't think you're trying hard enough. You don't care enough."

"What? I'm not in control of who gets roles!" said Ryan, indignant now. "Is that what our relationship is based on?"

Kim didn't respond but walked out, slamming the door.

Soon after that, she had moved out. Ryan was nominated for an Oscar for his supporting role as a hopeless drug addict in the movie *Wasted*. Instead of basking in the glow of his achievement, he received emails from Kim threatening to tell police he used his apartment as a drug den if he didn't help her get parts. Ryan had never used drugs in his life – he couldn't stand the feeling of being out of control. He also had seen too many peers ruined by drug use to even consider trying it. Ryan responded to her emails by challenging her to prove it, but he also knew she could doctor photographs. Kim was a photography major in college. Nothing came of her threats, but he couldn't relax during that time. When another actor won the Oscar, Ryan was actually relieved, hoping Kim would back off. However, it took months and hiring a detective to trace her movements before he finally got rid of her.

He sat in his car in a panicked state, willing his body to relax. *Not this again. Please God, not this again,* he prayed.

Ryan's thoughts returned to Christine, the first of his two serious relationships that ended and devastated him. His heart continued beating at a rapid pace. He had told Buddy the truth: he never saw Christine again, and when he tried to find her, she had disappeared.

Could Christine have gotten pregnant? If she did, why didn't she tell me? Why wait so long and then attempt to blackmail me? He shook his head, unable to fathom that this was the Christine he once knew and loved.

Spitting image of you, the letter read. Could this actually be true? In a total turnaround, he laughed, thinking of his mother's reaction.

Ryan contemplated his extreme emotions – from terror to joy, wondering if he was having some kind of breakdown.

CHAPTER TEN

Los Angeles

Buddy's initial concerns dissipated when his mind turned to his money troubles. Swelled with pride, Buddy Catalano leaned back in his leather chair and downed a shot of Scotch.

He shook his head, smiling. *Money talks. I'll save our condo in the city yet. Lucy will think of me as her hero again, just like back in the day when I swept her off her feet and married her.*

He took out a mirror to make sure his appearance was impeccable; he was as good as he ever was. But he frowned when he noticed his receding hairline. Grey flecks of hair were sprouting up on his scalp. His comb-over no longer covered his bald spot. He sighed.

OK, OK, I can still be her middle-aged hero. When we first met, I was young and muscular but with only two hundred bucks to my name. There's always some give-and-take in life.

His phone buzzed.

Shana informed him an Ozzy Dick was on the line and needed to speak with him right away.

Buddy rolled his eyes. "What does that loser want?" But being in a beneficent mood, he decided to take the call.

"Yeah, what can I do for you, Ozzy? I already told you weeks ago I don't have any open positions. No freelance work either. Hey, you told me you can't even afford to move to LA."

"Tsk, tsk! What an ungrateful man you are, Buddy. I sent business, big business, your way, and I could take it away from you just as quickly."

"Now what the hell are you talking about?" He reached for his coffee.

"Let me spell it out for you," Ozzy continued. "I was the one who sent Ryan Monti that blackmail letter. I knew he would go to you right away because you're known as the best private investigator in LA."

About to guzzle down the remainder of his coffee, Buddy instead spit it out and had a coughing fit. "W- what?"

"I see I have your full attention now, Mr. Catalano. I sent business your way, but it comes with a cost. If you don't give me half of what Mr. Monti pays you, I am going to call him and say you were the one that put me up to that blackmail letter."

Buddy's triumphant demeanor vanished. He was leaning forward on his desk with his eyes bulging. "But I didn't know you sent it! You can't pin this on me, Ozzy!"

"Watch me," he said. "Are you going to cooperate with me or not, Buddy? Send me Ryan Monti's original receipts and payment for half of whatever he gives you."

"But I also have to pay my private investigators who'll fly to Boston to find evidence. And you know damned well that all the business I conduct with my clients is absolutely confidential," Buddy protested. "This is why I have a sterling reputation!"

"I don't care, Buddy. You need money, but I need it more."

"But I told you about people who could get you gigs in Boston," Buddy insisted.

"They had nothing for me. You were just sending them to me to get rid of me. I'm not playing games, Buddy. I need the dough, and if you try to undermine me, I guarantee you'll be sorry. Very sorry. I can contact Monti right now. I paid a bounty just to get his contact information."

Buddy bowed his head. He didn't see a way out. "All right. I'll work with you."

"Good," Ozzy said. "You can start by sending me the first receipt, a copy of the amount he paid you, and my half. By tonight. No games. You know me well enough, Buddy."

"Yes, yes," Buddy said, capitulating. "I know you do what you say you're going to do. You'll have it by the end of the day."

"Good. We'll be in touch." Ozzy hung up.

Buddy slammed the phone down, regretting the day he met Ozzy, even though his efforts were now leading him to financial solvency. Buddy couldn't believe a nothing like Ozzy was able to manipulate him. Or even have the nerve to do so. He cursed the day he had needed to hire the sleazy reporter for a scandal in Boston involving a very wealthy but very impatient client.

He buzzed for Shana.

She walked in and, seeing Buddy's scowl, she said, "What's wrong? You looked like you were ready to start dancing only five minutes ago."

"Things change," he replied tersely. "I need you to do something for me. I got a call from someone who helped me in a pinch once." He gave Shana the instructions. "Shana, I don't want to go into the reasons why I'm doing this, but we'll just keep this to ourselves. You know what I mean, don't you?"

Shana shook her head. "Buddy, everything that goes on here I keep to myself."

"As it should be. I don't pay you a good salary for nothing. Now go, get it done."

Buddy knew Shana was rolling her eyes as she headed for the door, but he could do nothing else but fume.

CHAPTER ELEVEN

BRIGHTON

*N*othing *like a good run in the early morning to clear my head,* Christine thought as she breathed in the cool, crisp morning air.

She wore her black-and-white spandex outfit as she jogged to the local park. Her ponytail swayed from side to side.

She passed Bob, the elderly gardener, tending to his flowers. His eyes lit up as she ran past him. He tipped his hat and displayed his toothless grin.

"Beautiful! I need to work on my garden!" she called out to him. To her surprise, he blew her a kiss and bowed his head.

Christine blushed. *My, is he getting more forward! I guess a widower in his nineties is entitled to do whatever he wants.*

Recalling dinner last night, her thoughts turned to Daniel. Her muscles tensed up. Christine stopped and put her hands on her knees, exhausted. She shook out her arms and legs and walked back home.

"We need to talk," she told her husband as he was putting on his jacket, his briefcase waiting nearby.

Before he could say anything, she added, "You need to be more up-front with me on a day-to-day basis. Daniel, I can't go on like this spending so much effort wheedling the truth out of you about what's going on."

Picking up his briefcase, he paused and stared at her. "You're absolutely right. I thought about it all last night."

He put his briefcase down again, and that's when Christine noticed her husband looked like he'd lost a little more weight. She felt like crying but held back – they needed to talk.

They sat in the living room, Christine on the couch and Daniel in a chair. They said nothing for a few minutes until Christine met his eyes. "You have to understand you're killing me with this secrecy."

"I know. I know. I realize I'm only making it worse by not telling you," he said, lowering his eyes to the ground. "I have an appointment with the doctor to find out the results of my test this morning. If you can get off work…"

"I'll be there. My calendar is empty this morning, but even if it wasn't, I'd still be coming with you. We'll face whatever this is together."

"All right." He looked up at her. "I wish I could protect you from any bad news, but I end up hurting the people I love most. I wish there was an easier way."

Christine's demeanor softened. "Sometimes, it's necessary to tell your family bad news. When you got laid off for three weeks, I remember it took you a week to tell me. Every morning you went to the unemployment office with your briefcase. Honey, I have to know what's going on. That's a big part of marriage. Sure, this is scary, but you just can't sugarcoat everything. Especially something like this," she whispered.

Daniel got up to embrace his wife and kiss her on the lips. "I don't know what I'd do without you." He gently put his hands on her shoulders and stared lovingly into her eyes. "I love you, Christine."

"I love you too. We're in this together. I do my best to concentrate at work, but it's getting harder for me to continue everyday life with this damn mystery hanging over my head."

"Of course, of course, I understand. I'm not being fair to you. You, Tim, or Trudy. The last thing in the world I would want to do is hurt you and the twins in any way. The three of you are my life."

Christine felt her eyes moistening, feeling very lucky to have a husband who cared so much.

Daniel picked up his briefcase, and she kissed him and said, "We'll take separate cars. What is the doctor's address?"

As she watched him get into his Toyota Camry, Christine wondered what she had done to deserve such a good man. *I don't know what I would ever do without him.*

She got into her Honda and followed him.

* * *

Once they arrived and were in the waiting room, Christine noticed Daniel couldn't sit still in the doctor's office. He drummed his fingers and was ready to leap up at the slightest sound.

"Daniel, try not to be so jumpy," she said, putting her hand over his.

"I've got a meeting in an hour. I told the receptionist that, didn't I?" he asked her while keeping his eyes glued to the clock.

"Yes, you told him that about three times already. Your job is fifteen minutes from here. You have plenty of time.

Daniel, try to think about something else. Something pleasant. Like walking on the beach in Hawaii. We're still going to do that dream vacation, you know. Close your eyes and think about it now. Pretend we're already there."

But instead, Daniel stared at the dark wood furniture in the office. He was breathing heavily and blinking his eyes – everything he did when he was tense. She tried to think of another tactic.

"So Tim called and told me he thinks he did well on his calculus test. He was having so much trouble, but you saved him."

Daniel lit up. "Yes, Tim was all confused, scribbling the calculations on paper but getting them wrong every time. I spent a lot of time explaining where he was going wrong." He smiled, adding, "I saw the spark of excitement in his eyes when he finally understood the concepts. I know Tim wanted to hug me for coming to his rescue after hours of struggling but felt it would not be a manly thing to do, even though we were alone."

Christine put her head on his shoulder. "Tim's lucky his father is such a math whiz."

Daniel chuckled. "Years ago, in high school, a guidance counselor suggested I become a math teacher, but in my naïveté, I thought the business world was beckoning for my talents." He turned to her with sadness in his eyes. "This small marketing company is my fourth job since I was laid off. Maybe I should reconsider. I still love math and want a secure job to provide a steady income for the family, but I think it's too late."

"What're you saying, it's too late? You're only in your forties, and you had a great job for many years until—"

"Mr. Goldberg?" A young nurse with a brown ponytail and a round face entered the waiting area. "Please come in. The doctor's ready to see you now."

Daniel jerked his head up in alarm.

"It's OK, honey. Let's go in." Christine stood up.

"Y- you're sure you want to go in?" Daniel asked, still remaining seated.

"Of course I am. Remember, we're facing this together. Come on." Christine gently pulled him up.

They sat waiting in the doctor's office. The only sounds were the passing cars outside. Daniel was unable to sit still. Christine took his hand.

Daniel nearly jumped out of his chair when he heard a gentle knock on the door. His solemn-faced doctor walked in. Upon seeing Christine, the doctor tried to put on a smile.

Dr. Sherman nodded his head and made his way to his seat behind his mahogany desk. When he got there, he folded his hands on top of the table and stared directly into Daniel's eyes.

"It doesn't look as good as we had hoped, but it's no death sentence either. It is acute myeloid leukemia," Dr. Sherman began.

Christine gasped. "Leukemia. Did you say leukemia?" Christine wanted to break down and cry, but her husband reached for her arm. She tried to rein in her emotions for Daniel's sake.

Dr. Sherman continued. "Mr. and Mrs. Goldberg, fortunately we are living in an advanced medical age where your condition is serious, but by no means untreatable."

"You mean if I had this fifty years ago, I'd be finished?"

"Exactly. Our chemotherapy treatments are more effective today in killing the white blood cells, but I'm afraid you're going to have to take a leave of absence from your job if we are to have any chance of beating this. You'll need regular chemotherapy treatments, which will leave you too weak to work."

Daniel slumped in his chair while contemplating the gravity of his situation.

Dr. Sherman spoke. "I know this is a lot for the two of you to process, but you can be assured I and my team of doctors will be there every step of the way. If we begin now, we'll have a better chance of beating this thing. Time is of the essence."

"Yes, doctor. He'll begin right away," Christine told him. She was holding her husband's hands tightly, struggling to keep herself together, at least on the outside. But inside she saw their lives falling apart at the seams. Images entered her mind from when she was alone, pregnant, and unmarried; living with her Aunt Ann until giving birth; then struggling in a Section-8 apartment and relying on food stamps to feed her twin toddlers, dependent on family to pay her living expenses. She had worked cashier jobs when the twins were old enough to enter school. By the time they were in full-time kindergarten, she had started as a receptionist at the modeling agency. Toward the end of their first grade year, she was promoted and was barely getting by with help from family when she met Daniel…

Christine snapped back to attention when Dr. Sherman began speaking again.

"We want to make you as comfortable as possible. Chemotherapy is not pleasant, of course, but we're going to be with you the whole way—"

"But still there are no guarantees I'll make a recovery," Daniel interrupted him.

Dr. Sherman's face fell. "We're going to do the very best for you, Daniel," he said firmly.

Daniel turned to Christine. "We'll have to find out if your insurance covers any of this. I wouldn't think so. My own insurance hasn't even kicked in yet," he said, gritting his teeth.

"Daniel, don't worry. We'll find a way to cover this. The most important thing is for you to get well."

"You're on board with this, aren't you, Mr. Goldberg?" Dr. Sherman interrupted their conversation.

He nodded slowly.

"Of course we are," Christine said.

"I'll have to take a leave of absence right away?"

"I'm afraid so."

Christine had secretly been hoping his extreme tiredness and weight loss were related to his trepidation about joining the start-up marketing company and the twins going to college. She refused to process that he was in a struggle for his life. He was sick, and the sooner she came to terms with this reality, the better.

"Let me speak with Dr. Collum and find out when we can start the chemo. Excuse me."

As soon as the doctor left, Daniel put his head in his hands. "I don't know if I can go to work today. Damnit!" He hit the arm of the chair. "I wanted to make this job work. Prove I'm a valuable member of this company."

"Maybe you shouldn't go into work. Let's both take the day off and digest the news and plan."

Daniel shook his head. "No, I can't go home. I've got to distract myself. And I don't want the company thinking I'm quitting on them. I've got to hang in there."

"But, Daniel—"

"No buts. You go on to work too, Christine. We've got to keep working. We've got to preserve the twins' college funds as much as we can. I can't bear the thought of all their hopes and dreams dashed because of me."

"They'll have to understand. Life throws everyone curveballs."

"They might understand, but I can't deal with ruining

their plans. Let me go to work and digest this. You should too, Christine. They're expecting you."

Dr. Sherman returned with Dr. Collum, and they set up a schedule.

Christine's legs were shaking when she stood up. The life they had so carefully planned for themselves and their children was spiraling out of control, but she knew she had to stay strong.

Daniel was also shaky when they left the doctor's office. Walking with him hand-in-hand, she wanted to comfort him, to say the right things, but was too much in shock to speak. The most she could do was hold Daniel's hand and try to keep herself calm with deep breathing.

"I'll see you," Daniel said, kissing her. He looked like he wanted to burst into tears as he turned around and got into his car.

"Daniel!" she called.

He turned sideways, not wanting her to see him choked up.

"Are you sure you can go in?"

He nodded and hung his head low.

"Be careful driving. I love you!"

"Love you too." He rubbed his eye as he entered his car, not able to look up at her.

She knew he wanted to cry. She did too. Christine got in her car and sobbed.

CHAPTER TWELVE

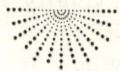

B̲RIGHTON

"Yes!" Ozzy pumped his fist after he hung up with Buddy. Instead of relishing in his victory, he decided to continue gathering further information. Ozzy wanted to jog around Brighton High School and try to engage in a conversation with the basketball coach or, even better, the boy himself. He ran to his dresser and found his old tattered jogging suit from years ago, but the pants tore when he put it on. He had gained considerable weight in the thirty-plus years since he had been in high school himself.

"Dammit!" he yelled. Ozzy realized he would have to dress in casual clothes when he made his next appearance there. He tried to smooth his red hair, but he had too many bald spots on different parts of his head. Giving up, he reached for his baseball cap.

He intended to discreetly park his car near the school and walk around a bit, but his car's engine screamed as he drove. Ozzy reassured himself that once Buddy sent him the money, he could at least begin to shop around for a new used car.

He reflected that at least he did not have to worry about housing. His late parents left theirs for him. Struggling to find work, he had long been frustrated about the dwindling number of jobs for reporters, so he was determined to break into private investigating. He had dreams of becoming a private investigator to the celebrities like Buddy Catalano. Ozzy read and collected pictures and articles about him at every opportunity – ever since Buddy had needed his help for a client in Boston. Ozzy was initially certain Catalano was impressed enough to hire him. After performing a small job for Buddy through a mutual friend, Ozzy called him numerous times for more job opportunities. Buddy finally told him to get lost. Ozzy then realized he had to create opportunities for himself, either through Buddy's cooperation or through blackmail. After all, he needed to survive. Spotting the boy at the high school provided his badly needed opportunity.

Ozzy got out of his car and strolled toward the high school's entrance. He checked his watch: 11:00 a.m. Students should be breaking for lunch soon, and that was when he hoped to gather information.

He heard the bell ring in the inside hallways of the building.

Perfect timing, he thought.

A woman in a navy blue suit opened the school's front door and addressed him. "Sir, can I help you?"

Think fast! Ozzy told himself. "Oh, good morning. I'm a new resident, and I was just checking out the school. My kids are high school age."

"Oh." The woman relaxed her rigid demeanor. "Have you made an appointment today?"

"No, I just wanted to look at the outside of the school

today. I'll come back and make an appointment to visit the inside another day. Thank you, ma'am. Have a nice day."

"You as well. It would be a good idea if you made an appointment first. We look forward to speaking with you," the woman said. She was smiling now.

Ozzy gritted his teeth. He knew he couldn't stay there. He was ready to turn and walk back to the car and formulate another tactic to obtain information, when lady luck shined on him: a man dressed in gym clothes was hauling gym equipment with a few boys.

One of them was the boy who was the spitting image of Ryan Monti.

Think fast! Think fast! "Um, excuse me, sir," Ozzy called to the man. "I'm new to this area. My children will be going to this high school, and I thought I'd look around. Could you give me directions on how to get to Washington Street?"

"Sure thing. Welcome to Brighton. I'm Coach Jim." He held out his hand.

"Steve Wellsworth," Ozzy said as he shook his hand.

Coach Jim gave him directions while Ozzy racked his brains, thinking of what else he could ask. Tongue-tied, he continued smiling as he thanked the coach and waved.

"Do you have a son that plays basketball?" a boy asked him.

"Why, yes!" Ozzy said a little too eagerly. "I have a son and a daughter."

"Cool," the boy said.

"Ah, do any of you have sisters here?"

The boys shook their heads. Only the one who resembled Ryan Monti spoke up: "I have a twin sister, but we're both graduating this year."

Ozzy's mouth dropped open. He was tempted to ask the boy's name when Coach Jim told the boys, "Let's get this equipment away. You boys need time to eat your lunch." He raised his hand at Ozzy. "Take care, Mr. Wellsworth."

Ozzy smiled and waved again, knowing he was being dismissed, but so elated he could barely contain himself. As soon as he reached his car, he began texting.

Oh, Buddy boy, I have more news for you. You are one lucky guy to have me on this case. Details to follow.

CHAPTER THIRTEEN

Pacific Palisades

R yan parked his Maserati at the curb. He was ready to meet with the producer and director of the film Phil recommended. He was an hour early – he found he could not stay at home with his mind consumed in memories, so he decided to walk around the town nearby and grab a coffee to distract himself.

But it didn't work. As he walked, those memories continued swirling around his consciousness. Seeing as he couldn't shake them, Ryan gave in and let them take over.

He was watching Christine as she was leaving her last college class for the day. Ryan was standing in front of his car. He waved and she smiled at him, a blush forming on her cheeks. He was taking her out for dinner.

What a sweet and beautiful girl she was! As he thought about her, he could almost smell the musk scent she wore. Musk was his favorite.

She was a thoroughly decent person who, in his mind, resembled a pure angel. Raised a strict Catholic, she wanted to remain a virgin until marriage. Ryan raised his eyebrows and shook his head in wonder: *Doesn't she realize what a knockout she is?* Every man who saw her stopped and stared, mouths hanging open. Her long, thick blond hair flowing over her shoulders every time she turned around, her long legs, perfectly shaped from cheerleading, and her thin, lithe frame – Hollywood actresses would kill for that body! Her big blue-green eyes and generous smile beguiled everyone who encountered her.

And she chose him!

He occasionally toyed with the idea of proposing to her, but he knew it was not the right time. He needed to work hard on his fledging career, and Christine wanted to finish college and possibly try her hand at modeling, in which he was convinced she would rise to the top. He admired her determination to be the first in her family to graduate college and work hard for a satisfying career. *She's trying to make it on her own without relying on anyone. What a find!*

In the midst of reliving the past, Ryan found that he was in front of the director's home. Checking his watch, he realized he timed it well.

Ryan had none of the usual feelings of anxiety about signing on to this role. In fact, he felt so confident he didn't need Phil to be there.

Let him enjoy his anniversary.

"Hi, there! Come in, come in." Richard Bowen, the producer, stuck out his large hand to shake Ryan's. Bowen's gleaming smile revealed he was more than pleased with Ryan's decision to play the film's leading man.

Ryan followed. The spacious hallway led to a wide-open living room. Framed posters of famous movies decorated the walls. On the couch sat George Tell, the film's director. Tell rose and walked over with his hand outstretched.

After engaging in a few pleasantries, Bowen handed him

the contract, along with a pen. Ryan signed and returned it to Bowen. When he looked up, Bowen glanced at Tell, who nodded. "Since we are so delighted to have you on board, Mr. Monti, we have decided to give you the option of choosing where you would like the movie filmed. We were able to secure locations in three big cities – New York, Toronto, and Boston. Which, sir, is your preference?"

"Boston," Ryan blurted out immediately.

"Boston it is," Bowen said. Both nodded. "Please let us know when you're ready, and we'll book a fine hotel for you to stay in while you research the role. How does next week sound?"

"Perfect," Ryan answered. "I'm ready to go as early as Tuesday."

"Excellent." Tell eyed the producer, and they both smiled.

"This calls for a toast, as they say." Bowen opened his wine bar. "Do both of you gentlemen drink champagne?"

"Oh yes, thank you," said Tell.

"Sounds great," Ryan added.

Bowen poured three glasses and handed one to each man before lifting his own. "May our upcoming film be a success and each one of us prosper from our Boston project."

"Hear, hear." Tell raised his glass high and sipped.

"Everything should go well in Boston," Ryan said, staring at the contents of the glass before imbibing. "Everything."

CHAPTER FOURTEEN

BRIGHTON

Christine drove home. After the doctor's visit, she went to work but couldn't concentrate. Every time she tried to read, her eyes glazed over to the point where the written words were all a blur. She started doing calculations in her head about how they were going to manage on her salary alone. Daniel's health was the first priority.

When the workday was over, Christine was grateful she managed to escape the office without having to stop and speak to anyone.

Contemplating going home to tell the kids about their father's grim prognosis got her so distracted that drivers behind her beeped their horns – the light had turned green, and she hadn't moved her car.

Taking off her coat, she went to work in the kitchen right away. Christine found that when she made dinner, constantly keeping her hands busy was a good outlet for her nervous energy.

In an hour, the smell of tomato sauce was wafting

through the house. Christina was cooking Daniel's favorite: meat lasagna. He walked into the house. There were bags under his eyes and he seemed out of breath, but when he saw her, he rushed over and kissed her lips and wrapped his arms around her. They embraced for a long time. They parted when Christine heard the timer go off, signaling the lasagna was ready to be taken out of the oven.

The front door opened. The twins were home.

"We'll talk to the twins after dinner," he whispered.

Christine closed her eyes and nodded.

"Hi, Dad." Tim came into the room all smiles. "Thanks to you, I got a B-plus on my calculus test."

Daniel looked at his son with admiration. "It was all you, Timmy. You're the one who took the test."

"I still say if this marketing company doesn't work out, you'd make an excellent math teacher." Christine eyed him lovingly. "You know, it's not too late. You'd probably only need to take a few courses to get your degree, or," she added, her eyes shining with enthusiasm, "isn't there a test you could take to automatically prove your aptitude in math and that would be it?"

Daniel breathed in and raised his eyebrows. "I'd still have to take teaching courses. Tell you the truth, I'd rather work in an office and just tutor my kids. With them, it's a labor of love."

Tim turned away, embarrassed by his father's show of affection.

"Guess what, everybody?" Trudy came in, still in her cheerleading uniform and carrying pom-poms. Her face was awash in excitement. "I've been promoted to head cheerleader."

"That's fantastic, honey! We've got to celebrate!" Daniel exclaimed. Christine sized up her daughter's tall, thin frame, just like her own; Trudy's long blond hair was pulled back into a ponytail. She often wondered if Trudy should forego college and start modeling, thinking for a fleeting moment that the extra income would help them get by.

Christine hugged and kissed her. "I'm so proud of you, sweetie! Wait till BC hears about your accomplishment!"

Trudy shrugged her shoulders. "Oh, Mom, do you think BC even cares about something like this?"

"Do they care?" Daniel asked his daughter. "Of course they care about a potential student demonstrating leadership abilities. Just keep your grades up and you'll be a shoo-in, Trudy!"

The oven timer buzzed a second time. Christine took out the garlic bread.

"Dinner's ready." Christine placed the lasagna and a huge green salad bowl on the table.

Christine frowned, thinking the children had to hear unbearably terrible news from their parents after delivering great news to them. But right now, she wanted the family to eat and enjoy. She tried to ignore the tightness in her chest and strove to maintain a cheerful facade.

* * *

The twins talked excitedly about their plans while the family was eating.

"Dad, when I'm in college, I'm not going to be a math major, but I'll still need your help from time to time. I'm sure I'll need to take some math courses."

Hearing talk about the future made Christine put down the glass of water she was about to drink. Daniel was in the middle of swallowing when his face turned red and he grabbed his throat.

"Daniel!" Christine screamed. Her hands shaky, she filled

his glass with water, spilling quite a bit onto the wood table, and handed it to him.

Grabbing the glass, he managed to finally wash down his mouthful of food.

"Daddy, are you all right?" Trudy said, concern in her eyes.

Tim was already refilling his father's glass.

"Don't worry! It washed down," he sputtered.

"Are you sure, Dad?" Tim asked, studying him.

"Yes, yes, I'm fine," he said, nodding.

Trudy got up and rubbed his shoulders. "You're sure, Dad?"

Christine, who by now had regained her composure, said, "I guess we're giving Dad so much exciting news all at once that we've got to let him settle down, relax, and eat." She got up and wiped the surface of the table with a hand towel. "After all, Dad had a very hectic day himself."

For the rest of the meal, the family ate in silence. The only remarks were requests to pass a dish or to remind Daniel to chew slowly.

Anxious to convince the twins he was fine, he ate while giving them reassuring smiles whenever they stared at him in concern.

After they finished eating, Daniel cleared his throat and said, "I want everyone to come sit in the living room. There is something I need to tell you."

Tim and Trudy looked at him and then at each other.

"I'm afraid I don't have such good news to tell you," he said once they all sat down. "I have leukemia."

The twins' jaws dropped, and their faces turned pale. Neither spoke as they absorbed the news, sitting as still as statues.

After answering the twins' many questions and convincing them the doctors were encouraged he would make a full recovery, Daniel grasped their hands and said, "We are going to band together and fight this thing. I know I have your full support."

"Absolutely," Tim said.

"No question, Dad. We're behind you all the way," Trudy added, tears forming in her eyes.

"And a big part of our support is being optimistic that Dad is going to get well again. So let's try not to have those long faces," Christine said, trying to take her own advice.

They nodded, but she knew they were not convinced.

"Now I'm sure you have homework to do. Dad and I need to talk."

Christine watched them head upstairs.

"We'll get through this, Daniel. I know we will," she murmured, taking his arm.

After they discussed their schedule for the coming days ahead, they embraced. Christine felt like crying but was determined to stay strong for her husband's sake.

* * *

That night, Christine lay in bed, staring at the ceiling. Even though temperatures were mild for October, she was shivering. A part of her regretted she had full knowledge of Daniel's illness, for it was more than she could bear. She knew the twins were trying to keep a brave front but were as devastated as she was. She overheard Tim sniffling and Trudy weeping as they spoke in whispers behind Tim's closed bedroom door. All she heard them say was they had to believe their father was going to beat this sickness and how important it was to remain hopeful.

Daniel was downstairs watching television. He said he wanted time alone and needed a distraction. Before going upstairs, Christine spotted a glass of liquor on the table next to his reclining chair. He almost never drank, often just holding a drink during social occasions.

She replayed the doctor's words in her head: that if Daniel followed his instructions, he had a good chance of recovery. Christine wished she could be more confident, but she was so scared. Life had become so much happier and more stable since she married him. She shuddered to think where she and the twins would be without Daniel coming into their lives. It was too painful to think about the possibility of losing her beloved husband, so she turned on her side and tried closing her eyes, but sleep would not come. She contemplated getting a drink to help herself sleep. Tomorrow was another workday, and the family had to manage to get through the day somehow.

She thought about the twins and their college plans. Even though they would be crushed if they couldn't afford college in the fall, perhaps it would be good for them to take a gap year – they would enter college a little older and more mature. Christine's mind drifted back to the other earlier trauma in her life when everything was tense, heartbreaking, and uncertain. She never thought her life would ever return to normal back then. She once thought she would end up raising her children alone and in poverty, and that no man would even consider dating a woman struggling with two babies. Their biological father's betrayal had sent her reeling, and she had thought she'd never be able to trust a man again until she met Daniel. Her thoughts about the past wearied her; her eyes closed as she drifted off to an uneasy sleep. She hoped the images of the past would vanish in a blur, but once she was asleep, they refused to disappear.

She remembered reluctantly grabbing her textbook that weighed as much as a brick, getting ready to study for her economics exam when her phone rang.

It was Ryan.

"I've missed you so much," he told her.

Christine felt her cheeks glow – an immediate turnaround in her mood.

"I've missed you too," she whispered. She touched her cheek – it was warm.

"How's school going?"

"Not so great," she choked out, fighting back tears.

"Oh, Christine, Christine, don't put so much pressure on yourself," he told her gently.

"Normally, I don't, but I'm in danger of failing. Usually, I don't have so much trouble in my courses – I mean, I can live with a C – but there are courses like economics where I just can't make heads or tails out of it, especially when they ask you to apply the information to example situations on tests! Oh, Ryan, I can't believe I'm telling you this, but I wish I had a smarter brain!" Christine sobbed quietly as giant tears rolled down her cheeks.

She kept meaning to make an appointment with a college counselor, but between running to tutors and cheerleading practice, she never got around to it. She had convinced herself if teachers and tutors couldn't transplant this information into her brain, she would fail economics for sure. Now she voiced all these fears and emotions to the most unlikely person: her boyfriend. Christine felt like kicking herself, convinced Ryan would now consider her a basket case and drop her, when she heard his calm, comforting words on the other end.

"I'd probably be in the same boat as you if I had to take an economics course. I admire your ability to try tackling it and sticking it out. Don't sweat it, honey. Most economists can't figure out what's going to happen anyway. Just take the class again if you need to – I can always ask around and maybe find somebody in Lowell who can help you pass."

His reassuring words warmed Christine all over. She was

amazed he could be so understanding given he kept auditioning and winning acting roles.

"I'm crazy about you, whether you pass or not. So we have something else in common – neither one of us gets economics."

Christine grinned through her tears. "So how's your latest movie going?"

"We're wrapping it up. Fourteen-hour days, six days a week. I just crash on my days off. I'm a little nervous too – at one point in the film, I play a teenager who is molested by different guys. The script is edgy and controversial, the way I like it, but I worry it may go a little too far and turn audiences off. I just hope this scene doesn't have a negative impact on my career."

"I'm sure it won't. That's what you're known for, taking chances. I am so happy you are getting all these offers."

Christine was delighted to be comforting *him* now, and to know she wasn't the only one wrestling with insecurities.

"I get Friday and Saturday off while they edit the film. Maybe we can get together on Saturday night?"

Christine was silent.

"Come on – a break will do you good, and I'll remind you how beautiful and sexy you are, and you'll forget about that dumb economics course."

She chuckled.

"And I need to feel like a normal man again after this role," he added. "What do you say? We both need a break."

Christine wound and unwound the telephone cord.

"I think I could spare a few hours. It'll be great to clear my head."

"I'll take you to Mancini's, the best Italian restaurant in town. Or do you feel like having something else? Chinese? Mexican?"

"Mancini's is fine."

"No really, Christine. I want it to be the place of your choice. You need a lift. Your wish is my command, my princess."

Christine put her hand to her cheek and felt her whole face turning red. "Actually, I've been curious about that new Chinese restaurant that opened a few towns over, the Chinese Garden."

"As long as it's upscale, we'll try it. Only the best for my baby."

Christine now held back tears of joy. Economics class no longer took the central importance it did only a few minutes ago. Passing or failing no longer dominated her thoughts; it receded to a small space in the back of her mind. Her excitement about seeing Ryan and the support of family and friends dominated her thoughts as she realized she had a lot to be grateful for. She'd do her best, and if she didn't pass, she'd simply take it over in the summer.

"Christine? Hello?"

Ryan's voice forced her out of her thoughts.

"I'm really looking forward to seeing you Saturday night, but now I've got to hit the books – how I wish I could do that literally," she said, giggling.

"I have an idea! In the winter, why don't we use them to build a fire? I could rent a log cabin, and then we'll make good use of them."

Christine's face was awash in smiles. "Excellent idea."

"I'll let you go and study – I can't be so selfish by monopolizing your time," he said. "I've got to give my baby room to work. I know how I have to hole myself up preparing for roles. If you get frustrated, just think of me nibbling your ear."

"OK, I will. I'll try to study and not go too nutty. I have Saturday night to look forward to."

By the time she hung up, she felt a warm glow radiating

all over her. She studied the phone as she put it back, reluctant to discard the instrument that brought her so much joy.

There was a knock at her door.

"Come in. Hi, Mom."

"Hi, honey. Were you just talking with someone?"

"Yes, Ryan called. He made me feel so much better. He's taking me out on Saturday night."

Christine's mother neither smiled nor spoke.

"What is it, Mom? We're just going out to dinner. Don't you trust me?"

Fran spoke in a quiet but firm voice. "It's not you I don't trust."

"Oh, Mom," Christine groaned. "I told you, Ryan's a gentleman."

"And he's also an actor who periodically goes to California and hangs around with God knows what kinds of characters. Please, Christine, please be careful."

"Of course I'm careful. I told him I want to save myself for marriage, and he respects that."

Lying in bed, Christine reflected on how naïve she was when she was young. Before everything went wrong. She ended up passing economics, but her relationship with Ryan turned ugly.

Staring at the ceiling, she felt a headache coming on. She got up to put a damp facecloth on her forehead and then went back to bed.

"Mom?"

"W- what?" Christine shot up in bed as if an imminent disaster was about to occur. The facecloth she had placed on her forehead plopped down to her chest.

"Mom, what is it? Is something wrong?" Tim cracked open her bedroom door an inch.

Christine breathed a sigh of relief, willing herself to stop shaking. "Oh, nothing. I just woke up."

"Oh, I'm sorry. It's still early, so I didn't think you went to bed already. Can I come in?"

"Sure," Christine said, rubbing her forehead.

Tim walked in, wearing a Boston College T-shirt. His newly trimmed hair made him look preppy.

"Bad headache?"

"Yes."

He sat at the edge of the bed. "I can't help thinking about Dad," he said, choking up.

Christine rubbed his back. "I know, honey. I feel the same way."

She made a concentrated effort to keep her tears at bay.

"It's not a hopeless situation, is it?"

"No, no. We're going to fight this thing, and he's going to get the first-rate medical care this city has. And we have to stay strong for Dad's sake."

"Do Grandma and Grandpa and Uncle Seth know yet?"

A wave of pain flashed across Christine's forehead. "I don't think so. We have to leave it up to Dad to tell them." With that, she sank back down into the pillows.

"Oh, Mom. I didn't mean to upset you more. Is there something I can do?"

Christine was touched by her son's concern, but she shook her head and smiled as she leaned forward and massaged his arm. "No. I'm going to take some migraine pills." She slowly sat up again and reached for the medicine on her nightstand, swallowing the pills with a tall glass of water. While they went down her throat and into her bloodstream, a thought occurred to her. Solemn-faced, she stared into her son's eyes.

"I know this is a lot for you and your sister to handle, but I know the two of you are going to do a good job staying strong. Try not to worry too much. We'll all get through this."

Patting his hand, she said, "I'm going to go to sleep. Good-night, sweetie."

"Goodnight, Mom. Give me a holler if you need anything." He got up and glanced her way for a moment before leaving the room.

He looks so much like Ryan, she thought.

She shut her eyes tightly, dismissing that thought.

"Mom?"

"Yes, Trudy?"

Trudy approached the bed, attempting to focus her eyes on her mother's but instead staring down at the carpet. "I know you don't like talking about it, but this might be a good time to try to get in touch with our biological father. He hasn't done anything for us, and maybe now we could use his help."

Christine opened her mouth to protest, but Trudy continued.

"You've told us he's not dead or in jail, so don't you think it's his responsibility to help us, Mom? If you loved him at one time, he might be a good enough person to want to help you." Trudy's eyes moistened. "Even if he never wanted to meet me and Tim."

Christine closed her eyes, and her head sank forward in defeat. "I've never put it that way, Trudy. All I can tell you is he's not father material."

"Still, I wish I could meet him just once. You always clam up whenever we bring him up. You know, someday we might want to meet him."

Now Christine's eyes were filled with tears. "When you become adults, that's for you and your brother to decide. But right now I can't deal with that too."

Christine reached for the tissues and felt her daughter's hand on her arm.

"Please understand, Mom. We are curious."

Christine nodded reluctantly as she wiped her tears.

"And if he could help us now, that would be great. Think about it, please."

"All right. I'll think about it," she said tersely. "Now please excuse me while I wash up."

She got up of bed and proceeded to go to the restroom without glancing at her daughter.

"Mom?"

Christine turned around.

"I hope I didn't upset you too much," Trudy said.

"No, no, you didn't," Christine said, but she could not even manage a smile as she walked away.

After washing up, Christine walked in the hall, where she overheard the twins talking in Trudy's room. Normally, she would never eavesdrop, but she could not help herself this time. She peeked through her daughter's almost-closed door.

"Every time I read a paragraph of *The Grapes of Wrath* for English, I forget what I've read when I get to the next paragraph," she complained to her brother. "Damn that Mr. Holden for assigning a term paper during senior year! I thought the last year of high school would be about having fun, not serious studying."

"Oh, really? Fun is the last thing I'm having now," Tim said.

"I know. Dad's leukemia diagnosis has effectively ended our carefree, easygoing life, but heavy schoolwork in our senior year shouldn't be adding to our pressures. Dad is so dedicated to us – a real a father if there ever was one. I can't stand this."

"I know what you're saying. I can't concentrate on a damned thing either," Tim said, sitting on her bed. "God! Everything was fine enough until now. And Dad's such a good guy. Why did this have to happen to him?"

"Eternal question because it's unanswerable. Grandma

Goldberg always said Y is a crooked letter," Trudy replied grimly. "The question is how to handle it."

"And it happened at the very worst time. Just when we're about to go to college. We can work, but how much can we make now without skills? Mom has to shoulder the whole thing."

"Believe me, I know."

"I wonder how we're going to manage with less money and Dad being so sick! It costs a lot to pay for doctors and hospitals." Tim put his hands over his face and shook his head.

"I wonder where our real father is. If he could help us out."

"Don't you ever let Mom hear you say that!" Tim looked up at her, aghast. "He's a good-for-nothing!"

Trudy sighed and met his stare. "To tell you the truth, we don't know anything about him, Tim. He's done nothing to support us. He owes us."

"Don't even go there, Trudy. Not yet. I don't think Mom can deal with that right now." He stared at her. "I hope you didn't dare mention him to Mom when you went into her bedroom after I did."

Christine could hear the scorn in her daughter's voice. Trudy would not admit it, but instead said, "I've tried for years to find out about him. Whenever I bring him up to Grandma and Grandpa Zarzycki, they immediately change the subject as if it's none of my business. Can you imagine?" She looked at her brother. "There's a wall preventing us from finding out about him."

"Oh, I know. The only thing Mom told us is that he's not a rapist or a murderer. You know I plan to see if I can find him in a few years, but I've been holding off so as not to upset her. She would go nuts, and as you know, this is the last thing she needs right now."

"I know it'll be hard for Mom, but the time has come that she's got to come clean about him. We've got a right to know who our biological father is. And if he can help us now."

"Trudy, believe me, I know what you're saying, but we have to find the right moment. One thing I do know is that now is not the right moment. Mom couldn't deal with this too."

"All I know is we're not on the same page about this, Tim."

"I'm going back to my bedroom. I have to read three chapters for tomorrow." He chuckled without humor. "The name of the book is *Things Fall Apart*. How apropos."

Christine had heard enough. She slipped quietly down the stairs. What she needed now was a good cup of coffee to help settle her nerves.

CHAPTER FIFTEEN

Los Angeles

The next afternoon, Buddy was pacing around his office, trying to decide if he should inform Ryan Monti about the text he had received from Ozzy Dick:

Boy, oh boy! You'll never guess what I found out. Ryan Monti not only has a son but a daughter too. Twins! Got this right from the kid's mouth. Haven't seen her yet, but looking into it. You don't realize how lucky you are to have me on his trail. Waiting for the next payment.

Despite his discomfort with being forced to include Ozzy in the investigation, Buddy had to look on the bright side: at least he was getting help with the investigation. He wished his own assistant investigators were finding out all this information. Buddy was much more confident they would find the truth to this paternity claim. He was still trying to process that there was not one child but two. Monti had an appointment with him in the early evening, and he wanted more solid evidence before relaying the news, not just relying on a screwball like Ozzy.

Buddy glanced at the clock. He figured Don Chin, one of his best investigators, should have come up with something by now.

He picked up his phone.

"Chin," Buddy said as soon as Chin picked up. "What's going on? Have you located this Christine Zarzycki yet?"

"Yes, I've been waiting for your call, Mr. Catalano. This woman married, and her last name is now Goldberg."

"Excellent work, Chin. What else did you find out?"

"She lives with her husband and two kids in a small house in Brighton, Massachusetts. She works every day. I managed to follow her to work. The Marie Cooper Modeling Agency. She is one of the representatives there."

"Great job! And about her kids. Ah, what would you say are their ages?"

"They both look like they're at least toward the end of high school. They get on the bus together every day."

"Y- you mean they might be the same age?"

"Yes, they're twins. I checked the records. They're both seventeen and are graduating high school in June. I was even able to see a copy of their birth certificates. Only the mother's name is on them. And they do resemble Monti."

Buddy let out a long breath. "Now I know you've discreetly spoken to people in the Lowell area where both this woman and Monti are from." Buddy paused to let Chin know the importance of this information, while praying he came up with something, anything.

"Yes, I was snooping around about the town for information about this Christine woman. Everyone was tight-lipped, but I finally found someone, this guy, who's lived there all his life. He had a crush on her at the time…"

"Yes, yes. Go on."

"He remembered when she was dating Ryan Monti. She always looked so happy. He knew he didn't have a chance," but one day she looked all upset when she came home to her parents, and she stayed in the house for weeks, not seeing anybody. This Monti guy tried to see her, but her father turned him away until one day she disappeared," Chin explained. "Her parents said she transferred to another college far away, but he never believed them. He then bumped into her a few years later, and she was walking with twin toddlers. She claimed she had gotten married but became uncomfortable when he asked about her husband. He knew something wasn't quite right..."

Bingo! Buddy thought. *This is the evidence I need when I speak to Monti.*

* * *

By seven, Buddy checked his watch: Ryan Monti was going to be here any minute. It was his last appointment of the day, and Buddy intended to give him the news as gently as possible.

His phone buzzed. "Mr. Monti is here," Shana said in a chirpy voice.

"Perfect. Send him in, Shana."

Shana had agreed to stay late. She sounded unusually cheerful despite working after hours.

I'd bet she'd work for free just to see that guy again, he chuckled to himself.

Buddy walked to the door to greet him. His assistant escorted Ryan. She looked like a young schoolgirl gaping at her first crush.

"Welcome! Come on in, Mr. Monti. Have a seat, please." He reached out to shake his hand. "Shana, that's all the help I'll need for tonight. You can go home now. Thank you."

"OK, Mr. Catalano," Shana said, still ogling Ryan. Buddy coughed a few times to signal his assistant to leave and close the door. She finally got the hint. "Good night, gentlemen," she sang with shining bright eyes upon closing the door.

Ryan got right down to business. "You found out something?" he asked, still standing.

Buddy returned slowly to his seat. "Mr. Monti, I want to share what I have learned with you. Please have a seat. You'll need it."

"What? What is it?" Ryan sat on the edge of his seat. "Well, go on. Let's have it. Forgive me for being so blunt, but you can do away with the formalities. What's going on? Are you trying to tell me this isn't a prank? Is it something horrible? What do you have to tell me?"

Buddy held up a hand. "No, it isn't something horrible. According to my most discreet investigator, it looks like you may be a father, Mr. Monti. I realize this is quite a shock for you to digest."

He was gazing beyond Buddy, and it took a moment before he was able to regain speech. "Are you sure?"

"Yes, the woman you told me about, Christine Zarzycki, mysteriously disappeared for a year after you two broke up. She now lives in Boston, is married, and—"

Ryan interrupted. "And she has a son. Maybe she met her husband soon after we broke up."

"Mr. Monti, we can look into a DNA test, but I've confirmed the boy looks just like you as the letter indicated and… that boy, ah, that boy has a twin sister. Your former girlfriend apparently had twins – a son and a daughter – and her husband is not the father. It's unclear who the father is. She left his name off the birth certificates. She gave birth about seventeen years ago."

Ryan nearly jumped out of his seat, his mouth falling open, unable to form words.

The only sounds were the cars driving past the private

investigator's building. Ryan was breathing hard and couldn't take his eyes off Buddy's face

"And she decided to send the letter now?" Ryan was finally able to speak. "And she wants child support now? After all this time? Please, do you have any more information about this and why she decided to blackmail instead of just tell me?"

Buddy struggled to keep his eyes steady on Ryan. "Mr. Monti, we're not absolutely certain she's the one who sent the letter."

Ryan turned to stare at the wall, not even listening. "I can't imagine the Christine I knew becoming a vicious blackmailer." He looked again at Buddy. "But I do know that blackmailers don't just stop after you pay them off. They always want more and more," Ryan said, clutching the arms of his seat. He shook his head. "Christine is now a blackmailer. My God! What happened to her?" His breathing quickened, and he was turning white. Ryan appeared overcome.

"Mr. Monti," Buddy said, sitting in his chair, hands folded on the desk. He knew he was interrupting Ryan deep in thought. "What can you tell me about your relationship with Miss Zarzycki?"

Ryan sat up. "We dated for eight months. She broke up with me so suddenly. I remember it was during the time my career was really taking off." He shook his head.

Buddy shifted uncomfortably in his seat. "Ahhh, do you remember why she broke up with you so suddenly?"

Ryan tightened his lips and gazed down. He turned away as if he wanted to block out the memory. Turning red, he said, "I, ah, would rather not go into it."

"Mr. Monti, I know I'm asking you a lot of personal questions, but" – Buddy lifted the confidentiality agreement – "you know if any if this gets leaked to the press, you could very well sue and ruin me. Whatever you tell me stays in this room." He paused, staring earnestly at his client. "Besides, we want to get to the bottom of this."

"It's… it's kind of embarrassing."

"You can rest assured it will not leave this room."

Ryan shut his eyes tight but began talking. "Christine was going to the University of Massachusetts. She was in her second year. Christine was raised as a strict Catholic and wanted to be a virgin when she got married." He opened his eyes and faced Buddy. "I respected that, or at least I did until one night when we went out together. I remember Christine had a very hard exam coming up. She was so afraid of failing. I wanted her to relax and enjoy herself that evening. I was commuting back and forth from LA at the time. I kept getting small roles on TV and in movies, and I was finishing up my biggest movie role and was back in Massachusetts."

Ryan hung his head and was silent.

"Mr. Monti," Buddy said gently, "please go on."

Ryan faced him and stared around the office as if he didn't realize he was still there.

He continued. "I took her out to dinner, and then I suggested we go dancing at a nightclub. She was reluctant at first because her parents didn't want her to be out late. They were very strict, but I convinced her she needed to have some fun, that she couldn't go into her exams being so wound up.

"We had a few drinks and were dancing to the music. I had never seen Christine look so happy. It was as if we were in a dream and nothing could ruin this moment, but when I noticed the clock read 11:30, I let her know we should leave. I didn't want Christine to have a problem with her parents. We stopped dancing, had one more drink, and then headed back to my car.

"I wanted to be responsible, I really did. But when we got

into the car, she put her hand on mine and before we knew it, we were in each other's arms. It felt so right. We were so happy being together. I guess we were both a little drunk and gave in to the moment. We stopped worrying and made love."

He eyed Buddy. "After we got together, Christine realized she was bleeding when she got out of my car to use the bathroom. That brought us back to reality real fast." He balled his hands into fists. "She was twenty years old, old enough to make her own decisions. It was so spontaneous we didn't think about getting protection. It was such a shock for her when she saw the blood. She started crying. I tried to comfort her. I even told her I wanted to marry her once I started working regularly."

He laughed mirthlessly. "I told her I was hoping this big role in the movie I had just finished might open more doors for bigger roles, and then we could start to think about a life together. In fact, a soap opera had actually approached me about playing a regular's son a few months previously. That would mean steady work. I promised her I would look into it, but nothing would placate her. She kept saying she promised her parents she would save herself for marriage – she wanted them to be proud of her, and she knew she let them down. Christine even spoke about going to confession. I honestly didn't know what more I could say. I then drove her to an all-night drugstore so she could get some supplies. By the time I got to her home, she was composed but wouldn't talk. When I brought her to her door, I took her hands and promised her I would look for steady work so we could get married. I told her she could finish college and also try modeling if she wanted. I hugged her, but she didn't hug me back. She went in, and there was nothing more I could do except go home."

Ryan had tears in his eyes. "Whenever we spoke on the

phone, she never had much to say, so I decided to invite her to Los Angeles while I was wrapping up a movie. She came out and things got better, at least for a while, and then there was a misunderstanding and I never saw her again."

He looked at Buddy. "And now you're telling me she had my son and daughter and never told me and is now trying to blackmail me?"

"As I said before, we're not sure she's the one who sent the letter," Buddy said as he stared at the carpet and cleared his throat. Conscious that Ryan was an actor and must know when someone was lying, he stayed still and forced himself to look into his eyes.

Ryan continued. "I was worried about her. The first chance I got as soon as I came home to Lowell, I went to her house, but her father came to the door and said in no uncertain terms that I was not welcome in his house, and if he ever saw me again there he would call the police. When I told him I just wanted to know if Christine was all right, he slammed the door in my face."

"Wow!" Buddy blurted out. "He wouldn't tell you anything else?"

"Nope."

After a moment of silence, Buddy spoke. "Mr. Monti, what can I do for you now?"

"I'm going to Boston next week to do research for a new role. I would like you to find out where I can find them."

"The twins?"

Ryan nodded. "And Christine."

"She did marry, by the way – her last name is now Goldberg. But don't you worry. I'll find out everything you need to know. I did get their home address, for starters."

Ryan nodded and with that, he departed the office with the only sound coming from the closing of the doors.

* * *

Buddy remained standing, leaning on his office desk. He knew Ryan was not telling him everything. He left a crucial part out. He would have to question Ryan again to get the full story of what had happened.

Buddy's ringing cell phone interrupted his musings.

"So does he know?" Ozzy asked by way of greeting.

"Yes, he knows," Buddy answered. "I will mail you half of his latest check, and I can take it over from here."

"So who's going to give you information?"

"My own private investigator, Ozzy. I appreciate your help and will continue to find people who may be able to hire you—"

"Not so fast, Buddy!" Ozzy yelled. His anger was so swift that Buddy almost dropped the phone. "I am going to continue getting payments, Buddy, or I'll tell Monti you were the one who concocted this scheme of blackmailing him."

"You wouldn't!" Buddy sputtered, sitting down and pounding his fist on the desk. "And why would he believe you? I didn't force him to come to me."

"But you're the number one private investigator to the stars, you know that. And I also know that business was slowing down for you!"

"How did you know that?" Buddy's face was red with rage.

"I told you, I am also an excellent investigator, and if you were smart, you would have hired me a long time ago! But since you didn't and I really need the money, you're going to continue paying me half. Now I'm quite sure Monti's going to want to come to Boston to see his kids for himself. If you miss a payment, well, I have my own sources for tracking him down and telling him that you put me up to this."

Buddy thought of paying Ozzy off for a moment, but

then dismissed it. There was no getting rid of him, so he'd have to play along, at least for now…

"I don't know how much longer he's going to need my services, but I'll give you half while he does and then don't even think of contacting me again, Ozzy. I have contacts of my own that I can use if you push me too far."

"Agreed." Ozzy hung up, and Buddy staggered to his chair. Closing his eyes and bringing his hands to his forehead, he wondered how he could get rid of him.

CHAPTER SIXTEEN

C hristine sat still in her chair, waiting for Daniel in the oncologist's office. He had insisted consulting with the doctor alone, and then she would be called in to join them. Christine suspected he did not want her to witness him frightened and trembling.

Christine tried not to shake her leg while sitting in the waiting room reading a months-old issue of *Glamour.* She rifled through the pages, showing scant interest in hairstyle recommendations, the hottest books recently published, or how Marion Cotillard balances her acting career and family.

Giving up on the magazine, Christine dropped it on the table and closed her eyes, hoping to relax. But instead, her mind traveled back to the days when she found out she was pregnant. She had been visiting Ryan in Los Angeles when he was wrapping up his latest film. Christine's parents booked her a hotel room and made her swear up and down, backward and forward, that she wouldn't sleep with her boyfriend. Her mother even contacted a childhood friend who had moved to LA and asked her to check up on Christine. If that wasn't enough, her parents were flying in toward the end of her vacation to spend the last few days with her before they all headed back to the East Coast.

Christine told Ryan in advance that being together that night was a big mistake, and they could never do it again until they married. Ryan had hinted he was looking for a ring, certain that this movie role would give him the financial stability necessary to marry her.

All was fine until she came to visit him at the studio where he was wrapping up a film. She discovered Ryan was having an affair with another woman. He was not the man she had trusted and fallen in love with.

Christine had wobbled out of the studio lot in a daze. When people involved in the production spotted her leaving, they must have thought either she was having a nervous breakdown or was drunk. They couldn't say or do anything but stop and stare.

Her face was tear-stained and pale, her eyes glazed over. She ran out and continued running until the wave of traffic surrounding her on Melrose Avenue slowed her movements. It was the lunch hour, and the streets were jammed with cars of all makes and styles. As car horns blared and people were shouting at her to get out of the way, Christine felt as if she were looking through a kaleidoscope – her vision was blurred, and her surroundings appeared twisted, not quite real.

Was she dreaming? In the middle of a nightmare?

She hobbled to an abandoned lot and threw up. Repeatedly.

Her head and joints throbbed. She feared she would never stop throwing up.

Christine had never experienced a headache like this one. She rubbed her temples, took deep breaths. Nothing worked.

Before she could even contemplate her future, she had to get rid of the pain so she could function again. Her eyes welled with tears as she tried navigating her way to the bus stop.

Clutching her head with her hands and walking bent over, as if she needed a cane, she continued inching forward. She could not even think about where to pick up the bus to go back to her hotel.

When she managed to get back to the busy street, people stared at her as she walked as if she were a curiosity from a circus.

A woman draped in black approached her and asked, "Child, do you need help?"

Christine's eyes traveled in the woman's direction, and she saw her flowing black robes. Her head rose as much as she could to figure out this woman was a nun. Her body was completely covered, except her round, ruddy face and her thick hands. The nun was elderly, and behind her rimless spectacles were eyes that stared intently at her with tenderness and concern. Even while experiencing relentless pain in her head, Christine could see that the nun was focused on her and nothing else mattered.

"There's a hospital a few blocks from here," the nun said. "Let me help you get there."

Slowly taking Christine by the arm, she added, "Whatever happened to you, believe it or not, you're going to get through it. This will not break you, I promise."

Unable to bear the agony, Christine allowed herself to be led, convinced an angel from heaven had come down to help her.

Gently holding Christine's arm, the nun led her to the hospital's receptionist and explained how she had found her.

"Dear, who can I contact to help you?" the nun gently inquired.

THE BOOK OF REVELATIONS

Christine was able to recite her parents' work numbers before she said, "I think I have to throw up again."

"She needs a plastic bag," the nun told the receptionist. She still held Christine's arm and appeared unruffled. "Don't you worry, dear. Don't you worry about a thing. We've all seen vomit before. It's how we rid the body of toxins."

The woman led her to the seats in the waiting area. Christine sat down with her hands still clutching her head. Someone put an open plastic bag in front of her. She heaved and tried to throw up again, but nothing would come up. The pain in the forefront of her head was so intense she felt like she was going to fall over and start crawling around like an animal screaming if the pain continued to throb at this rate.

Fortunately, she was able to throw up three more times.

"That's it, dear. Now you'll feel better." The nun rubbed her back. "Now you're going to start feeling better. The worst is over."

At this point, the receptionist resumed asking her questions.

"What is your name?"

Christine struggled with blurry vision as her head continued to throb. "C- Christine Zarzycki."

The nun continued rubbing her back.

Christine vomited into the bag in response to the receptionist asking for her address.

She answered after heaving several times.

The throbbing in her head and joints dulled. Determined to put Ryan out of her mind and life forever, she concentrated on getting herself together.

"Miss?" A nurse approached and asked her in a kind voice, "Will you follow me please?"

The nun helped Christine slowly rise and walk with the nurse. She clutched the nun's hand in an awkward attempt to thank her. She wanted to say, "Thank you. You've been an angel," but feared she would throw up again.

Christine woke up to a warm, calm sensation circulating throughout her body. She was snuggling under a thin white blanket when she opened her eyes. She didn't recognize her surroundings. A monitor stood a few feet from her, and an IV with a bag was dripping a few feet away. She heard beeping noises and saw medical staff in blue uniforms wheeling patients in hospital gowns. She caught a glimpse of the nurse's station and spotted medical staff conversing, overhearing a hearty laugh – someone must have told a joke.

Her eyes traveled to scan her small room. Seated against the wall were her parents. Worry lines creased their foreheads. Both were pale and wore shocked expressions, their bodies tightly wound with tension.

Oh! At least my parents are here when I need them the most! she thought.

Her head still groggy, Christine tried to sit up, but an IV bag attached to her arm restricted her movement.

"Don't try to get up! We're here! How do you feel?" Her mother came rushing over.

"I can't believe it! I thought I knew him! And I came all the way here to visit," she said, biting her lip and directing her tear-stained face toward the ceiling. She began sobbing.

Her mother tentatively touched her daughter's hair, as if she were not sure she knew her own daughter. She and her father remained silent.

Eventually, her father slowly asked, staring at her, "What happened when you went to visit Ryan?"

"Oh, Dad! You were right! You were so right about him."

Her father stood and gritted his teeth. "Why that piece of sh—"

"How are you feeling now?" The doctor came in and, seeing Christine crying, he said, "Now, don't get upset. You had a very bad migraine headache. That was why you were vomiting and your vision was blurry. That's all over with now. We gave you chlorpromazine to treat it. You'll be feeling better. You need to calm down and rest."

"The doctor's right, Christine," her mother said, shooting a warning glance at her husband. "It's not good for you to get all worked up. Think of the b—" Instead of saying the last word, she covered her face and sobbed. "Oh, Christine!" she wailed.

"What? What? What are you talking about?" Christine looked up, trying to understand. "Tell me! Please!"

"Now, you need to calm down. You're going to be fine." the doctor said.

She continued staring at her father. "Dad, what's going on?"

Despite her mother trying to signal her father to be quiet, he asked, "What happened with Ryan?"

"He was busy making out with his costar!" She moaned and covered her face with her hands as she burst into tears again.

Christine forced herself to stop crying and faced her father again. "Dad, what were you going to say? What are you trying to tell me?"

By this time, her father rose and with steely, determined eyes, his body shaking with anger, he said, "I'm going to beat the brains out of that pretty face! I swear he's never going walk again!"

"Christine, Christine, you're pregnant," her mother told her in a strained voice, tears streaming down from her eyes.

"What? I don't understand! How could that have happen —" Christine stared at him, perplexed.

Her mind flashed back to the night she and Ryan made out in his car, and she remembered finding blood on the car seat. Her face turned white.

"Christine, don't be upset! Everything is going to work out all right, I promise. Just don't get upset. We're going to take care of everything." Her mother held her hand until she closed her eyes and settled down, too dejected to remain conscious.

Her father was facing away from her, but she could still hear him say in a low voice, "We wanted you to finish college and find a nice man to marry. That's all gone now."

"Mrs. Goldberg?" the nurse said in a soft voice, almost a whisper. "The doctor is ready to speak with you now."

Christine's eyes popped open. For a second, she forgot where she was. Her memories had completely taken over her consciousness once she closed her eyes.

"Are you all right, Mrs. Goldberg?" The nurse approached her and felt her forehead. "You're pale."

"I'm all right. I'm coming, thank you." She quickly got herself oriented to the present.

She entered the doctor's office as Daniel sat in front of the desk balling and unballing his hands into fists.

"Hi, honey," Christine said as she lightly tapped her husband's shoulder. Daniel, a faraway look in his eyes, almost jumped out of his seat.

"I'm sorry, honey. Forgive me." He put his hand on her arm and blinked his eyes as though awakening from a trance.

Christine sank into the chair and gripped the arms as if to brace herself for more bad news, but Dr. Sherman spoke gently, putting her at ease.

"Mrs. Goldberg, I was giving your husband the results of the needle biopsy he went for a few days ago. I'm afraid it confirms he has acute myeloid leukemia," he explained. "His test showed an abnormal white cell count."

Christine froze in her chair, trying hard not to gasp in horror.

"As I was telling your husband, the medical profession has

made great strides in the treatment of leukemia. Chemo-therapy is required, and Massachusetts General Hospital is one of the best in the country for treating it. He'll be in the best hands."

Christine cleared her throat. "What about the prognosis?"

"It's fortunate we caught it early," Dr. Sherman began.

Her mouth became a thin, tight line. *Stop stonewalling me, Doctor!* she yearned to say out loud.

The doctor must have sensed her rising impatience. He added, "There are no guarantees, but to fight this disease, we must meet it head-on. Daniel will go for chemotherapy sessions in the hospital and stay there in case he requires blood and platelet transfusions if there's an inadequate level of healthy blood cells. The goal is for Daniel to be in remission. Now there may be side effects—"

"You mean I'm going to go bald." Daniel sat up, coming out of his stupor.

"I don't know about that. But you'll find you'll be losing hair. In most cases, it grows back."

"Lord, who cares, Daniel? As long as you stay alive." Christine stared at her husband incredulously.

Daniel looked back and forth from the doctor to his wife.

"If I got sick and lost my hair, would you have a problem with that?" Christine asked.

"No, of course not! It's just… it's just…"

"Just what?" his wife asked.

Daniel sank in his chair, touching his mane. "In high school I was voted best hair."

The doctor put his hand over his mouth to conceal a smile.

"It will grow back," Christine said as she touched his cheek.

"Patients also find they have less energy, need more rest, and have a reduced appetite," Dr. Sherman said.

Christine reached for her husband.

"We're all going to deal with this as a family."

Daniel shot up again. "But I won't be able to work." He turned to Dr. Sherman. "Our twins are planning to go to college in the fall." He looked from one to the other and then sat back with his hand over his eyes. "God, this couldn't be happening at a worse time!"

"Daniel, we have to take one day at a time. So if the kids get into BC or go to the state school, they'll have to take out more loans. They're hard-working, mature kids. We'll work it out. Even if they have to postpone college for a year. That's no catastrophe."

"You're right, you're right, of course. As long as they're healthy," Daniel said, sitting up. He turned to the doctor. "I'm sorry. You don't need to hear this."

Dr. Sherman smiled. "Daniel, it's all right. I understand."

"We'll talk more about this later," Christine said, forcing herself to smile. She placed her hand on top of his and said with more conviction than she felt, "Don't worry, it will all work out."

Her words seem to placate her husband. Daniel smiled and gave her hand a gentle squeeze. Turning to the doctor, he said, "She's my rock. I would be lost without her."

Dr. Sherman nodded. "She sure is. You're lucky to have her. Listen to everything she tells you." He turned to Christine. "You're looking a little pale. Be sure to also take care of yourself. Don't neglect your own health at this time. You get some rest too."

Christine beamed and clutched her husband's hand. "I will, Doctor. Thank you. We have our work cut out for us, but we're working together as a team."

CHAPTER SEVENTEEN

Hollywood Hills

Before starting his engine Friday morning, Ryan checked his cell. Megan had called, but he was in no mood for apologies or romantic conversation. He left a message for Buddy that he was traveling to Boston on Tuesday. He started up his Maserati and headed over to his parents' house. Ryan found himself trembling with excitement thinking about his twins and possibly seeing them in Boston. It still didn't seem real. Would they even accept him if they knew he was their father? Would they be just as confused as he was that they hadn't met him until now? Would they even give him a chance?

Ryan kept conjuring theories as to why Christine had those babies without telling him. He recalled the moment when she had walked in on him. It was a misunderstanding, and she never gave him the opportunity to explain. But surely, if she had gotten pregnant, she could have used his support. Endless theories kept swirling around in his mind by the time he parked his car and proceeded to walk up to his parents' front door. Sadness descended on his high spirits when he thought about Christine withholding knowledge of the twins from him. Did she think he was some sort of monster, shielding them from their own father? His pace slowed as he hung his head in shame.

Beaming, his mother opened the door before he had a chance to put in his key, but her smile vanished when she noticed all his features turned downward.

"Ryan, what's wrong?" Sara creased her eyebrows and put her hand to her cheek. It was early, and she was still wearing her robe.

When he didn't respond, his father, wearing the purple silk robe Ryan had bought him the previous Christmas, rushed to the door. "Son, what's happened?"

"I got into a fight with my agent." Ryan mumbled the first excuse that came into his head. "I don't want to discuss it."

He didn't want to reveal what was going on. At least not yet.

"Well, Phil has always made great decisions when it comes to your career. We'll discuss it when you're ready, but don't make any hasty decisions. Son, I've got a lot of confidence in Phil. When you hired him, your career really took off," his father said.

"Let him sit down and relax, Jerry," his mother scolded her husband. "I know after Ryan eats, he can think more clearly. She turned to her son. "I just made hash browns and sausages. Let me make French toast, just the way you like it. Come and sit down."

"Thanks, Mom." Ryan fell heavily into a kitchen chair. "So what's going on with you two today?" he asked his parents, hoping to change the subject since they now wore worry-stricken expressions. Although they were his most reliable confidants, he wasn't ready to divulge his news. Besides, it could still wind up being some crazy mix-up.

THE BOOK OF REVELATIONS

"Well, I signed up to take mah-jongg lessons. I'm starting later today," his mother responded after an initial pause.

"That's great," Ryan said weakly, not even attempting to drum up enthusiasm.

"Your mother needs to stop puttering around the house," his father added. "She's got to go out more. Be with other ladies. She'll find she has lots to talk about with them, won't you, honey?"

"I suppose. I can't be a homebody all the time," she said.

The family sat down in the kitchen, and Sara served breakfast.

"And I decided to take a drive out in my favorite car today," Jerry said, winking at Ryan.

"Dad, how do you manage to keep that car in pristine condition? I bought that for you years ago."

"I remember how proud you were to buy Dad a car. It was after you made a few movies. Dad couldn't afford another car when his broke down, but you saved the day, son!" Sara recalled, her eyes sparkling.

"I drive it about twice a week, wash it once a month, and make sure everything is up to date," his father declared. "I'll always remember you bought me that car on my forty-fifth birthday. I remember only buying you a birthday cake and a small gift for your birthday that year." Jerry smiled sadly. "Money was tight back then."

"Dad, you bought me a new suitcase for traveling that year. Don't you remember?"

Jerry waved his hand. "It was nothing compared to a car."

"But you shopped around in a lot of stores until you found the suitcase you thought was spiffy enough for Ryan to bring to Hollywood," Sara said. "And you bought it just in time. Ryan's old suitcase had just fallen apart."

"You bought it for me just when I needed it. I didn't have time to buy a new suitcase when they asked me to audition for that soap opera," Ryan said. His father looked happy again, but Ryan's smile vanished.

"Ryan, what's the matter?" his mother asked.

He hesitated before asking, "Do you remember the girl I went out with at around that time? Her name was Christine Zarzycki?" He studied his parents' faces as they turned their heads and stared at each other, trying to recall her.

"Oh, I remember that girl. We met her a few times. She was sweet and beautiful. A strict Catholic, right?" his mother recalled, her eyes lighting up.

Ryan nodded and stared down at his meal.

"I was very surprised you two found each other. We were never religious, but I remember the two of you were so in love. I saw it in your eyes and how you smiled every time her name came up," Sara remarked. "I thought for sure you two were going to get married. I wondered then how many grandchildren I was going to have." Sara laughed a bit and then turned serious. "I never saw you so in love since. Then Kim came along, and you were interested in her for a while, but it was never the same."

"Oh, don't even mention that evil girl," Jerry remarked. "She tortured Ryan for months. He couldn't even enjoy his nomination for an Academy Award. Thank God you finally got rid of her!"

"More like she knew she had nothing on me so she quit trying to blackmail me," Ryan said, heaving a sigh. "She was a nightmare."

"And you never pursued a serious relationship ever since," Jerry said, shaking his head. "Every year it's been a different woman."

"What about the one you're seeing now, Ryan?" Sara asked.

"Megan Riley."

"She's a working girl, I understand?" his father inquired as he raised an eyebrow.

"Yeah, an insurance company."

His father nodded and winked. "Sounds good. Sounds good."

"She's going to have a big birthday party in two weeks, but – oh, I almost forgot to tell you. I'm going to Boston next week."

"But you were starting to tell us the problem with your agent—" his mother began.

But Ryan waved his hand. "Nothing we can't fix. I get a little worked up every time he tells me about a role. No big deal."

"Do you have to leave for Boston so soon? Why not put it off, Ryan? I'm sure Megan will be disappointed. Maybe this one will turn serious," Sara said. "Wouldn't that be wonderful?"

"I already told her I wasn't going to be here for the party. That was when I was going to take another role, but I dropped it for this new one that came up."

Sara shook her head and was about to lift her fork when she asked, "You can't put off Boston?"

Ryan closed his eyes and shook his head. "No, I can't."

"Oh, Ryan, you have so much clout in Hollywood. I can't believe you can't tell them you need a few more weeks." She held up her hands in exasperation. "How are you going to get married if you keep letting women down?" she exclaimed.

"Mom, I've got a lot on my mind, and I really feel it would be good to get away. I'm not sure about my feelings for Megan right now. I can't give in to her demand I be there. I'm sorry."

"But, Ryan, that's what marriage is all about," she said, her expression turning downward. "It means being there for your spouse."

IDELLE KURSMAN

Ryan held his hands up. "Maybe I'm not so in love with her that I want that."

"I don't have enough fingers and toes to count how many women you've gone out with in the last few years. I don't think you're ever going to get married, Ryan," she whispered in a pleading voice. "When your father and I are gone, you'll be all alone, son. Don't you realize that?"

Ryan was tongue-tied. She was right. When his parents were gone, he would be alone. Ryan knew he didn't want that. There was a pause; he stood up, took out his phone, and said, "Excuse me," to his parents.

"Of course," they responded together.

As Ryan walked into the living room, he began losing his earlier enthusiasm for making this call, wondering if this was what he really wanted.

"Whittier and Hall Insurance," the receptionist chirped into the phone.

"May I speak with Megan Riley, please?"

"And who's calling?"

"Bill Smith," Ryan said. This was his code name that he and Megan made up between them so as not to cause a stir.

"One moment."

"Hi, babe! I thought you'd never answer my call!" Megan gushed on the phone. "And I'm really surprised you'd call while you're eating breakfast with your parents."

"You know my schedule well," said Ryan. "I'm calling you back when I finally have a moment to catch my breath. I'm going over a new script after breakfast. I'm feeling real good about this movie role. It – but here I go again, rattling on about me. Tell me how you're doing?"

Ryan could detect a pleasant laugh in her voice. "Working on some accounts to seal the deal. My clients are coming later today, and I'm just doing research to find out how best I can serve their needs."

Ryan glanced back in the kitchen. His father was sitting at the table, and his mother was at the stove, cracking eggs for French toast. His plate of hash browns and sausages was covered. His mother always did that with his warm food whenever he had to leave the table.

"Listen, I don't want to keep you. I want to take you out again before I leave, just as I promised you. What about tonight?"

"Sounds great. I'll call you if I'm running late, but I so look forward to seeing you. Enjoy your day, babe."

"You too. See you later."

Upon returning to the kitchen, his mother rose and said, "I'm preparing French toast for you. W- was that your girl-friend you were talking to?"

"Yes, Megan. We're going out to dinner tonight."

"Oh, wonderful!" A glow appeared on his mother's face, and her eyes sparkled as if this was a major breakthrough.

"Ryan," his father began, "don't you think you can ease up a little at this point in your career?" He shook his head. "When you're on top, don't sweat over every script, son."

"You're right, Dad." Ryan uncovered his plate as he heard bread sizzling in egg batter on the stove.

Dad doesn't understand how a flop can seriously damage a career, he thought.

The smells of his mom's cooking calmed his mood, and he looked forward to a relaxing meal with his parents. He decided to put his feelings about Megan on hold for now.

CHAPTER EIGHTEEN

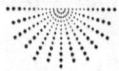

Boston

At 7:00 p.m., work was finished and she could go home, but Christine still lingered around the office, making sure her files, pens, and notebooks were all in place. She would have vacuumed the carpets if she could have, but the maintenance man did that in the morning and the vacuum was locked in the utility room.

Tonight was *the visit*. She and Daniel were going to tell his parents about his illness. Christine was sure his parents had been anxious ever since Daniel called and said they were going to pop over to their house tonight.

He had already called Seth. His brother was extremely distraught but swore he would let Daniel break the news to their parents himself. Daniel offered to go over his parents' house alone, but she insisted on accompanying him. He told her she didn't have to put herself through this, but she wouldn't back down.

It's the least I can do after he rescued me and the children from a life of misery, she thought.

As she straightened the chairs in her office for the tenth time, Christine had a nauseating feeling in the pit of her stomach every time she thought about the visit.

She knew she also needed to deliver the news to her own parents. To this day, her mother, Fran, would still hint that she was selfish when she got pregnant all those years ago. Didn't Christine know what could happen? Why did she take that chance having relations while she was still single? She had promised them she would take the traditional path: get married to a nice Catholic man and then raise a family. Though they melted and swooned whenever they saw the grandchildren, their expressions betrayed their disappointment in her.

Christine sat down. She put her elbows on her desk and her hands over her face. Years afterward, both her parents suffered health ailments. Five years ago they retired to Florida. When the twins were younger, they used to stay with her parents for one week every winter. As time went by and they saw how well she was bringing up the twins, they began calling her once a week. They slowly became more affectionate toward their daughter once again.

Now they've got to hear this. Christine shrank deeper in her office chair just thinking about it. She dreaded calling them and decided to put it off until she was ready.

She was not to remain in her private agony for long. Her desk phone rang.

"Christine, don't hurry home. I know you had a long, hard day. I'm going to my parents' by myself."

Christine sat up, trying to object, but she couldn't find the words.

"But, but—" she began.

"You've been wonderful, but I think this is above and beyond the call of duty. You go out and have a relaxing meal. I ordered a pizza for me and the kids. This is something I'd rather do alone, and I don't think it's fair to put you through it – especially after a long workday. Go out to dinner and relax. I rested all day. I'm prepared."

She felt bad, but her relief inside was palpable.

"Are you sure?" she asked, furrowing her brow.

"Definitely. I love you."

"I love you too."

Hanging up the phone, Christine let out a heavy breath, as if she had just averted being run over by a car.

As much as she would have loved to follow her husband's advice, Christine knew she owed it to him to do the right thing. By the time she got into her Honda, she resolved to grab a quick bite, call her own parents, and then meet her husband at her in-laws' house in Brighton.

* * *

Sitting in her car, Christine had just finished a fish sandwich and a salad from McDonald's, grateful for the invention of fast food on such a hectic day. She took out her phone and dialed. Her father answered.

"Hi, Dad."

"Hi, Christine. Are the twins all right?"

"Yes, they're fine. Why?"

"Because I know you're usually on your way home from work at this time."

"Dad, I have to talk to you. It's about Daniel."

"What about him?"

She had been so determined to keep her voice even but couldn't. She said, sobbing, "He's really sick, Dad. He has leukemia."

"Oh, Christine, that's terrible! I know we haven't called you in a while. Mom has been slowing down lately, and I've been busy with that. But we have been thinking about you and the twins. What is the prognosis?"

"He needs to start chemotherapy right away if there is any chance of remission. Tonight we're going over to his parents' house to break the news to them."

"Oh my God! How horrible! We'll be in touch more, Christine. How are the twins handling it?"

"They're upset, of course. They love their father dearly. They may have to put off college for a year and work, but they're trying to stay strong for their father's sake." She checked her watch. "I'm afraid I have to leave now, Dad. I'm meeting Daniel at his parents' house."

"We'll have to come up, Christine. All of you are going to need help. I'm going to break the news to your mother, and we'll get back in touch with you. Let me know if the twins need anything right away. Oh, and you too."

Christine hung up the phone. *My parents' main concern is the twins. I'm nothing more than an afterthought.*

She closed her eyes, willing the bitter thoughts to disappear. She had more important things to do and think about. Christine started the engine and headed over to Brighton.

* * *

Christine spotted Daniel walking up the steps to his parents' house. She parked her car behind his and called over to him. Daniel turned around, his initial surprise turning to relief.

He proceeded down the steps. "You came," he greeted her.

"This is going to be a tough meeting. I figured you'd need support."

"You figured right, as usual." Daniel couldn't help smiling. "I'm so glad I have you on my team."

They held hands as they proceeded up the steps together.

"Hi, Daniel! Christine. Come in! Come in!" Judy rushed to

the door, opened it, and gave her son a hug and kiss. She touched her daughter-in-law's arm lightly as she gave her a peck on the cheek.

All three stood, wooden, in the hallway.

Finally, Judy broke the ice. She attempted a chuckle and said, "Come on in. You two know your way around here. How are you and the family?"

Daniel struggled getting his words out. "The family's fine." He spoke so quietly it came out as a whisper. "How are the two of you?"

"We're fine, no complaints," Judy said while reaching to take Daniel's coat.

"No one wants to hear them anyway," Harry quipped as he walked in. He shook his son's hand and kissed Christine.

No one laughed at his joke. An eerie silence filled the room.

"What about you, Daniel? Is there something wrong?" Judy asked faintly, staring intently at her son and massaging her arm.

Daniel and Christine glanced at each other. "Maybe we ought to sit down," he suggested while Christine looked down.

"No, I want to hear it right now. What's wrong, Daniel? I know something's going on with you, and I want you to tell us already!" Judy spoke in a sudden shrill voice.

"I've been seeing Dr. Sherman. I've got an illness," Daniel said, looking down at the floor.

"You saw Dr. Sherman!" Harry said with a start. His face paled. "Now we noticed you've been losing weight and looking more drawn, but I thought you said it was because you were nervous about starting the new job. Dr. Sherman is an oncologist! What's going on, son? What has been going on?"

"I have leukemia. I didn't want to tell you" – he glanced at Christine – "or anyone else until I knew for sure."

"Why not? Why didn't you tell us?"

Daniel put his hands in his pockets and stared at his chest in shame. "I didn't want to put you through another nightmare until I was certain."

Judy closed her eyes, slouching, appearing ready to cry. Harry put his hand on his forehead and looked away for a moment before looking into his son's eyes and saying, "Daniel, we're a family. One of the purposes of family is to support each other when problems come up. Whether they're real or turn out to be nothing."

"I know. I know. What happened in college – don't worry, Christine already knows," he rushed to say as his parents' eyes traveled to their daughter-in-law. "That took so much out of you two that I had to be sure I was as sick as I feared."

His parents now appeared shriveled and weak. Daniel said, "Let's all sit down."

Harry nodded and slowly and gently led his wife to the couch. Once seated, he said, "We'll come up with something. A plan to beat this thing. You're a fighter, Daniel. We're behind you all the way."

Christine's eyes grew moist. Her normally outspoken mother-in-law looked ashen. Judy said nothing and let her husband take over. She noticed Daniel gripping the seat of his chair, trying to control himself, but he couldn't and broke down. The three of them jumped up to console him. Daniel said through his tears, "I've been keeping this inside for so long."

"You don't have to anymore, Daniel," Christine said quietly as she wrapped her arm around him and gently placed her hand over his shaking one.

"That's right, Daniel," Judy said, looking at her daughter-in-law as if she just had a revelation. "We and your wife are here to support you all the way. Listen to us. Our friend Gregory had leukemia, and now he's doing just fine."

"But I have an acute case. Myeloid leukemia."

His parents stood with their mouths open and stared at each other. Harry looked away and put his hands over his face. Judy put her fists near her mouth. Then she put her arms around her son's shoulders.

"Oh my Daniel! My poor son! What you have to go through!" she wailed. "You don't deserve this tsuris!"

"Judy, stop talking about suffering," Harry insisted. "Daniel's going to do whatever the doctor tells him to, and we've got to think positive. He'll make a full recovery."

"You mean a remission, Dad," Daniel choked out.

"You'll have a remission because you're going to do everything the doctor tells you," Christine said. She was also crying.

By the time they left the house, Christine felt so depleted that she wished she were home and could collapse into bed. But she wanted to make a show of strength for Daniel's sake. They held hands as they walked to their respective cars.

"Are you sure you're up to driving?" Christine asked her husband. "We could pick up the car tomorrow."

"No, I'll be fine. I actually feel more at ease when I'm driving and thinking. I don't know, it just calms me down." He turned to her. "This was the hardest. Telling them."

"I know. But it had to be done."

Daniel nodded. They kissed and embraced before getting into their cars.

Daniel drove out, but Christine lingered in the driver's seat. She pulled her car out but parked it again after driving only a few blocks. She didn't want her in-laws to see that she didn't feel able to drive yet.

Her mind turned to the dreadful scene eighteen years ago. The worst scene she had to witness in her life. The ultimate betrayal. She could not relive this memory and drive at the same time.

Christine had taken a bus to the movie studio where Ryan was wrapping up filming. She had exciting news to share – she had passed her economics exam! The one she was convinced she would fail for sure. What better way to celebrate than tell the news to the man she loved and who believed in her.

Once she got off the bus, Christine had no trouble getting into the studio. Ryan had taken her there yesterday and introduced her to security. They waved her in with no problem.

"Hi, Christine. How're you doing?"

"I'm fine, Mr. Brennan." She smiled widely at the cameraman. "How are you?"

"Great! We're just about wrapping up here," he said. "You must be looking for Ryan."

"Yes, I am."

"He knew you were coming?"

"No, I thought I'd surprise him."

Mr. Brennan's eyes lit up. "Well, you have excellent timing, my dear! He went to his trailer at the break. I'm sure he'll be thrilled when he sees you."

He pointed to the general direction Christine would find his trailer.

I'm so happy I feel like skipping like a little girl again. I feel like everything is coming together for us! I'll continue college, Ryan will keep making movies, we'll get married...

She was at the front door of his movie trailer. Christine would have liked to run to the bathroom first to make sure her hair and clothes looked just right, but she was too excited.

Christine knocked. Silence.

"Ryan? Ryan? Are you there?"

She was going to turn around when she heard what sounded like moving furniture. Christine knocked louder this time. She turned the door handle and found the door was open, so she walked in.

Her exuberant mood was shattered, replaced by shock. Christine felt her legs give way. She clutched a wall to keep from falling. She couldn't believe the scene before her. "Oh! Oh my God! Oh my God!" Christine screamed.

Ryan shot up.

Christine stood there paralyzed with her hands covering her mouth and her eyes bulging in disbelief.

Ryan turned red, his mouth hanging open. He was in the arms of a beautiful woman wearing a thick coat of black mascara and lips painted a deep red. Her dress was cut low and her bra strap had slipped down one of her arms. Christine and Ryan stood transfixed, simply staring at each other.

"What? Who is this, *amor*? Your girlfriend?" the woman asked as she struggled to cover up.

Christine began rocking unsteadily.

"Christine! Christine!" Ryan called out. He reached for his clothes, attempting to dress.

Christine struggled for the door, her vision blurry, trying to find her way out.

"Christine! Wait! Please!" Ryan called. "I- I'm sorry! We've gotta talk! Wait! Christine!"

But wait she did not. She dragged herself out the door.

Christine wobbled out of the studio lot in a daze. When people involved in the production spotted her leaving, they thought either she was having a nervous breakdown or was drunk. They couldn't say or do anything but stop and stare.

Her face was tear stained and pale, her eyes glazed over. She ran out and continued running until the wave of traffic surrounding her on Melrose Avenue slowed her movements.

Was she dreaming? In the middle of a nightmare?

Her phone rang.

"Christine! Are you all right? Are you stuck?" Daniel sounded near hysteria.

Christine took a deep breath. "No, sorry, honey. I just stopped at the convenience store to use the bathroom. I'm coming right home."

"Are you sure you're all right? I was about to come looking for you."

"Don't worry. I'll be home in five minutes."

She hung up and checked the rearview mirror. She wished she could go into a convenience store and wash up but feared people would stare at her. What if there was someone she knew in the store? Christine wiped her face and headed back home, hoping the redness in her eyes would go down by the time she arrived.

Her family was dealing with so much now; she couldn't afford to fall apart.

CHAPTER NINETEEN

LOS ANGELES

Sitting in his office and making plans to go home, Buddy found himself in an untenable position. Clients considered him a genius for devising strategies to get out of compromising circumstances, yet he was now at a loss on devising a plan for himself to escape Ozzy's blackmail scheme. How could that nitwit come along and jeopardize the sterling career he had spent years building? If he didn't comply with Ozzy's demands, could his life's work unravel? And what would Monti do to him if he found out Buddy knew who was blackmailing him all along? Monti was an actor; how long could Buddy lie to him without giving himself away? Buddy had spent the last few hours calling contacts in newspapers, social media, and private investigation, hoping to find Ozzy a solid, well-paying position so he'd leave him alone while he continued working on Monti's case. Unfortunately, he couldn't find anything lucrative or long-term enough anywhere that would even tempt him.

Ozzy would make more money splitting Ryan's fee with him.

Buddy found a pencil on his desk and broke it, wishing it were Ozzy's body.

Maybe I should take a chance and forget about him. Why would Ryan Monti believe a screwball like Ozzy?

But Buddy knew he dare not consider taking that risk.

His cell phone sounded. He checked his watch. His wife, Lucy, must still be playing mah-jongg. His clients knew they couldn't call him after hours unless there was an emergency. Maybe someone had found a way to get him out of this mess. Buddy picked up the phone.

"So what's going on?" Ozzy barked into the phone.

Buddy sank in his chair. "What do you mean?"

"What is Monti doing now? Is he coming to Boston or he is trying to make this go away? He can't, you know."

Buddy sighed, forcing himself to say, "He knows. He'll be leaving for Boston shortly."

"When is shortly, Buddy? Stop messing around with me."

"Sometime next week," Buddy answered. He jerked up. "Why? What do you mean to do when he's in Boston? Ozzy, I want you to keep your distance from him. The worst thing you can do is interfere. You don't want him to drop me, do you?"

"The last cut you sent me was much smaller. You're not fooling with the numbers on those payments, are you?"

Buddy turned red in the face. "No, I am not changing the amount. The initial payment is higher, and then he sends me payments in installments. I'm barely covering my expenses with half the payments now."

"Send me the information where Monti is staying and what you know about his schedule."

Buddy wished he could grab Ozzy by the neck and

strangle him. He said with gritted teeth, "I told you this won't work for either of us if you interfere in the investigation."

"Sorry, Buddy, these payments aren't going to go very far. I need to buy a new car and be kept abreast of developments. As long as you're giving me half those payments, your investigation won't be compromised. Who knows? I may help you uncover more in the process and you'll even want to hire me as one of your star investigators."

Buddy stared at the phone. *Is he out of his mind? I want nothing more than to get rid of this good-for-nothing,* he thought.

But nuts or not, Buddy needed to play along. At least for now.

"So let me know the details," Ozzy continued, "and if I find out that you aren't telling me what you already know, I'll blackmail Monti myself. I may be out of work, Buddy, but I have tremendous resources of my own for finding out what I need to know. Double-cross me and you'll soon find your client suing you for everything you have."

Buddy's mouth dropped open. Images of Lucy berating him when they were forced out of their two homes flitted through his mind. The rich and famous eyeing him, the once "private investigator to the stars" brought down, penniless, his adversaries relishing his fall. Wannabes scrambling to replace him. His head pounded as he recalled bringing many of his clients' opponents to bankruptcy and even jail. Would he find himself in the slammer? Abandoned and disgraced, the subject of ridicule?

"He's leaving Tuesday next week," Buddy blurted out.

"Very good, Buddy. Much better. And where is he staying?"

Buddy sank within himself. The pressure on him proved too strong to bear. "The Mandarin Oriental," he huffed out.

* * *

Midnight. People were inside, most of them asleep. Don Chin saw very few lights on. He had picked the right moment.

Chin slipped out of his black car and closed the door as quietly as he could. He was parked on the Goldbergs' street, under trees fives houses down from where they lived. Dressed all in black, he slithered down the street until he was close to the Goldberg house. Chin could hear an occasional passing car on the main street. He was relieved they lived on a side street far from the city center. He crept in front of their house and, wearing thick, heavy gloves, opened one of their garbage cans. Chin heard a dog barking in the distance and crouched down, but the barking was far enough away that it shouldn't disturb the neighbors on this end of the street.

Chin rose again and rifled through the garbage contents. Napkins, crumbs from leftover meals, and wrappers. Nothing useful.

He grimaced and retied the garbage, gently putting the cover back on. Fortunately, there was another can beside it. Chin didn't know what he would do if he couldn't find anything. He needed some objects to test the children's DNA. His boss, Buddy Catalano, was counting on him. Buddy always referred to him as his number one investigator. Chin stuck his hand in broken glass – fortunately, his gloves protected him. Discarded pens. A tube of toothpaste. Four toothbrushes. Finally! Chin was sure two of them must belong to the twins.

He whipped out a plastic bag from his jacket pocket and deposited the toothbrushes in it. Then he crept back to his car, careful to make a minimum of noise.

Upon getting into his car, he heard the dog bark once again. This time, Chin closed the door shut as he normally would and drove away at twenty miles per hour, checking his rearview mirror for lights turning on in houses or heads poking out windows. Noticing nothing of the sort, Chin picked up speed once he turned on the main road.

CHAPTER TWENTY

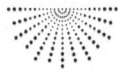

Los Angeles

*I*f there's someone I can always rely on, it's Mr. Don Chin, Buddy thought as he lit a cigar. His feet were atop his desk. A good night's sleep and making the last few months' payment on his Tribeca condo gave him a great feeling of satisfaction. It enabled him to push away any lingering anger at Ozzy. Lucy was pleased and even promised she would cook him his favorite dish for tonight: veal cutlets and spaghetti, with piping hot garlic bread and a Caesar salad. Buddy felt more relaxed. Maybe someone would come through to enable him to get rid of Ozzy. He began wondering why Ozzy couldn't find a job if he had as many resources as he claimed. But on the personal front, he felt relieved the pressure was off him.

Yep! Ryan Monti's indiscretion years ago helped get me back in the black!

His phone rang.

"Don Chin's on the other line, Mr. Catalano," Shana told him in a low voice.

Buddy knew she was disappointed it wasn't Ryan Monti.

"I'll take it, Shana. Thanks."

"Last night I went through their garbage cans and found the kids' toothbrushes," Don said, in his usual style of getting straight to business. "I brought the samples to a local lab for testing."

"Excellent! So you've been following this Christine woman and you've found out she is a recruiter for a modeling agency. How would you describe her?"

"Looking at her, she looks like a top model herself."

"Yeah, Ryan's got good taste," Buddy said as he puffed on his cigar.

"She's married to a man named Daniel Goldberg, who just began working for a marketing start-up company. He worked for close to twenty years at Smith Marketing, but since the company folded, he's gone through three jobs. Struggling."

This interested Buddy enough to take his feet off his desk. He placed the cigar in the ashtray. *So maybe this Christine Goldberg is hard up for money and is shaking Ryan. Figures he forgot they slept together.*

"College age," Buddy said and thought, *God, they must need money now!*

"The only other thing I found out was the husband's been taking a lot of days off work. I don't know why yet. When I've watched them at a distance, none of them looks too happy."

"Ohhhhh! You did good, Don! Keep digging. I know you'll get to the bottom of this."

When Buddy hung up, he resumed puffing on his cigar and put his feet up again. They were getting somewhere. As he thought about this, the cigar smoke he puffed out formed into dollar signs in his mind. He even thought of people who owed him favors that just might find a way for him to get rid of Ozzy.

He sighed. "It's always money," he said aloud, dispensing the cigar's ashes in the ashtray. The priest at his church came to mind. Buddy was ambivalent about religion, but his wife insisted they attend. Whenever Father John received a big donation, he would shake that parishioner's hand longer and more warmly than the others, telling them he would gladly help them out if they ever needed anything. Buddy used to get those handshakes until he began experiencing financial problems.

He shook his head as he stamped out his cigar in the ashtray. "It always comes down to money."

CHAPTER TWENTY-ONE

BOSTON

R yan's thoughts were a blur on the plane. He kept forgetting he was also doing research for a new movie. He blamed it on not being able to sleep all night. Neither could he rest on the flight. He remained stiff in his first-class seat – unable to eat, drink, or sit back and watch the movie. Once he got off the plane, he couldn't help scanning every teenager he saw. *Would his twins magically be waiting for him, their biological father, at the airport? Would he be ready to meet them? How would he react?* Ryan dismissed these fantasies and looked for the driver the studio had arranged to take him to the hotel. He spotted the black town car with the sign bearing his prearranged code name, but not before he was recognized.

"Is that Ryan Monti?" shrieked a teenage girl with long thick, black hair and a mousy face to her friend as the pair stopped walking and gaped at him.

"Yeah! Yeah! I think so!" said her friend, who had braces

and brown hair in tight curls. They started giggling and pointing, jumping up and down.

When they approached his car and called to him, Ryan stared straight ahead and was oblivious to their efforts to get his attention. He neither glanced their way nor acknowledged them.

"Man, what's with him?" the girl with braces said to her friend as the car drove away. "It's as if he didn't even know we're here! Is he deaf or something? He acted like we're invisible!"

And to Ryan Monti, they were. He heard their words, but he failed to register they were talking about him. His thoughts were miles away as he recalled the time Christine saw him in his movie trailer eighteen years ago.

Finishing the last day of work on the set, Ryan couldn't wait meet up with Christine when it was finally over. He and costar Felicia Montero had to complete a lengthy intimate scene that final day. A budding star in her native Mexico, Felicia and her agent were determined to spread her fame to the United States. Ryan saw her potential to hit it big: she had dark, beguiling eyes surrounded by thick black eyelashes. When she sauntered around the set, people couldn't help gaping at her hourglass figure.

During their sex scene, Ryan was surprised Felicia did not feel self-conscious or awkward as actors normally do for these scenes; on the contrary, she appeared to relish snuggling up under the sheets with her arms embracing him. And when they needed to kiss, she kept her lips locked on his far longer than necessary. Cast members and crew snickered. Sheepish inside, Ryan couldn't help enjoying it.

"We can do this off the set too, *amor*," Felicia whispered in his ear between takes. She winked and smoothed his chest for added emphasis.

"You like Ryan, yes?" she said when he failed to respond.

His eyes were shining, and he merely grinned until the image of his girlfriend came to mind.

But Christine. What about Christine?

Ryan decided that when this scene was completed, he was going straight to his trailer to escape Felicia's seductions.

When the scene was finally completed, Ryan rushed to his trailer without looking or speaking to anyone. He put on jeans and a black T-shirt. Combing his hair, he wondered if Felicia was serious when she whispered she wanted to get together with him or if she flirted with all her costars.

Who cares? I'm dating Christine.

Ryan sighed and shook his head. Filming had been more arduous than usual. He would need a month's break at least. His head was still spinning from creating his character's words and movements over and over again for all those takes.

What I need now is a tall mug of beer, he thought. *Or an extra smooth glass of wine.*

Opening the door of his trailer, he found Felicia there, holding a bottle of wine and two long-stemmed glasses.

Her long thick black hair was loose; full, lush eyelashes hooded her eyes; and red lipstick greeted him with an inviting grin. Felicia wore a tight-fitted, low-cut black leather dress that allowed a glimpse of her tiny black lace bra, causing her breasts to burst out. Her red nails glinting, she offered Ryan a glass of wine.

"For you, *amor*," she whispered. "The film is almost finished. Time to celebrate." Her lips had a velvety-red heart shape.

Ryan's mouth hung open, and his knees became weak. He wanted to walk past her but couldn't, so he stood as still as a mannequin, staring at her. He had never been so overcome with desire, and she was ready to give him what he wanted.

Before he knew it, she stepped forward, and he could do nothing else but step back into his trailer.

"Come, *amor*, I'm told we have one more love scene together, so we practice."

"Here – alone?"

Felicia grinned and winked. "Precisely. This way we can make the scene more authentic, yes?"

"Ahhh, I have a girl—"

Felicia placed her finger to his lips. "Shh, say nothing. Drink."

He obeyed as if he were under her hypnotic spell.

The wine traveled through his bloodstream, and he began to relax. She gently led him to the couch while she sipped her wine, never taking her eyes off him.

"I must leave for Mexico tomorrow, but when will I see you again?" she purred as she batted her eyelashes and her mouth pouted. "When we did those love scenes, I felt something special between us, *amor*. As if we were meant to be together. Come to Mexico with me," she whispered in his ear. "I have a lot to offer you. Come with me. You won't regret it."

Spellbound, Ryan started to protest, but Felicia put her hand over his mouth.

"Shh," she said again. "Don't think, *amor*. Just enjoy. Yes, you can enjoy."

With that she brought her luscious lips to his mouth.

Ryan lost all resistance. He closed his eyes and melted in her grasp.

"Wait," she said as she rose.

Ryan was breathing heavily. His body shivered with excitement.

Felicia turned off the lights and crawled back into his arms, her breasts brushing against his mouth.

He wondered if this was what the heights of heavenly

ecstasy felt like. In the back of his mind was a nagging worry about protection, but this overwhelming feeling of bliss overrode any concerns. No intrusion was worth interrupting this extraordinary interlude.

Why must such exhilarating pleasure be forbidden? he ruminated as his tongue found its way into Felicia's mouth.

This moment couldn't be spoiled.

Then Ryan heard a soft knock on his trailer door.

"Ryan? Ryan? Are you there?"

It was Christine. He couldn't believe it.

Ryan felt his brain exploding.

The knocking continued. Felicia appeared oblivious and held him tight with the lovemaking unperturbed, but an epic battle was raging inside Ryan's head. Whenever he tried to disengage himself, Felicia clung to him tighter, more urgently.

But they both stopped upon hearing Christine open the door.

Felicia had forgotten to lock it.

"The Mandarin Oriental, sir," the driver announced.

Ryan jumped as if a cobra were beside him in the back seat.

"Whoa, whoa! Hey, man. I didn't mean to startle you," the driver said as he held up his hands.

He stepped out of the car, and one of the hotel employees in a crisp uniform rushed to grab his luggage.

Police sirens wailed in the distance. A car's tires squealed as the driver narrowly avoided hitting the car in front when traffic came to a standstill in order to allow police cars and an ambulance to rush through. The smell of charcoal-grilled burgers wafted through the air, coming from a large restaurant across the street. He was oblivious to it all.

His thoughts turned to Megan. Could he whisk her away from LA for a little while? She indicated that she couldn't take any more time off. What if he took her to the Boston Harbor Hotel for a romantic weekend? He doubted she would have any objection. All he knew was that he needed a distraction from his mind dwelling on the past. He feared it would only get worse now that he was here in Boston.

For the first time, a creeping feeling of guilt touched his conscience that he had not been faithful to Megan. That he had never been faithful to any of his girlfriends since he dated Christine and Kim. He didn't bother examining those new feelings now but rather shrugged them off. He had too much to worry about right now.

Ryan was still trying to ward off the past when he arrived in his penthouse suite. The furniture was in warm tones of magnolia and grey. The suite featured a four-poster bed, a marble bathroom with a Jacuzzi bath, and a garden terrace.

The luxurious, inviting setup calmed him. He felt like he had entered another world. Ryan proceeded to unpack but decided what he needed most was a glass of wine and a short nap.

The hotel phone rang.

"A Mr. Chin is here to see you," the receptionist in the hotel lobby informed Ryan.

Ryan felt an instant shudder go through his body. "OK. Send him up."

It was Buddy's special private investigator. Ryan's hand shook so hard that he almost dropped the phone.

Could Christine have been with someone else? Could this still be some mistake? There has to be another explanation. Ryan squeezed his eyes shut and began pacing the room. *Is there a chance this might after all have nothing to do with me?* He was surprised to realize that he would actually feel a pang of disappointment if those twins weren't his. *Ryan, are you losing your mind? What's wrong with you?* he reprimanded himself.

There was a knock at the door.

Ryan stared at the door a moment before walking over. He wondered again if Chin was there to tell him this was all a mistake and he should forget about it. He told himself that at least he had come all the way to Boston for the movie preparation.

Don Chin was a man in his late thirties. He was thin, about five four, and had short, jet-black hair slicked back with hair gel. He wore a serious expression and nodded his head when Ryan opened the door. He was carrying a compact black briefcase.

Ryan invited him in and shook his hand stiffly. "Sit down." Ryan motioned for him to sit at the custom-made dining room table. Ryan sat across from him, at the edge of his seat, willing himself to stop shaking.

Finally, Don Chin spoke. "There was no father's name on the birth certificates," he said, getting right down to the subject at hand. "She gave birth on December 27, 1990. When did you two stop seeing each other?"

Ryan's hand reached for his gut as if he had just been punched.

"At around the end of May."

Chin nodded and said, "Mr. Catalano said it's up to you."

"What do you mean, 'it's up to me'?" he demanded.

"Do you want me to give you a DNA test?"

Ryan studied him, confused. "Wouldn't you have to match the results with the kids? How are you going to get their DNA?"

"I already did, Mr. Monti. I went through their garbage and found toothbrushes from every member of the family," Chin said in a calm, even tone.

Ryan, on the other hand, slicked his hair back while his eyes darted in all directions. "OK," he said with a slightly shaky voice. "I'll do it."

Chin's expression revealed nothing as he opened his

briefcase and took out a cotton-like swab. "Open your mouth wide, please."

Chin took the swab and rubbed it against the inside of his cheek. Ryan felt nothing as he kept his gaze on the swab until Chin deposited it with ample care in a plastic bag. The bag disappeared into his black briefcase.

"Mr. Catalano will be contacting you imminently about the DNA test results. In the meantime, I am assigned to dig deeper into the family."

Ryan nodded. There was an uneasy silence in the room.

Finally, Ryan cleared his throat as he asked, "So do I pay you?"

"No, you pay Mr. Catalano directly for my services. You will get the results very soon."

Ryan grabbed the dining room table in an effort to rise. The detective took his briefcase and nodded, having nothing more to say.

Ryan walked Chin to the door, and they shook hands. When he closed it, he leaned his head on it, closing his eyes, trying to process what Chin might find out and its implications for him.

Ryan rubbed his eyes; he now wasn't certain how he felt. He yearned to shut off his mind and slink into bed for a nap, but he was determined to continue unpacking. Once he finished, he decided to walk the streets of Copley Square but instead gave into his urge to crawl under the sheets and fall asleep into oblivion.

CHAPTER TWENTY-TWO

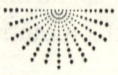

BOSTON

When Christine arrived at work to attend the mid-morning monthly meeting, she felt so depressed she wished she could crawl under the table. She and her team were deciding which young women the agency would take on as models. It was like any other meeting until they showed a video of one potential model who spoke of her heartrending decision to give up her baby when she got pregnant at sixteen. It was highly unusual that a young woman interviewed would make such a startling confession.

"Well, she certainly made a distinct impression," said Greg, a mid-level manager. He chuckled nervously, twirling a pen between his fingers.

"I am impressed by her poise and maturity as she told her story." John, the assistant manager, spoke up. "Personally, it shows me she can handle herself well on camera."

"I don't think this was an appropriate venue to share such a personal experience," Lynn, an interviewer, observed. "She's applying to be a model. This isn't a confessional or group therapy. And with the abortion issue such a hot topic, I think she was trying to push her pro-life agenda. Another no-no when you're applying for a job." She turned to Christine. "Christine, don't you agree?"

Christine turned pale when all eyes fell on her. She had been mulling over the young woman's words and not listening to her coworkers' conversation. Raised as a strict Catholic, she wouldn't have gotten an abortion, but she had considered the possibility of giving up her twins for adoption. Her parents convinced her to keep the children – after all, they had argued, she could still find a good Catholic man to marry who would be willing to adopt them.

The struggle back then overwhelmed her. When Christine wasn't working, she was taking care of the babies. Sometimes she couldn't work because the babies needed her and her parents were also working. They helped fund her studio apartment in another town. That was preferable to living with her parents and exposing her shame to the church community. Her parents had told people Christine had married and was now living in California. In the meantime, Christine was always busy and stressed, and she rarely enjoyed the luxury of a full night of sleep.

Daniel saved her. She had thought she was going to bring up her children in poverty, always struggling to provide for their basic needs.

Christine looked up. Everyone was waiting for to contribute to the discussion. Since she had barely been listening, she merely shrugged her shoulders.

Come on, Christine, you're at work! You've got to appear somewhat professional! She recalled bits and pieces of the conversation.

"I don't know why she had to relay this information, but I have to respect her reasons for the decision she made," she said quietly, her eyes focused on the table.

Everyone else was silent, staring at Christine and then at one other.

Sophie, her boss, was the only person in the room who knew about Daniel's illness as well as his adoption of the twins when Christine got married. She cleared her throat and said, "I agree with Christine. However, I don't find this relevant to our decision about whether to hire her as a model. I would prefer candidates not to offer these revelations at the interview stage."

"She would make a great guest on *Dr. Phil*," Greg said. Everyone chuckled.

"I agree with you, Sophie. Hiring her would set a bad precedent," Lynn said. "Save those life stories for TV talk shows."

Everyone around the table nodded their agreement. Except Christine. She stared out the window and ceased listening to their discussion. When she realized it was all quiet, she pulled out of her own thoughts and found the team was studying her.

"Excuse me." She rose, realizing she had to go out and compose herself.

"Christine, when you come back, we'll show the video of the next candidate," Sophie called after her.

Christine glanced back quickly and attempted to smile.

"Let's hope the next one sticks to the standard interview questions and is not already trying to make a name for herself," Greg said.

"Boston is extremely divided when it comes to abortion. She would've have had more luck with her story if she were interviewing in the South," John added.

"Still, not good form in an interview. Actually, a little creepy, come to think of it," Lynn added.

Christine, meanwhile, hurried into the hallway while the others continued conversing. The sounds of their voices faded as she rushed to the ladies' room. Once inside, she put her hands on the edges of the sink and slowly faced the mirror. She wondered if she would even recognize the young woman she was eighteen years ago. It felt like it happened in a different lifetime. Images of that night crept up in her mind and refused to leave.

She shook her head – she had been so naïve back then.

Christine's shoulders sagged at the memory of the Saturday night in Ryan's car.

She had failed to live up to her own standards but realized they both went too far because they were young, carefree, a little drunk, and in love. She lowered her head and stared into the white ceramic sink, reminding herself that Tim and Trudy were conceived that night, and after all the turmoil that followed, they proved to be two of the greatest blessings of her life. She loved and adored them more than life itself – indeed, life would lose all meaning if she didn't have them. She considered raising and seeing them turn out so well as the greatest accomplishment of her life.

At that moment her boss stuck her head in the ladies' room.

"Christine – where are you? Are you all right? Christine, what's wrong?" Sophie said, rushing to her side.

Christine snapped out of her time warp, as if coming out of an out-of-body trance. "Oh, I'm sorry. I- I just have a headache. Don't worry about me! Oh my God! I'm not holding up the whole meeting, am I?"

Her boss said slowly, "Christine, I know you've been having problems—"

Christine started to protest, but Sophie raised her hand. "We are a business, but we realize our employees have lives of their own."

The tears flowed down Christine's face. "Sophie, my husband has leukemia. My twins are getting ready to go to college." She sobbed and fought the tears. "I'm sure they'll understand they're going to have to put it off. But it's going to be a rough road ahead for all of us," she said, wiping away tears; they kept flowing down, and she finally gave up trying to stem the tide.

Sophie, who always kept up a professional demeanor, melted upon hearing the news. The tall brunette came closer and put her hand on her shoulder. "Christine, perhaps we can work something out…"

Christine finally stemmed the tide of tears by squeezing her eyes shut and breathing in deeply. She put her shoulders back and said, "Thank you, Sophie. I just appreciate you lending your support. I'm a strong person, and I have to stay strong for my family."

She responded to her boss's concerned stare by adding, "I'll keep you posted. I promise."

Sophie tried to smile. "OK. You know, my husband had prostate cancer two years ago. If you remember, I had to take a leave of absence. I've been there, Christine, if you need to talk."

Christine turned her head sideways and creased her lips into a small smile, touched and gratified that her boss was so sympathetic. She nodded. "Oh, yes, I remember when you went through that. I'm sure it's a time you'd rather forget." She paused. "I'm ready to go back into the conference room. I feel better, but wait – let me just freshen up a bit."

Sophie gave her arm a gentle squeeze. "Sure. I'll see you in there."

Christine stood still, watching Sophie exit the ladies' room, the door slowly closing.

Here I am thinking about the unexpected pregnancy when my dear husband is fighting for his life, she reprimanded herself, shaking her head. *Christine, why are you dwelling on the past at a time like this?*

Because then you won't admit how scared you are about the possibility of losing Daniel. A small voice inside her gave Christine the underlying answer.

Turning to the mirror, she saw her mascara had streaked down to her cheeks and her eyes were swollen. She washed her face and expertly retouched her makeup. After a quick comb-through, she stared into the mirror.

Almost as good as new, she thought.

Years ago, a therapist had told her she was a survivor.

And a survivor I'm still going to be, she told herself upon exiting the ladies' room.

CHAPTER TWENTY-THREE

BOSTON

R yan was in a deep sleep.

He was six years old. He and his parents were vacationing at Will Rogers State Beach near Santa Monica. Ryan was kicking the water because he loved making it foam with white bubbles. When the tide of the sparkling blue water came racing toward shore, he loved kicking the foam to make even more foam, even if it was only a few more bubbles. Ryan always thought that was when he first discovered his creative nature: making more foam in the ocean. From then on, he loved making things: pictures, sand castles, and creating and pretending he was a totally different person, which he would invent inside his head.

His parents pointed and laughed at little Ryan kicking the waves while they enjoyed the sun. Encouraged by their attention, he continued kicking, determined to make as many bubbles as he could. Without realizing it, he headed deeper into the water. It was only when an approaching higher-than-normal wave knocked him down and pulled him underneath that he became scared.

Ryan tried shouting for his parents, but ocean water filled his mouth. He couldn't see underneath the water and lost track which way was toward his parents and the shore. Unable to control what was happening, he struggled to come up for air, but the pressure of the tide prevented him. He couldn't make sense of what was happening. He couldn't scream, rise above the water, or get back on his feet.

This was the first time he felt completely alone and helpless. Forces out of his control were taking over, and he couldn't do anything about it.

When he thought he'd never see his parents again, his father scooped him up out of the water. Ryan's small hands clutched his father. Crying, he never wanted to let go.

"Is everything all right here?" the lifeguard asked as he rushed over.

"Oh, yes, fine! My son went in a little too deep. We've got to watch him more carefully," his father conceded as he held Ryan. He rubbed his little son's back, still shaking from the panic, in an effort to calm him. "Now, it's OK, son. I've got you." He kissed his son's head and said, "Soon, you're going to be a big brother, and before you know it, you'll have to help watch your little brother or sister."

Ryan's mother approached, her hand clutching her heart.

"He's fine, Sara, don't worry."

"Oh, that was so scary, Ryan! You've got to be more careful in the water."

Hearing his mother's voice, Ryan immediately released his father and held out his arms for her. She took him and rocked him, humming his favorite song until his crying turned into quiet whimpers.

"Tonight we're going to buy you a lollipop and a toy, Ryan. Would you like that?" Sara spoke in her son's ear.

Ryan nodded, sniffling.

Everything was going to be all right.

Ryan's eyes popped open. He sat up and looked around his plush bedroom in the penthouse suite.

The dream was so vivid that he felt it was really happening again. He was usually filled with so much energy that he could never sleep during the day unless he was sick. While wondering what had come over him, Ryan had a realization: children are a blessing, and he wouldn't want to go through life without them. Of course, raising children was hard, but to be able to hold and cuddle another human being of your own flesh, watch them grow, and have them in your life until the very end was priceless. He knew in his heart that the twins were his; the DNA results would simply be a formality.

His parents lit up every time they saw him. He was never without their love and affection. After his younger brother was born a stillbirth, he remembered the dark cloud that descended over their expressions whenever he was mentioned. His parents still mourned him today, a life they conceived but were never able to enjoy. The family still visited Robbie's grave on his birthday every year.

Ryan attempted to shake himself out of his musings and his memories. He went over to the desk and picked up the list of locations where the movie scenes were supposed to be filmed. There was a seedy bar in Dorchester his character frequents, the police station on Gibson Street where he often gets thrown in jail, and a corner in downtown Dorchester where he buys drugs and first encounters the beautiful single mother he will romance.

Ryan turned to his iPad, loaded with videos of a real person whom the character was based upon. He was supposed to watch them and study the man's physical traits and behaviors.

But he stayed where he was, not even attempting to make an effort to begin preparing for the role.

For the first time in his life, acting was not his central concern.

Instead, his mind drifted off once again to one of his dates with Christine, recalling his feelings of love and happiness with her despite her parents' reservations.

He was remembering her parents. He had met them long ago. He recalled they were flattered a budding young actor was dating their beautiful daughter, but they were also wary of him. He could read it in their unsmiling eyes, the furtive glances they gave one another.

"We're thinking of going on a picnic on Sunday morning," a nineteen-year-old Christine said as she turned to her parents that day.

Her mother's unsteady smile vanished. "Christine, you always come to church with us."

Christine looked up at Ryan. "Would you like to come to church with us?"

"Oh! Of course, you're welcome to attend with us!" her father interjected.

Ryan, a nonpracticing Catholic who only stepped into church at weddings, christenings, and funerals, shuffled his feet, trying to think of a good excuse to get out of it. Finding one, he said with a smile, "Oh, well, I always go to my parents' house for breakfast on Sunday morning. My parents go to church on Saturday night."

A little white lie. Actually, the last time they attended church on Saturday night was ten years previously.

But Christine brightened and had an idea of her own. "I'm going to church on Saturday night instead of Sunday so Ryan and I can go on our picnic."

Ingenious, Ryan thought to himself. *Do I know how to come up with the right answers or what?*

But Christine's father was scratching the back of his neck, and her mother was clearing her throat. "Well, I guess you could do that, Christine," she said.

Christine's mother opened her mouth to say something

else, but her husband gave her the eye and she remained silent.

As these memories played out in Ryan's mind, his cell went off.

It was Richard Bowen, the movie producer.

"Hey, Ryan," he said. "I hate to tell you this, but the city is doing some renovation work right near where we're filming the beginning scenes. It's so loud and chaotic you're going to have to wait visiting the area for a few weeks. We've heard you scout out the area of an actual scene while you're researching a role. Of course, we'll be more than happy to reimburse you for the extra time you're spending here."

"Oh, I see," Ryan said. He was at a loss to say more. He glanced at the unread script on the desk.

Maybe this is a blessing in disguise. I haven't even picked up the script yet.

The producer continued, "Hey, George Tell and I would like to take you out to Balanchi's tonight. Are you available?"

"Sure," he forced himself to answer.

I've got to take a break from all these recent developments and step out of myself.

"Great! How about we send a car to pick you up at 7:00 p.m.? This restaurant was voted the best in Boston by a landslide. You won't be disappointed."

"Good, good. That sounds real good. I'll see you then."

As he ended the call, he remembered his mother always saying that good food is the cure for whatever ails you.

Ryan knew what his next step was now that he didn't have to worry about researching the new role. He pulled up a contact on his phone and connected a call.

"Mr. Catalano's office," Shana chirped into the phone.

"May I speak with Buddy?"

"And who's calling?"

"Ryan Monti."

"Oh, I'll connect you, Mr. Monti. Hold on one moment, please."

Ryan noticed her voice perked up and she was barely able to stifle a giggle. At any other time he would have been flattered, but now it had no effect on him whatsoever.

"Yes, Mr. Monti." Buddy came on. There was also a chirp in his voice.

"Is Chin still in Boston?"

"Yes, he is remaining there awaiting further instruction. That is, if you need his help."

"Tomorrow I want to see the children. Now I know the DNA results haven't come in yet. But I am curious. I just want to see them. Is there any way he can find out where I can locate them?"

"Of course! Just like you told me earlier, you wanted to find out where they live, go to school, extracurricular activities, and jobs. Chin has already gathered some information, but I'll have it organized for you later tonight. I'll call you back in a few hours. Is that acceptable for you, Mr. Monti?"

Ryan knew Buddy was working extra hard to satisfy him, but he needed his help.

"I'll wait for your call," Ryan told him and hung up.

* * *

Ozzy alternated between eating a McDonald's double cheeseburger with fries and peering into his binoculars at Ryan's hotel. He didn't care that his binoculars were getting greasy and his car seat dirty from eating – he was already looking for a new used car. He was glad Buddy had provided him with the information he needed to track Monti down. Now he was going to decide how best to blackmail Monti himself – he no longer needed Catalano's assistance. He had

Monti right where he wanted him: in Boston, his own territory.

Ozzy checked his cell. Zoe had texted him a few times. He was too excited to contact his girlfriend. When he missed her, he called to see her. She was an odd woman who wore heavy makeup and had especially thick hair. It was only after sleeping with her that he found out she wore a wig. Zoe wore colorful, tight clothes and seemed happy with the trinkets he bought her whenever they were together. She was never demanding, but Ozzy still couldn't wait to tell her he was coming into some big money.

Who knows? he thought. *Maybe we could even move in together.*

But for now, Zoe would have to wait.

CHAPTER TWENTY-FOUR

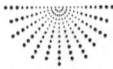

Brighton

Christine came home and went right to the kitchen to prepare dinner. She was grateful the twins had not come home yet. She kept checking her face in the mirror, making sure all traces of crying and sadness had disappeared. Daniel was resting upstairs. She hoped he had taken the sedative Dr. Sherman had prescribed but knew he wouldn't be able to stop thinking about beginning chemotherapy tomorrow. Neither could she.

A half hour later, the front door opened. Tim and Trudy were arguing in low voices, but Christine still overheard their heated exchange. She peeked through the kitchen door.

"You know life isn't over," Tim was telling Trudy.

"I've been looking forward to college for years. Now it's been taken away. What's left?"

Tim snapped at his twin sister, "What's left? What the hell do you mean? We want Dad to stay alive."

"I didn't mean it that way," Trudy said. "Shhh! Shut up! Dad's probably up there now, you idiot! I just don't know what I'm going to do now! Every day of high school I've worked with one objective – to get into BC. I don't have any skills to get a decent job. Minimum wage is nothing!"

"Things change. I don't think Mom planned on getting pregnant without a father around. She wanted to graduate college. Plans get derailed."

"OK, Mr. Know-It-All, then why did you attend the college fair anyway?" she snapped.

"You know just as well as I do that all college seniors were required to attend the fair," Tim said, jolted by his sister's anger.

"Oh, really? Seniors going to trade school or the army were told they could go out for the period as long as they came back after lunch for class." Trudy kept blinking to feign surprise that her brother didn't know this, but her tight smile had anger written all over it.

"I just wanted to see what the colleges were offering, not like you who just went to wallow in your misery," Tim replied with gritted teeth.

Christine decided now was the time to stop their arguing and walked out of the kitchen. "Shh, Dad is upstairs sleeping. What's going on?"

"Today was the college fair," Tim replied. "We didn't want to go, but everyone was going and we didn't want to stand out by skipping it. At least quite a few community colleges were there."

"I know it must have been hard for both of you," Christine said, her shoulders drooping.

She heard a noise at the top of the stairs, and they watched Daniel walking down in his bathrobe, his hand gripping the bannister.

"Daniel, honey, I told you I'd call you when dinner's ready. You need to rest."

"Yeah, Dad. It's OK. We're doing fine," Tim added. "Go get some rest."

"It's hard for me to rest when I know how much the two of you had your hearts set on Boston College," he said. He looked even thinner, and his shoulders also sagged as he stood before them. He turned to Christine and spoke quietly. "Christine, I've got to get my affairs in order."

"Daniel, please don't—"

But he shook his head. "How are you and the kids going to live? I want to make sure you can stay in this house."

"Mom," Trudy said in a soft voice, "maybe we all need to sit down and talk about this."

Christine said in a strident tone, "What do you mean? What is there to talk about? Dad is going to take a leave of absence and then when he feels stronger, everything will continue as it was. You and Tim may have to delay college, or at least college full time, but then you can pick up and join your friends at school. *We'll be able to manage.* Dad's health comes first."

"Nobody is arguing that, Mom," Trudy said. "But I think we have to come up with a plan."

"Oh, we certainly will. I've been thinking about that a lot. You don't have to worry. You and Tim can take jobs. I'll see if I can take on more work at the modeling agency—"

"Mom," Trudy said slowly, trying to mask the impatience in her voice, "what about our biological father? Aren't we at the point where he can help us? Mom, you can't put this off any longer. We have a right to know who he is, and we're going to need his help."

Christine just stared at her daughter. A part of her wanted to slap her daughter's face. She considered that topic off-limits. She yearned to say she had made a big mistake back then, but she held back; she didn't want Trudy and Tim to think they were mistakes too.

"Can't he help us, Mom?" Tim asked.

Daniel was staring at the floor. "Christine, maybe it's time," he whispered.

Christine turned to him with her eyes bulging and her mouth half-open, as if this was the ultimate betrayal. She combed her hair back and fought the tide of tears waiting to spring forth. She was still so mad at Ryan she couldn't even imagine confronting him. She didn't want his history of dating lots of women and partying to influence the twins. Christine couldn't help occasionally following his career and life. Movies. Tawdry sex scenes. She could just imagine what he did in his personal life. Every time she saw a picture of him in the media, it was always with a different gorgeous woman on his arm. *He is a little, immature boy in a man's body. Deceiving and lying to women just like he did to me. My parents told me he couldn't be trusted; I should have listened to them.*

I don't want him and his pathetic life near my children! He'd ruin their lives. I wish I could make them understand how awful he is.

She cleared her throat as she regained her composure. "I- I don't think that's a good idea—"

"Why not, Mom? Is he some horrible, evil person?" Trudy demanded.

"Trudy," Tim reprimanded her, "you're coming on too strong, and we have enough going on already."

"That's right!" cried Trudy. "We could use the help! Help us. Help Dad. It's the least he can do after all these years." Turning to her mother, she said, "Unless he's in jail or dead."

"Trudy, that's enough," Daniel told her. "Don't keep pushing your mother."

"We'll talk about it when I'm ready, Trudy—"

"If not now, then when? When, Mom?"

Christine closed her eyes, willing herself not to scream at

her daughter. "Look," she said, "give me a few days to think about this. I need some time."

She could no longer stand there and take her daughter's recriminations. "I'm going to continue making dinner now," she said and turned to go back to the kitchen.

"Mom," Tim and Trudy said at the same time.

Christine didn't turn her head – she couldn't. She needed a few moments to sit at the kitchen table alone before going back to preparing the meal. Although Trudy's words shocked and hurt her, she realized for the first time she believed what she had said. She and her children *would be able to manage*. She had been working at her job for many years. She had demonstrated she was competent and professional. She knew Sophie would give her more work if she needed it. It wasn't like it was years ago when the twins were babies and the three of them were basically relying on family to take care of them. She had grown and matured and would help her family manage no matter how long it took for Daniel to recover. She had to convince them of that now.

Christine was rubbing her eyes when Trudy entered the kitchen and gently pulled out a chair across from her mother.

"I'm sorry if I upset you, but you have to look at it from our point of view. It's not only for help. Please understand, Mom, we need to know who our father is. We've been waiting for you to be ready for a long time."

"I understand," Christine whispered. "Please, just give me a little more time. I need to settle this in my own mind. I haven't told you because it's for your own good. He's not a bad man, just not a father for you and Tim." She gave a little laugh and stared at the ceiling. "I've always been grateful and proud of your dad and thought that should be enough."

"I agree. We have the best dad in the world, but I'm afraid

that isn't quite enough. We need to know who our biological father is."

Christine nodded and turned away as she rose and headed to the stove to pour a vegetable sauce over the chicken breasts. Some of the mixture ended up on the counter because her hands were shaking. She knew now was the time to face what she had refused to discuss. Christine wished she could run away. She yearned to run to her car and escape. She couldn't face talking to the twins about Ryan now. She wanted to take care of Daniel and somehow manage until he became well again.

CHAPTER TWENTY-FIVE

BOSTON

Ryan woke up the next morning refreshed and optimistic. He was able to enjoy dining out and talking with the producer and director at the restaurant last night. The movie industry was a fascinating business. The deals, the actors, the hunt for the right role, and the chemistry among cast members and crew were subjects they discussed for hours. The wine was also a great help. He savored every bite of the food last night – he even made a mental note to go back to Balanchi's again. Ryan wished this restaurant was located in Los Angeles. As he was getting dressed, he decided to call his parents and maybe Megan after he ate.

Ryan was even contemplating visiting the hotel's famous spa when his cell rang.

"Mr. Monti? Good morning. How are you?" Buddy said.

"I'm fine. You have any news for me?"

"It's about the DNA tests."

"You got the results back."

"Yes, Mr. Monti. The twins are your children," Buddy told him.

Ryan sank onto his four-poster bed. Not even his warm, inviting luxurious penthouse suite could calm the chill that swept throughout his body. This was no longer a possibility – it was real. He was a father.

"Hello? Are you still there, Mr. Monti?" Buddy sounded alarmed.

"Yes, I'm still here. I'll have to call you back."

"Of course! Call me if you need anything at all. Mr. Monti?"

"What is it?" Ryan needed time alone to digest the news.

"For what it's worth, my wife and I tried to have a child for years. It never happened. Not everyone gets so lucky. Just think of that, OK?" He chuckled. "I don't know why in the world I'm telling you this – I guess it's the first thing that came to my mind."

"OK. Thanks, Buddy," Ryan said and hung up.

He forgot about breakfast, the phone calls, the spa. Ryan walked over to the terrace and stared at the people down below. There were two human beings out there in this town that came from him. He never thought it would actually happen. After Kim, he had unconsciously resigned himself to the single life, thinking he would never have a lifelong commitment to anyone. Instead of joy, he felt numb inside. *What do I do now? I'm not ready for this, am I?*

Ryan stared at everything and nothing. His mind was a haze. He knew he couldn't stay like this and had to do something. So he returned to the suite and retrieved the information Buddy had sent him last night.

* * *

Ryan drove a rented Honda Accord and parked in the

Brighton High School parking lot. He found his hands were shaking, and it took him a while before he had the courage to get out of his car. The high school seemed like a massive, intimidating building. Would they allow him to see his children? He made up his mind he was going to pretend he was supposed to substitute teach there tomorrow, and he wanted to see the general layout of the school because the last time he substituted somewhere else he kept getting lost. Would they buy that? Would the thick glasses and baseball cap be an adequate disguise?

He stepped out of the car wearing dark sunglasses, feeling uncertain. Ryan decided to treat the situation as if this was only a role he was preparing for. It wasn't easy, but he forced himself to remember a character he had played who was a teacher, and pretended he was on that movie set again. This helped him get closer to the school building. He glanced at his watch.

Three o'clock. Was he too late for today? Ryan had made numerous attempts to drive to the school, but he kept turning back, worried he looked too much like a movie star, he wasn't dressed like a teacher, or he was dressed too casually. Ryan had finally settled on a tailored checkered shirt and cotton twill black pants that he purchased at a store next to the hotel. By that time, it was nearly two o'clock.

Now he felt foolish arriving to the school so late. When he saw the line of buses in front, he cursed to himself.

I'll have to wait until tomorrow.

Ryan turned around to walk back to the car, angry at himself when he heard the dribbling of a basketball. He glanced at the boys, thinking there was no chance his son would be there until he spotted a teenager with the same dirty blond hair he had. He did a double-take. Buddy had sent him photos and information from Chin. Then he heard another boy shout to the teenager, "Tim, right here!"

There was no doubt in his mind. It was his son.

He made his way to the basketball court. He prayed no one would recognize him or ask him any questions. He simply wanted to observe. There were only six boys playing. He clutched the fence separating him from the basketball court as if he wished he could dismantle it.

Ryan's eyes traveled wherever his son ran. Ryan felt his insides swell with admiration and wonder. A light feeling of pure happiness overcame him. Did he actually have a part in creating this boy? He did!

He's a better basketball player than I am, Ryan noted right away. *His moves are more polished, more skilled. I think he's had better training.*

It looks like Christine has given him a good life. Ryan watched him interacting with his friends and thought that Tim appeared well adjusted. He had a ready smile and played hard. At times he rubbed his forehead, which indicated to Ryan that something serious was on his mind that he was trying to forget about. He had no idea what that could be. He looked happiest when he was playing.

Ryan yearned to knock the fence down and go right over to his son, put his hands on his shoulders, and stare right into his eyes – the same eyes he had. But that would only shock and scare him away.

The son of my flesh, he thought.

He wiped a tear and laughed at himself. *I'm actually getting biblical now.*

He continued staring at his son. He was grateful for his large dark sunglasses because the tears started to flow.

He slumped and looked down for a moment. *Christine, why didn't you tell me? Why didn't you even give me a chance to get to know them?*

He turned his anguish aside and continued observing his son. It was as if his younger self had come alive again. Ryan couldn't help feeling proud of him – tall, blond, handsome, athletic.

Instead of clutching the fence, he opened his hands as if he desired to reach out and touch him for the first time but knew he couldn't.

Ryan noticed another boy coming over to his son when they took a water break. He thought they glanced in his direction but wasn't sure. He knew instinctively he should leave, yet he couldn't budge from his spot. A few other boys glanced his way. He had no choice – he couldn't stay.

He hurried away. He knew neither one of them was ready for an encounter.

At first he was walking backward, unable to peel his eyes away, but when a boy kept staring at him and walked over to the fence, he turned and jogged away.

By the time Ryan reached his car, he said out loud, "My God!" He felt light-headed. His mind was swirling, and his body felt waves of sensations he never experienced before: a contentment and fulfillment that even his successful movie career and giving his parents an easier life had never brought him. He wanted to look back at his son but was afraid he would burst into tears and yet wasn't exactly sure why.

Ryan also felt heavier; he no longer had only himself and his parents to worry about. He had a son now, and his mind became paralyzed by the thought that something bad could happen to him. What if an actual deranged stranger came over to the school and harmed him? He shook his head, not even understanding these protective feelings – they hadn't even met each other, and his son could probably take care of himself. *Unless the stranger carried a weapon,* Ryan told himself. He put his hands over his face to dispel this fear.

Ryan! Ryan, what the hell's wrong with you? What a crazy thought! he chided himself. *Get a grip!*

Ryan sat in his car without starting the engine. He had to

see his daughter now. He tried to figure out how he could make sure they were all right – that the kids had everything they needed. Ryan noted his son's sad expression when he wasn't busy in the game and wondered if he could help him in any way. There was also someone else he was burning to visit. A mere sighting would not be enough – he had to confront her, to understand why she did what she did and hid the twins from him all these years.

Just then he heard a loud engine roaring. He looked up and saw an old Saturn race by, the driver huddled at the wheel staring in the opposite direction so Ryan couldn't see his face.

* * *

Half a mile away, the man watched with his binoculars while sitting in his old car. Ryan returned to his car but simply sat, not turning on the engine. Ozzy put away his binoculars and crouched in his seat. He raced out of the parking lot, looking the other way so Ryan couldn't see his face, hoping no school official or policeman caught him speeding. As his car entered the street, Ozzy smiled.

This is working out perfectly! Better than if I had planned it, Ozzy thought. *Besides getting a new car, I should shop around for a condo in the city so I can live with Zoe like royalty!*

Time to put pressure on him. Tell Monti to give him two million or this would be front-page news. Ozzy licked his lips. *And I'm sure no one will mind this time if I embellish some details.*

CHAPTER TWENTY-SIX

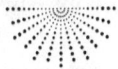

C hristine, her brother-in-law, Seth, and Daniel's parents accompanied Daniel to the outpatient center for his first chemotherapy treatment. Energy depleted, Daniel lay in the bed. He was so weak and nauseous that he threw up numerous times. Nurses had to hold him while he retched. In a few hours, he would be ready to go home. Judy could not stop herself from sobbing while Seth helped Christine get Daniel from his wheelchair into the car. Harry stayed back and wore a twisted, anguished expression. Seth resembled a ghost, and his weeping mother reached out to Daniel and came close to knocking him over. Fortunately, nearby staff prevented her from knocking him down. Daniel had remarked that he now only weighed as much as he did when he was a teenager. By the time they arrived home, Christine and his family had to help him into the house, for he no longer had much strength.

Christine's overwhelming depression deepened. Daniel's seventy-year-old mother seemed stronger than he was. She didn't dare tell him that she saw clumps of hair on his hospital bed.

They wanted to sit beside Daniel when he finally managed to get into bed, but he said that felt as if they were keeping vigil. Daniel insisted he needed some time alone, and Christine sat with her in-laws downstairs in silence. No one felt like going over the schedule for the next chemotherapy treatment.

Christine announced, "I'm going to see how he's doing. I'll be right back."

They nodded. "Let me know if he needs me," Judy said.

"I will."

Christine walked up the stairs and stopped in the bathroom to check her appearance in the mirror. She wanted to make sure she looked cheerful and well groomed, not depressed and overwrought. Daniel was lying flat on his back in the bed and wore a stricken expression as he stared at the ceiling.

"How's my honey?" Christine was determined to act natural and not shocked by her husband's weakened state.

"Christine." Daniel's eyes brightened upon seeing his wife. He tried to lift his limp hand, but it barely rose an inch. "Now it's only you that can come home and bring the bacon."

Christine chuckled as she said, "Don't let your mother hear you say that. Bacon's not kosher."

Daniel grinned as Christine hugged him and kissed him on the cheek. As she sank down on the side of the bed, she said, "I remember when your mother found out we were engaged – she felt she had to keep reminding me you don't eat pork or shellfish. She was afraid I would actually serve it to you."

"She had nothing to worry about. You don't even bring that food into the house. You and the kids only eat it outside the home. You're more observant than most Jews," Daniel said, his hand wrapped in hers. "That's my wonderful, beautiful Christine."

Despite his pain and exhaustion, Daniel's expression was full of adoration. "I've never regretted marrying you, and I couldn't live without you and the twins."

Christine lay gently next to her husband in bed, making sure she didn't put too much weight on him. She didn't feel like talking – she wanted to be near him, to feel his body and convince herself he was staying with them. She was blessed to have Daniel. She smiled as she closed her eyes, pondering this, hoping and praying he would recover and they would continue their lives again as usual soon.

It's a miracle I found such a wonderful man. I was on my own with twin toddlers, and he still married me and even adopted them – it was a miracle. Maybe, just maybe, a miracle could happen again. Daniel will get well, Christine prayed.

They lay together, gently holding hands. They wanted to cherish this quiet time alone. Not even his family downstairs would cut this moment short.

CHAPTER TWENTY-SEVEN

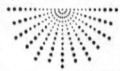

NEWTON CENTER, MASSACHUSETTS

As soon as he entered the Whitestone Creamery, Ryan, wearing his sunglasses, smelled the hot fudge. It was a small store with five round tables, four chairs surrounding each one. Giant posters of tantalizing ice cream concoctions draped the walls. He saw one customer sitting and devouring a large sundae.

Ryan loved ice cream and would normally treat himself if he wasn't preparing for a film that required him to slim down. However, ice cream was the last thing on his mind. Buddy had sent him a report that his daughter Trudy worked here a few days a week after school. Today was one of those days.

Ryan's body was rigid and tight – even the aroma of hot fudge wafting through the air failed to tempt him; he was here on a mission.

Just then, he heard an employee come out of the double doors on the other side of the counter. Ryan was too nervous to even move his head, but out of the corner of his eye, he saw it was a boy putting in more tubs of ice cream flavors.

Losing his nerve, he headed into the men's room.

He found his hands were trembling as he washed them in the sink.

Why is seeing my daughter more nerve-racking than seeing my son? he wondered.

It's because this is more up close and there is a much greater chance of interaction with her, he answered his own question.

He grabbed a paper towel harder than usual, angry with himself.

You're a man now, not a frightened little boy! It's time to act like one! Closing his eyes and breathing in, he eyed the men's room exit.

Upon reentering the main room, Ryan staggered, fighting off the urge to rush back into the men's room.

Wiping the tables was his daughter. He recognized her right away.

"Hi, do you need some help?" She cocked her head and asked him with a brightness in her eyes and smile

"Chocolate sundae, please," he managed to blurt out before his throat constricted.

"Chocolate ice cream, hot fudge? Would you like whipped cream or any kind of toppings?" Trudy had stopped wiping and was giving him her full attention.

"Whipped cream and Reese's Pieces," he answered without thinking.

As she doled out two scoops of chocolate ice cream, Ryan sat at one of the tables and studied her features. She looked just like her brother. He noticed they both had his and his mother's expressive eyes and dirty-blond hair. She had his Roman nose and Christine's long legs and slim figure. When she spotted him looking at her, she displayed her mother's easy smile and warm, friendly expression.

She was about to serve him the sundae when another customer demanded her attention.

"Hey, miss? You didn't put enough hot fudge on my sundae. You were real stingy with the hot fudge!"

Ryan turned. The man was wearing old, faded clothes and slurring his words. He smelled the faint odor of alcohol on his breath.

"Oh, I'm sorry! I wish you would have told me before," Trudy answered, turning red and not knowing what to do with her hands.

"I want a partial refund 'cause you gave me only a smidgeon of fudge," the man yelled as he slammed the table with his sundae glass and dirty napkins.

Ryan could see Trudy trying to summon up her courage. Her mouth fell open and no words came out, but then she put up her shoulders and met the man's eyes. "If you would have told me that before, I would have gladly put more hot fudge on your sundae, but since you're telling me after you ate it, the sundae will have to remain full price."

"What?" the man roared, causing Trudy to jump. "I demand a partial refund for only a little hot fudge! Why did you give me such a measly amount, girl?"

She attempted to walk over to the register, but he stepped in her way.

Ryan, a few inches taller than him, did not give him a chance to approach Trudy any closer.

Whipping off his sunglasses and wearing a menacing expression, Ryan stepped close to him and said through gritted teeth, "Hey, buddy, if you don't leave her alone, hot fudge is going to be the least of your problems."

The man, who hadn't even noticed Ryan, eyed both him and Trudy, his eyes turning from one to the other. The disgruntled customer regained his composure and snapped at Ryan. "And who the hell are you? Why're you butting in?"

Staring right into the man's eyes, Ryan nearly said, "I'm her father," but thought better of it. He fumbled a moment before lifting his shoulders high and proclaiming, "I'm a concerned customer."

A man in his forties, overhearing the heated exchange, rushed out of the double doors from the back and said, "Is there a problem here?"

The irate customer eyed the three of them and, realizing he was making a scene, slapped money on the table and left without another word.

"You're... you're... my God, I can't believe it. You're... Ryan Monti! The big actor!" The man who'd rushed in wore a pin labeled Store Manager on the side of his shirt. His eyes were alight as he said, "That was a great movie you were in last year about that human trafficking ring. I loved it."

"Oh, I'm glad you enjoyed it," a flushed Ryan said.

"Yeah, I saw it twice."

Trudy stared with her mouth agape. Her shock turned into a wave of delight as she clearly forgot all about the difficult customer and blushed upon realizing a famous person had come to her aid.

"Thank you, Mr. Monti, for helping me," she gushed. She tentatively held out her right hand. "Thank you so much!"

Ryan's eyes locked with hers. He wouldn't look down. Instead, he pretended not to notice her extended hand; he actually feared he would experience a rush of emotion and hug her instead. He turned to the manager and said, "I- I just saw this man being unreasonable to this young girl working alone, and I felt I had to say something."

"Ah, Mr. Monti," the manager asked, "would you mind taking a picture? I have other celebrities' pictures on my wall." He waved his hand in the direction of the photos. "It would be an honor if you would join them."

"My pleasure." Ryan forced himself to smile. He stifled his

emotions as he resisted the urge to embrace his daughter, to touch his own flesh and blood to make sure this wasn't a dream.

"I've got a camera, boss. The two of you stand together!" The young man who had placed tubs of ice cream behind the counter rushed out the double doors with his smartphone.

"Perfect, Jorge!" The manager's face was all smiles. He shook Ryan's hand in a tight grip as if they were old buddies. "I'm Tom, by the way! It's a pleasure to meet you, Mr. Monti!" Welcome to Whitestone Creamery!" He then put his other arm behind Ryan and mugged for the camera.

"Ready!" Jorge worked hard to adjust his phone at just the right angle and distance.

Despite his initial shock, Ryan worked on adjusting his paralyzed mouth into a semblance of a smile.

After the camera flashed, Tom said, "Trudy, you join us for the next picture. Stand on Mr. Monti's other side."

Trudy giggled. She studied her appearance in the wall mirror for a few seconds, rearranged her hair a bit, and came over with a deep blush. She didn't know what to do with her hands, and Ryan had the same problem. He felt like embracing her yet knew he couldn't. He was afraid if he touched her he would burst into tears. He imagined Tom would think he was harassing his employee if he lost control and wrapped his arms around her. So for the picture, they both kept their hands to their sides. He yearned to place his hands on her cheeks and study her face: she was his daughter, his little girl. Together with her brother, they were his most precious possessions. Ryan was at a loss to understand his instinctual paternal feelings.

At that moment, Ryan knew his life would never be the same. He felt as if he had been given two blessings – blessings he never thought he would ever experience. He could never go back. After Jorge took the photo, he strived to keep his eyes off Trudy, shook hands with Tom and Jorge, and glanced at his watch.

"Actually, I'm running late. Could I have that hot fudge sundae to go?"

"Of course," Trudy said, running for a cover. "Extra hot fudge at no extra charge!" she announced giddily.

"No charge at all!" Tom proclaimed, asserting himself as the boss. "We're going to put those pictures on the shop wall. You take care of yourself, Mr. Monti. It was a pleasure meeting you."

"Thank you. Same here." Ryan chuckled, feeling like blushing himself.

When Trudy handed him his takeout bag, their fingers touched, and Ryan felt a chill run through his body. That touch alone made him want to break down and cry, but he blinked and stiffened, working hard to maintain his composure.

He waved unseeingly to the crew and left.

Ryan couldn't bear to look at his daughter's face again, for as he turned away, he felt tears welling up in his eyes. He took out his sunglasses and quickly put them on again.

* * *

Ozzy Dick grinned as he peeked from outside the store, hiding at the edge of the window. Fortunately for him, everyone was too busy to notice him lurking around.

Ozzy glanced at his reflection in the door window when he was confident the people he was watching in the store were sufficiently distracted.

I'm no Ryan Monti, he thought morosely.

He drove away that thought. Dwelling on his shortcomings did him no good whatsoever. Self-pity did not help him get jobs. Or anything. He only elicited sympathy from the psychologist he was seeing. Or seeing until his insurance ran out.

Ozzy recalled what he had witnessed moments ago.

The customer he had seen shoveling ice cream into his mouth was confronting the young female worker. He looked angry.

Sitting down waiting for his order, Ryan approached the man, looking equally angry.

Ozzy peered into the window. It looked like Tom was hailing Ryan as a hero or something. Next thing he knew, they were standing together and mugging for the camera. Ozzy knew Tom; in fact, he patronized the Whitestone Creamery often. He brought Zoe there a few times; she would buy the biggest sundaes and eat with such relish she reminded him of a little girl.

Tom's always looking for publicity. He wouldn't let this moment pass him by, Ozzy thought. *He'd bring in a dancing monkey if he thought that would give publicity for the ice cream store.*

Ozzy frowned at this thought. If he was still working for the *Boston Herald,* he'd be hurrying in there taking photos and interviewing everyone.

He felt like braining himself. *Why the hell did I have to make up those details for the story? Why didn't I just report the boring facts?* But Ozzy already knew the answer. He wanted to make a name for himself. It would've been great if he hadn't screwed up.

Ozzy hid his face when he saw Ryan leave the store. The smell of the hot fudge when the door opened beckoned him inside.

Ah, what could it hurt if I go inside now? He turned to the workers in the store, laughing and talking animatedly. *I can find out what happened in there. Who knows? Maybe something significant, something I could use.*

If only I could work for a celebrity detective and make shitloads of money. Have a few homes and go to all those exclusive parties. Have the ear of all those Hollywood big shots.

Like Buddy Catalano.

Upon walking into the Whitestone Creamery, Ozzy took one look at Trudy and spotted her uncanny resemblance to the famous actor immediately.

He froze. Then he smiled. Everything was working out. He'd have no problem blackmailing Monti.

Don't fret, he told himself. *My luck is changing. Soon I'll be on top too.*

CHAPTER TWENTY-EIGHT

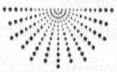

BOSTON

Ryan drove back to his hotel awash in happiness, exhilarated at being alive and in awe of the unexpected surprises life had handed him. He got out of his car with a spring in his step, enveloped by a wholeness and contentment he had never experienced before. He felt giddy – he wanted to laugh but was afraid strangers would look at him as if he was deranged. He recalled not even feeling this complete happiness when he was nominated for an Academy Award.

Ryan viewed the world through different eyes. For the first time, he actually noticed and smiled in appreciation of the young children he saw on the street. He never contemplated having his own. The twins were already grown up, but so what? They were still his.

He had to hand it to Christine – she had done a phenomenal job raising the kids.

Christine. Ryan ceased smiling, and his countenance

turned serious. He needed to meet with her but at the same time dreaded the prospect.

He had to see her again. He shuddered at the thought but reasoned that she must have sent him that letter. She apparently was no longer the sweet, beautiful Christine he remembered. Life must have hardened her. He couldn't even speculate how this could have come about. Would she want to reminisce about the old days, revealing why she had failed to inform him about the children's existence, or would she be demanding and bitter, rehashing fresh accusations about his supposed unfaithfulness eighteen years ago?

She was probably desperate for college tuition money, he figured. But two million dollars? Ryan had no reason to learn about college costs, but could they have gone up so high? They must have, judging from all the headlines about the increasing cost of college that he read about but never bothered to investigate. Why else would she inform him of their children's existence now? It had been many years, but their children would forever link the two of them together and she expected him to help out. Of course, he would have done so anyway – all Christine had to do was contact him. Why her need for deceitful blackmail?

Ryan's head was swirling in a mixture of anticipation and fear. Would they have a confrontation? Would she stoop so low as to threaten to blackmail him if he didn't pay up?

But then again, the blackmailer threatened to inform the press of the twins. He concluded Christine must be a loving mother. It didn't make sense for her to do that.

If the blackmailer wasn't Christine, who could it possibly be?

Ryan's whole body stiffened. He was forced to stop walking and take a seat at an outdoor cafe. The waiter rushed over to take his order, and Ryan thoughtlessly ordered an espresso, the first drink that came into his mind.

He stared at the heavy traffic – drivers trying to maneuver ahead despite the congestion, the pedestrians with their shopping bags from major retailers and famous Boston storefronts.

Placing a glass cup of espresso before him, the waiter interrupted his thoughts. He stared at the hot drink as he recalled the fresh, kind faces of his twins. They seemed like good, well-adjusted kids. Nothing sinister, devious, or desperate about them. Pressure was pounding in the back of his head as he contemplated flying out of Boston and returning to Los Angeles and his old life.

The life he was satisfied with.

His career at the forefront of his life.

Staying close to his parents.

Fewer complications. The only pressure was the search to star in a hit movie.

Yes, his inner voice told him, *return to your old life. You were happy, and this would invite a host of complications. Suppose your children reject you?*

But as he brought the hot drink to his lips, spilling a few drops as he weighed his inner battle, Ryan knew he couldn't do that.

He was going to jump into unknown territory – meet the children he'd never known he had – and then be forced to face the consequences.

There was no going back now.

He took out his phone and checked his calendar. He was due in Christine's office at 9:30 a.m. tomorrow.

As Ryan took a few sips of the espresso to calm his jittery nerves, he stared at the car parked across the street. It was the same car he had noticed at the high school, an old blue Saturn with a dented front passenger door. His eyes narrowed. Then he sat up, frightened, nearly spilling the whole cup.

Is this person following me? Who could it be? Is it the blackmailer?

* * *

Ozzy felt a creeping terror when Ryan stared at his car for an inordinate amount of time. He wanted to sink in the driver's seat, but there wasn't enough room.

What can I do? He felt himself heating up. *How am I goin' get another car right away?*

When Ryan turned away, Ozzy realized that somehow, some way, he would have to be more careful.

He had been too confident, believing the endless flow of Boston traffic would be the perfect cover.

I've gotta think of something. I know I'm close to breaking a big story. I can feel it.

CHAPTER TWENTY-NINE

BOSTON

Christine was actually relieved to go to work. Her in-laws were home with her husband, and she knew she deserved a day that distracted her from Daniel's leukemia with all the accompanying sadness and worry. She was staying strong for her family, but it proved draining. Sophie texted her saying she had a sudden, surprise appointment at nine thirty. Sophie didn't give her any more details but promised her she would be pleased and excited. Christine certainly needed that.

But as she got out of her car in the company parking garage, she experienced an eerie feeling. She glanced around. She did not see anyone, but still a tinge of fear shot up her spine.

It must be all the stress I'm going through, she reasoned, shaking off her fears. *Just relax and put everything out of your mind,* she instructed herself. *Today will be a better day.*

As she proceeded to the building, Christine heard a low voice.

"Christine, Christine!" the voice whispered insistently.

She jumped as she whirled around, dropping her briefcase. Christine gasped and stood still as she made out the man approaching her. She blinked and shook her head in an effort to deny the presence of the man she saw in front of her.

Ryan Monti – her boyfriend of eighteen years ago and the biological father of her twins.

Christine opened her mouth, not sure if she should scream or get in her car and drive away.

"Christine! Christine! We need to talk, please!"

She said nothing, standing still with her mouth open, unable to move.

Finally, he spoke. "I'm sorry I frightened you," he whispered.

Recovering from her shock, she exclaimed, "H- how did you get in here?"

"I have an appointment," he said slowly, still staring at her.

"An appointment? Why do you have an appointment here? With whom?" She almost laughed at the incredulity of his answer while trying not to shake.

Ryan glanced down and then slowly faced her as he said, "With you."

"With me? With me? Why the hell do you have an appointment with me?" She glanced around as she spoke.

They were still alone in the parking garage.

"If I approached you in the office, you'd be in shock when you saw me, the way you are now. I wanted you to keep your composure in front of everyone."

Christine shook her head, unbelieving. "Ryan, I don't understand. W- why are you coming to see me now? Why now? I- I've got a lot of important things to do today." She felt herself getting hotheaded as she retrieved her briefcase from the ground. *How dare he just waltz into my life at his convenience? Who does he think he is?*

Ryan wrinkled his brows in puzzlement. He looked at her sideways and asked, "You sent me that letter?"

"What letter? What the hell are you talking about?" she demanded. She felt like stamping her foot in exasperation. Or slapping his face. Or choking him. "You idiot! I've got quite enough on my plate now without you popping into my life!"

"I need to speak with you. It's urgent. Why else would I be coming here out of the blue?" he shot back.

From his heavy breathing and wild eyes, Christine could see he was incensed and offended.

Finally, he looked at his watch and said, "Don't you have to be in your office soon?'

"Shit," she murmured as she looked at her own watch, seething in anger. She felt like pulling her hair and sinking into the black cold pavement of the parking garage, scream-ing, *I can't deal with anything more! I've had it! I'm falling apart!*

Noticing her distress, Ryan said, "Christine, I'm not trying to give you a hard time. I just want to speak with you." When that didn't calm her down, he added, "Would it have been better if I surprised you at home with your family?"

His last statement shook Christine from her seething rage. She stopped and stared at him as if seeing him for the first time: he appeared reasonable and nonthreatening. Ryan had aged well. He had a few wrinkles at the corners of his eyes, but his hairline had only receded a bit since his youth. She recalled the way his hair kept falling over his forehead. Ryan had a slightly fuller frame instead of the lanky young man just coming out of his teenage years. The years had treated him well.

As she gaped at him, he came closer and said, "You go in

now. I don't want to go in before you get there and make you look late. Then we'll talk, OK? Just talk. I'm not trying to do anything to hurt you." He then hurried away.

Unable to move, Christine watched him. She wondered what had brought Ryan back into her life and what it portended.

He's always traveling around the world for his roles, always being seen with a different beautiful woman. What could he want with me?

Forcing her legs to move forward and trying to thaw her brain that had become frozen with shock, Christine began walking toward the door to get into the building while attempting to process what was happening.

Whenever she saw an advertisement for one of his movies, she quickly turned away and focused on something else. She recalled that when he starred in *Beguiled* seven years ago, a blushing Trudy confessed he was one of the most handsome men she had ever seen. This left Christine speechless, and Trudy thankfully changed the subject. Sensing her mother's discomfort, she finally said, "Don't worry, Mom. I'm not into older men."

Christine remembered nodding with her mouth still agape.

As she reached the door to the building, Christine felt a shudder ripple through her body as she turned the door-knob. *Did Ryan find out about the twins? How could that have possibly happened? Everyone who knows has been sworn to secrecy!* Her mouth went dry as another prospect loomed over her: *Would he want to meet the twins? Have a relationship with them?*

She scoffed at the idea. *No way! I am quite sure he enjoys his carefree playboy lifestyle. Why would he want to be saddled with the responsibility of worrying about kids?*

Christine always took the stairs in lieu of the elevator,

taking advantage of any opportunity to exercise. Going up the stairs relaxed her. *Could he just want to hire a new young model for a film role? Was that supposed to be an actor's job? Maybe he looks into modeling agencies if he sees a model he's interested in meeting? Who knows? Did he see my name and want to reconnect to talk about the old days when we were young and relatively innocent? Did he want to take this opportunity to do a little bragging about how far he's gone in his career? I always knew he'd get somewhere.*

But deep down, she knew those reasons couldn't possibly be why he was there.

As Christine entered the office, Linda came rushing over to her, her eyes dancing, her cheeks pink, and her smile wide.

"Christine, you'll never guess," she whispered loudly while hurrying over to her. "A big actor in Hollywood made an appointment to see you! Ryan Monti! Can you believe it? First thing this morning! Oh my, I can't... he's a little late," she said, glancing at the clock, "but that's OK. You're just a few minutes late too. No problem." She waved her hand. "You go into your office and get ready. Sophie has an early meeting today. After she's done, she's coming over here to greet him." Her hand went to her chest and then both her hands fluttered to her cheeks. "Oh my! This is so exciting! Wait until my family hears about this! After he meets with you, I'm hoping to get a picture with him!"

As she rambled on, Christine stood there woodenly. When Linda finally finished gushing, she mindlessly headed to her own office, where her assistant was too excited to notice her expressionless face.

Her intuition sharpened at the realization that the only reason Ryan wanted to see her again had to be because he somehow found out about the twins.

She closed her office door as Linda began prattling on to coworkers passing through. Christine dropped her briefcase and leaned her head on the door, struggling to steady her nerves and calm the rising nausea in her stomach, gasping to breathe, attempting to stifle her growing panic as she recalled what Ryan had said.

A letter. A letter? What letter? Who sent him a letter?

CHAPTER THIRTY

As promised, Ryan did not go into the building right away. He paced the parking garage, wishing he had a drink. It was obvious Christine saw him as another problem in her already stressed-out life. He had been convinced Christine must have sent him the letter, but after encountering her, he was confused, pondering if someone had a vendetta against him. Ryan wasn't confrontational, and he could not think of anyone who despised him to the extent that they would blackmail him. Kim had not been in his life for many years. He thought, for the first time in a long while, that perhaps he should have Buddy check her whereabouts.

Ryan returned to his car to check himself in the mirror and regain his composure. Sitting in his car, he fought the impulse to drive away and pretend this encounter had never happened. But no, he'd come this far. He'd seen his children.

There was no going back now. As a big Hollywood star, he acknowledged to himself that he was not used to being treated as nothing but a nuisance. No time to think about that now.

Ryan combed his hair. Stretching his knuckles in and out, he glanced at his watch. Ten minutes. He would give her ten minutes to get herself settled.

Exiting his car, he meandered to the building, dreading to enter. Her boss had offered him a parking space in the garage for convenience as well as keeping in mind his desire for anonymity. He took pains to compose himself. Ryan breathed deeply and shut his eyes to slow down his beating heart: this life-changing meeting could not be delayed any longer.

* * *

In the eerie silence of the parking garage, Ozzy witnessed their whole exchange.

At first, his heart raced with excitement. He felt his jacket pocket for his cell phone to take pictures, but although the woman was surprised and Monti looked uneasy, all they did was talk for a few moments, not even allowing him to get his camera into position. He had hoped something scandalous would have occurred – Ozzy relished the thought of Ryan Monti summarily dethroned and blacklisted from his Hollywood elite status by the afternoon. This brick of gold had fallen into Ozzy's lap, and the media the world over would be covering his findings on Monti's visit to Boston. He envisioned investigative journalism jobs pouring in – everyone would want him. But he nearly dropped his cell phone when he saw the woman walk away and Ryan pace around before heading back inside his car. She didn't ogle him – she apparently *knew* him, albeit was dismayed to see him.

The song "Shattered Dreams" began playing in Ozzy's head.

IDELLE KURSMAN

No! he told himself. He had to follow the actor further and uncover what he was doing there.

CHAPTER THIRTY-ONE

BOSTON

"Ms. Goldberg, your nine thirty appointment is here to see you," Linda Page said in a high, merry voice.

"Send him in, Linda. Thank you," Christine responded. She forced herself to rise from her chair at her desk. Her legs and arms felt heavy and stiff. She checked her face in her bathroom mirror to make sure she looked calm and normal. Christine approached the door as if awaiting her doom. She had applied a little blush because she had looked so pale in the bathroom mirror, but upon opening the door, she greeted an equally pale Ryan.

"Mr. Monti, welcome to the Marie Cooper Modeling Agency. Please come in." They smiled and shook hands as if they were meeting for the first time.

Standing in the hallway, Linda was blushing like a love-struck teenager. Christine took pains to hold her shoulders up high and appear in her usual impeccable professional mode. She thought inside that she must be a born actress –

she planted a small smile of satisfaction on her lips as if she had achieved the apex of her career.

But once they were alone, the acting was over.

"What are you doing here? And what kind of excuse does an actor make for having to make an appointment with a modeling agency, for heaven's sake?" Christine asked with gritted teeth after she closed her door. She motioned for Ryan to sit down.

He said nothing but simply stared at her once they were both seated. He appeared to be studying her.

Christine began another question but didn't finish it as she became caught up in studying him.

Their eyes locked, and again they were in their early twenties, shy and awkward, dating, searching for the right things to do and say. Then Christine turned away as she made an effort to return to the present.

"You're still as beautiful as you were at twenty," Ryan said. He then looked down as if contemplating what might have been. He looked up again and said, "You still wear your signature musk."

Christine's temper eased, and she actually smiled. Ryan continued, "I'm sorry. I didn't know the best way to approach you. I was going over in my mind a thousand other ways, but nothing worked. I was afraid you would be shocked if you didn't find out I was coming in. I thought about calling your house but just couldn't bring myself to do it. You know, it isn't always easy being famous."

"You could've made an appointment under a pseudonym, you know."

"But you still would have been shocked once you recognized me. And we would have had lot of explaining to do to people in your office who saw your reaction."

Christine could not argue with that.

He continued. "I needed to see you immediately, and I

didn't want to cause any problems with your job... or with your husband."

Christine straightened at the mention of Daniel. "Ryan," she whispered gently, "why are you here? How did you find me?"

It took time for him to face her. He slowly met her eyes and told her in almost a whisper, "I saw them."

He paused. Neither spoke.

"I saw them, Christine. I saw our children." He stared at her with pleading eyes. "Why didn't you tell me?"

She glanced down at her desk, studying it and looking as if she were about to cry. Putting her elbow on the desk and covering her eyes with her hand, she whispered, "Ryan, I caught you with another woman, remember?" She removed her hand and faced him. "Tell me the truth. If you knew about them, you would have wanted me to get an abortion. Isn't that right?"

Ryan did not respond right away, staring down at the carpet. He slowly nodded, his head falling on his chest. "Yes, I'm sure I would have wanted that... I wasn't ready to be a father."

"Being a strict Catholic, I would never have agreed to that. You were disloyal to me, you cheated on me. That was unforgivable. But those babies needed to be born – they deserved a chance. If you weren't on board, if you were unreliable, what good would it have done them or you to find out?"

"We were dancing and drinking too much that night. I guess we got carried away. We weren't thinking about our reality... or your parents."

Christine wrinkled her brow, puzzled as to why he was changing the subject. But she closed her eyes and was forced to acknowledge how it had occurred. "Yes, we forgot ourselves in the moment."

"I was in love with you. I wanted to marry you, remember?" Ryan stared into her eyes, waiting for her reaction.

"I felt the same way." Her eyes grew moist, and she shook her head. "Ryan, you cheated on me. I never dreamed you would betray me. How can you sit here and tell me that?"

"Hey, wait a minute. It didn't exactly happen like that!" He stood up. "You don't know everything that happened! Y- you see, it's like this…" He paused a moment, bringing his fist near his mouth. "She came to my trailer to seduce me. I didn't invite her."

"It appeared she was succeeding marvelously," Christine said acidly, her arms folded.

Ryan's eyes narrowed. "Christine, I'm just a man—"

"I know. A weak and helpless creature," she retorted, rolling her eyes.

Ryan's shoulders sagged. "She was a beautiful woman. I tried to resist her, but she practically threw herself on me."

"And did you start dating her?"

"No! Of course not!"

"Have you kept in contact with her?"

Ryan was baffled. "That was the last time I ever saw her, Christine! I was furious with her. Her machinations broke us up! She was seducing me to further her own acting career."

"I never read about her after that movie," Christine observed, searching her brain for her other movies.

"Her career went south after that. She really didn't have talent. Last I heard from another actor on the set, she divorced her fourth husband and was starring in underground porn movies."

Christine looked up and met his eyes. *Did I totally misread the supposed liaison? I never gave him a chance to explain after witnessing the damning scene.*

She rubbed her forehead. "She upended my whole life."

"She upended mine too."

"What do you mean? You went on your merry way and starred in more movies – became a big Hollywood actor!" she huffed, staring at him as if he were out of his mind.

"But I lost you."

"You got over it," she answered, biting her lip to prevent tears from flowing.

"Not like you think. I missed you," he whispered.

"If you knew I was pregnant, we'd have been fighting over whether I should get an abortion, which I think you would have wanted. Insisted on."

Ryan's face dropped. He knew she was right.

"But you ran away so hurt. I tried calling you, sending letters. I even went to your house once. Your parents wouldn't let me in."

Christine's mouthed dropped open. "When was that?"

"It was a week after you saw me on the set. They told me in no uncertain terms that if I came over again, they'd call the police."

Christine's mind was racing. She'd had to stay in the hospital. Her parents feared she'd have a breakdown. She remembered them admonishing her that she was selfish, ungrateful, and irresponsible. A disappointment. She then began screaming and pulling her hair. The doctor had to sedate her, and she spent two months in the psychiatric unit. Only her parents visited her.

Then she had to go away. She spoke to her friends on occasion before they slowly dropped out of her life. Her young life came to an abrupt end, and she was forced to start anew.

The tears flowed. She hid her face and stood. Ryan also stood up and approached her, but she said, "Let me go to the bathroom so I can compose myself."

She felt his eyes pine after her as she hurried away. This

was not the time for him to comfort her. She needed to regain her composure.

She sat on the toilet and proceeded to fall apart. She yearned to have a good crying session but tried to hold back for fear someone would hear her. She wept softly, the tears flowing like a faucet that had been stopped up for so long it finally burst open. This was the first time she had ever cried so much since she found Ryan with another woman and then found out she was pregnant.

Christine needed time to herself but knew she wasn't going to get it. Amid her crying, there was a gentle yet insistent knock on the door.

"Christine? Christine?" he kept saying.

She reached to lock the bathroom door, but it was too late: Ryan opened it with tears streaming down his face. Heartbreak was etched across his features. Christine knew he was not acting – those tears were real.

Yearning to embrace him, she held back. It would be disloyal to Daniel. Then a thought struck her: Where was he all these years? No matter how shattered he now appeared, Ryan had lived his life in ignorant bliss. She was the one who cared for their children, stayed up late into the night when they were sick, comforted them during their disappointments and rallied them on. Meanwhile, he was gallivanting from woman to woman, from one critically acclaimed role to another, traveling the world in luxury.

Clearly, he had no place in their lives then or in the present. After all, with all his wealth, he could have searched for her these past eighteen years if he had really wanted to find her. She viewed his pleading eyes and tear-streaked face as nothing more than his being a lightweight, weak man. To Christine, he could turn right back to his shallow Hollywood lifestyle of parties and women. She had more than enough on her plate.

Drying her eyes, Christine forced herself to rise and confront him. "Ryan," she said sharply, "you know you could have tried to track me down all these years if you had really cared for me. I was fortunate to find a man decent and strong enough to help raise the children. I don't see why you need to come into our lives now, especially at this time—"

He interrupted her. "And don't you think I was actually hurt when you wouldn't let me explain what happened? You wrote me off completely, and I thought your parents had convinced you to dump me – but I'm here now because of that letter."

"That letter – you keep mentioning it. Please show it to me. I want to read it. I can't imagine anyone I know would have the audacity to send it to you and betray me."

Ryan felt his pockets. "Damn, I didn't bring a copy with me! The letter said I am a father and that I better pay two million dollars or the news would be all over the media."

Christine froze. "You have no idea who sent you that letter?"

"None. I have a private investigator helping me find out."

"And has the private investigator found out who sent the letter?"

Ryan said nothing. He appeared to be mulling over her question. Finally, he said, "No, and you know, that's a very good question, Christine."

As they made their way back into their seats in her office, Christine stared hard at him. "Is someone following the children? Are they in danger? That's what you should find out. But in regard to the children, Ryan, please just leave well enough alone with the kids."

His contemplative expression vanished, and he lashed out. "Why?" he said, aghast. "Don't they have a right to know their father?" His eyes narrowed to slits. "What have you told them about me? Did you say I abandoned them or I'm dead?"

His vicious retort startled her. *What if I told them the truth? That you most likely would have wanted an abortion?* she was tempted to say out loud.

"I- I really never went into it with them." She gave a humorless laugh as she pushed her hair to the back of her head. "Even when they grilled me. I couldn't go into it. We always emphasized that my husband was their father." Her eyes narrowed. "He was the one who was always there for them."

Ryan studied her. "And what did you tell your husband about me?"

Christine bit her lip and shut her eyes. "That I went too far with a boyfriend and had to move away when I found out I became pregnant. I had to practically start my life over again."

"And you never went into any more details with him?"

"No, my husband realizes people make mistakes. I was very young when it happened." She glanced down and then met his eyes. "He's been my rock ever since. I don't want anything or anyone to jeopardize that."

Ryan shook his head. "You mean to tell me he doesn't know I'm the father?"

She shut her eyes and shook her head.

"Man, you've been keeping a big secret from them."

"I do what's in the best interests of my family," she declared obstinately.

"In their best interests or yours?"

She glared at him, then realized she had hurt him needlessly. "Look," she said, "this has been as big a shock to me as it has been to you. At least you were prepared for today. Just know that the twins have been loved and cared for. Believe it or not, there is a lot going on in my family right now. My husband has an illness, but I'd rather not go into it now. Let's both digest all that happened today, and when things are less hectic for us..."

Christine paused in the realization of the futility of that argument.

How would they continue? Would her family ever forgive or understand why she had never revealed the identity of the twins' biological father? Had his unfaithfulness, or more accurately, being a victim of a seduction, eighteen years ago prevented them from knowing the truth?

Contemplating the other emergency situation in her life, Christine resisted the urge to cover her face with her hands and order him to leave until Daniel got better. Terrifying thoughts soon assailed her: Suppose her family would now feel she had betrayed them by concealing the truth and turn their backs on her? She would have to tread carefully with Ryan and deal with him as reasonably and unemotionally as she could. She feared losing everything near and dear to her.

There was a knock at the door. Christine and Ryan nearly jumped out of their seats, their eyes locked and mouths open.

"Please give us a minute! We're going over some papers!" Ryan tried to keep his voice even, but he sounded hoarse.

"Oh, of course! Take your time! Take your time, please!" Sophie, Christine's boss, said through the door.

Christine glanced from the door to Ryan and back again, her face turning pale.

"We've got to play it cool. We're in a business meeting. We have to look professional," he told her.

She couldn't help noticing that he was faster to recover from the surprise than she was. She closed her eyes, lifted her shoulders, and breathed, determined to regain her composure.

"Do you want some water?" he asked, leaning toward her solicitously.

She nodded again, not finding her voice to speak.

He stared around, and she pointed to the Poland Spring water cooler in the corner.

Handing her the water, he whispered, "Despite what you may think, I'm not here to ruin your life. I'm not going to stay long. I don't mean to upset you, but we have to talk… about the future… come to some agreement that's right for both of us and the kids. This isn't the time to reopen old wounds. We both have to continue living our lives."

Christine took a long sip and said, "I agree. Is my color back?"

"Yeah, it's coming back."

"She can come in," she said, waving her hand. "Let's get this over with."

He nodded and opened the door an inch. "Uh, sorry for the delay."

"No problem! I'm sorry I'm interrupting," Sophie apologized. Christine noticed her boss's eyes were glittering in excitement although she tried to maintain her professional demeanor.

Christine found herself at a loss for words, but Ryan interceded immediately. "Actually, I'm confused about dates, so we've decided to wait before we agree on anything. Afraid I'm suffering from jet lag… I just came back from vacationing in Indonesia and am a little confused about when I'll need the models for my next movie set."

"No problem! No problem at all!" Sophie walked in and shook Ryan's hand. "I must say it is an honor to meet you, Mr. Monti. We get so many people from Hollywood but rarely an actor."

Christine forced herself to not roll her eyes, thinking, *since when do we get Hollywood people here? There have been probably one or two in the all the years I've worked here.*

"I am actually doing a favor for a friend of mine. I am

getting ready to do a film in Boston, and he asked me to find some models from the East Coast for a photo shoot."

Sophie raised her eyebrows and smiled in delight. "Oh, what kind of photo shoot?"

"A calendar for college girls," he said evenly.

Christine was impressed that Ryan didn't miss a beat.

"Well, we at the Marie Cooper Modeling Agency are always happy to help. Feel free to call us at any time. We have an abundance of college-age models. I'm sure we can find your friend just what he needs... and what is your friend's name?"

"He actually would rather not give his name out until a contract is signed. I hope you understand. He's in great demand and already has more contacts than he can handle. He has found remaining anonymous in the scouting stage to be the easiest approach."

Christine wanted to roll her eyes. *What an artful liar!*

"I understand," said Sophie. "Please let him know that we are here to facilitate his selection process. As I'm sure he already knows, we have been in business nearly fifty years."

"He knows, and that's why he requested I come here first."

Sophie's eyes were dancing now as she asked, "Is there anything else you need, Mr. Monti?"

"No, we're fine now, thank you," Ryan said quickly. Christine smiled and shook her head, grateful that the spotlight was on Ryan while she was recovering from her outburst.

Sophie fumbled, "Then I'll leave you two alone to continue on with your work."

"Great!" they both answered.

As soon as Sophie closed the door, Ryan collapsed in his chair.

Christine and Ryan breathed sighs of relief.

"Would you mind telling me what we're supposed to be

working on?" Christine asked. "And what movie set are we talking about?"

"All right, all right. I'll have to figure something out," he said. "I'm scheduled to star in a movie here, but it's been delayed."

"And I remember you telling me that you never had a problem with jet lag." Christine's eyes were sparkling as she teased him.

Ryan smiled. "I'm happy to see you got your sense of humor back."

Despite forcing herself to regain her composure rather quickly, Christine felt calmer. All hope was not lost, and Ryan had promised to be reasonable.

"Let's just exchange contact information, and then I'll be on my way."

Christine was reaching for her mobile phone when her office phone rang.

"Christine?" Daniel's voice sounded unusually low and weak.

"Honey, what is it? Are you all right?" She clutched her phone tighter and stood up.

"I'm all right" – he paused – "I hate to bother you at work…"

"It's all right. Tell me what's wrong!"

"The doctor said I'd feel a little stronger today, but I feel a lot weaker."

"Have you been trying to be active? You're supposed to get rest."

"Except for a light breakfast, I've spent the whole day in bed."

Christine forced herself to smile even though she looked like she wanted to cry. "Daniel, you'll feel better soon. We're all rallying behind you!"

She failed to notice that Ryan was observing her and sat as still as a statue.

"I'm sorry, but I just started with the chemotherapy and I- I don't want to continue. It's taking every bit of strength I have out of me. I feel like I'm being whittled down to the size of a pretzel."

Christine stifled her sobs and said, "Now, Daniel, you listen to me. Yes, you are going to beat this disease!" The moment she said it, she glanced at Ryan and put her hand on her temple, regretting the admission. She couldn't worry about that now. "I'm going to come home as soon as I possibly can. I already told Sophie that I'll be here on Saturday. But, Daniel, you can't get discouraged. We all love and need you."

"You don't need to hurry. My parents are on their way. My mother's losing it, and you don't want to be here when she breaks down. My father said she's tottering."

"I see you've inherited your mother's optimism," she said dryly. "She doesn't need to come if she's just going to discourage you."

"I know. I just couldn't stand being by myself in my own thoughts. A few minutes after I called them, Trudy called and said she's coming home to keep me company instead of going to cheerleading practice. She'll be here in two hours. You stay at work, Christine. You'll be better off there. Trudy's good at calming my mother down." He paused. "I shouldn't have called you."

"That's OK," she said quickly. "I was just about to call you."

There was a pause before he said, "I just think I should prepare you. I don't want you to get your hopes up that I can overcome this when I know I'm not going to make it."

Christine knew from his voice that he was holding back tears.

"I'm going home right after work unless you need me sooner. It's been an interesting morning." She glanced at Ryan.

He was pale and looked anguished. He was moving in his seat as if he wanted to say something but kept silent.

"You go ahead with your day and forget about my calling you. I see my parents' car parked in front of the house."

"Our bedroom is in the back of the house. Are you out of bed?"

"No... yes," he conceded. "But they'll be here any minute. I'd turn on the TV for a distraction, but I'm afraid I won't hear them come in."

"Put the TV on low," Christine told him with a faint smile.

"I love you, honey," Daniel said. She overheard a news show on low.

"I love you too, Daniel. Call me again if you need to."

Christine closed the phone while holding back tears. She shut her eyes, not even wanting to face Ryan.

Ryan finally broke the ensuing silence by clearing his throat and asking, "Was that your husband?"

No, it's one of my many lovers! she was tempted to snap. Out loud she said, "Yes. Listen, Ryan. I've got lots of work to catch up on. No offense, but I've gotten nothing done this morning." She sat back down in her chair and regarded him coolly. "I'll be in touch."

"Christine, is there something I could do?" He rose when she did and met her with earnest eyes and a grave expression.

Christine fought to maintain control. "No, of course not. There's nothing you can do. Like I said, there's a lot going on in my life right now. I'm even coming in on Saturday to get work done in case I have to take a day or two off next week."

He did not reply, but his eyes never wavered from hers.

"Let's somehow think of a quick way to deal with my

boss. I'm sure she'll want all the details of what you want to do."

They both glanced at the door.

"Can you give me your phone number?"

She stood silent.

"I'll give you mine," he said, taking paper and a pen, scrawling it down, not bothering with his cell. "I'd hate to have to meet up with you again like we did in the parking garage."

Christine flinched. She stared at the paper he handed her and said grimly, "We'll be in touch."

"Life can be very unpredictable. What we plan doesn't always materialize the way we intended."

"That's for sure," she agreed. "I was raised to be a virgin until I got married," she said wistfully.

"Life happens, you know. We try to do everything right and something falls askew."

"That's right, but I don't regret having the twins."

"I don't either. I saw them. They look like great kids."

"They are."

"You did a marvelous job. They couldn't have had a better mother. Looking at them I felt so proud, and yet I had nothing to do with it."

"Oh, I wouldn't say that," she said with a chuckle. "You were responsible for them coming into existence."

"But you did all the work."

"And a lot of work it was," she agreed. "But they're definitely worth it." She then grew serious, adding, "My husband adopted them when we got married, and he's been the most wonderful father."

"D- did you have any more children?"

"No," Christine said, shaking her head. "Daniel is unable to have children..." She hesitated before adding, "Besides, kids are expensive, you know. Especially when you have two at a time."

"I'm sure." Ryan coughed into his hand.

"Do you want some water? Or coffee?"

"No, no." He waved her suggestion away. "I want to talk about the children. What are their names?"

"Timothy and Trudy."

There was silence.

"I can just imagine how your parents reacted when they found out you were pregnant. Their attitude was more the mainstream fifty years ago."

Christine closed her eyes. "I realize that. They were as shocked as I was. They looked at me as if they didn't know me. I didn't know myself either. It took a while before I understood what had happened... until then, they stopped trusting me... I stopped trusting myself. Of course, I had to drop out of college immediately. I was sent away to my aunt in Boston, where we told people I had gotten married to an army man and he was stationed in Iraq."

Christine frowned as she recalled the memory. All levity in her face disappeared. "They whisked me away to my Aunt Ann's, and I stayed with her until I had the babies. That way, no one in our town knew about my shame."

"Christine, I'm so sorry." He reached out his hand and then withdrew it, as if knowing his care and sympathy were too late now.

"Yeah, there was no chance I was going to become a model then," she answered bitterly. "Or graduate from college. After they were born, I expected to work a low-end job to support us. If I mentioned I wanted to return back home, my parents told me they would have to move so they wouldn't have to endure everyone's questions and stares. After all, they were very active in their church." Christine sighed. "But the truth was I would rather have collected welfare and lived in a shelter than go home again." Christine was studying her nails.

"And all that time you never tried to contact me? Why not?"

"I saw you making out with an actress. I felt I didn't know you... and I didn't want you near the babies. I felt you would do more harm than good, being such an unfaithful jerk."

She stared right into his eyes accusingly.

"Well, I hope I gave you a full explanation of the circumstances. I admit I should have been stronger when she came on to me like that, but it was unexpected and I was unprepared for her. I've had nothing to do with that woman ever since. Would you agree we can rest it at that? Do you have any more questions for me about her? She was an actress on the set, and I never saw or worked with her again. You were the one I was in love with and wanted to marry."

Christine breathed in and started shuffling papers, avoiding his eyes. "OK, I can accept that. It was a misunderstanding, and it's well in the past." She looked at him. "We've got to deal with the present. There are more people involved now instead of just the two of us."

"Yes, our children."

"And my husband, who needs my attention now."

"All right. I promise I'll give you some space."

They stood in silence for a moment. Then Ryan cleared his throat. "D- do you need any help? Financial or otherwise?"

Christine glared at him. "I am not that young helpless girl you remember who lacked strength and confidence. I can stand on my own now and handle my own problems."

Ryan tapped the top of the chair he had risen from. "I know that, Christine! You always did have that stubborn streak! I want to make things easier on the children... and on you, believe it or not. All of you are intimately tied into my life, and I want to help."

Christine stared down. "We are going to handle it, but thank you for the offer."

"Then we'll be in touch." Ryan made his way out the door.

When he had left, Christine sat back in her chair, slouched in defeat, not knowing how she was going to share her family with Ryan. It wasn't just the kids she was worried about. She wanted to make every effort to keep him on the sidelines and not allow Daniel to feel threatened. Christine feared this extra stress would wreak havoc on her husband's health as well as on her own.

CHAPTER THIRTY-TWO

BOSTON

Ryan left the office shaking his head. Linda, Christine's assistant, who appeared to have put on makeup since he last saw her, opened her mouth to speak to him. But he mumbled his thanks and left.

Christine is still as proud and stubborn as ever, he thought, shaking his head. *Some people never change.*

Despite his fame, status, and wealth, she knew how to put him in his place.

He recalled a disquieting point she had brought up to him: Had the private investigator found out who sent the letter?

What had Buddy done to find out who sent it? He was a well-seasoned investigator. He must have run into this situation before. Getting into his car, Ryan took out his phone.

"Good afternoon, Bud—" Shana began.

"I need to speak to Buddy. This is Ryan Monti." Ryan did not have the patience to be polite.

"One moment, Mr. Monti."

"Yes, Ryan. What's going on?" Buddy answered.

"Buddy, have you made any efforts to find out who sent the blackmail letter?"

Silence.

"Ah, well... my efforts have been focused on finding out about your children, Mr. Monti," Buddy said in a low voice.

"Well now, I found the kids. I want you to focus now on who sent that letter... unless I have to call the police to track down this person. Someone has been following me in Boston, but I haven't been able to get a good look at him."

Again silence. Then: "I could make some inquiries so we can nip this in the bud before getting the police involved."

Ryan noticed Buddy was not talking in the same confident tone that he normally did.

"That blackmailer has no power over me anymore, but I still don't want the kids or Christine under the media's glare. I want to handle this whole thing at my own pace – that is, whatever is in their best interests."

"Did you get in touch with Christine yet?"

"Yes, we just spoke. She thought I cheated on her years ago and that I wasn't trustworthy enough to have the kids in my life. I believe we cleared up that misunderstanding, but I have to get that blackmailer off my back. I'll give you a day or two to see if you can come up with something, anything, about him. He told me he would give me more details, but I haven't heard from him. If you can't find out anything, I'm getting the police involved."

"I- I'll get on this right away, Mr. Monti. You'll be hearing from me," Buddy tried to reassure him, but he was breathing hard.

"Good. We'll be in touch." Ryan hung up the phone.

As soon as he hung up, Ryan was tempted to call Buddy back to instruct Chin to find out what was wrong with Christine's husband. Christine had let him know that it really wasn't any of his business, but if it was going to affect his children, it certainly was. He vowed the next time they met he would ask her to bring him a photo album of the twins growing up and tell him more about their lives. He would also demand a meeting with them.

Upon starting his car's engine, he stared down and studied his car keys as he thought, *No, Christine has taken care of the children all along, and her husband is now sick. It's best to let her decide when they should meet me. After all, she made it clear she doesn't want me intruding in their lives now.*

Phil had texted Ryan and suggested that since the movie project had been postponed indefinitely, he ought to fly back to LA and look into a few other movie proposals. Ryan also owed his parents a phone call, and he hadn't called or heard from Megan in days.

Ryan started his engine. He wasn't going to leave Boston.

When he entered the lobby of the Mandarin Oriental, a female receptionist said, "Good afternoon, Mr. Monti. This letter came for you."

His name was typed in the same extra-large size on the envelope as the first from the blackmailer.

Ryan felt instant sweat on the back of his head. His stomach lurched as he took the envelope and almost forgot to thank the young woman. His mouth dry, he was tempted to go to the wine bar, but he was too anxious to find out the contents of the letter. With shaky hands, he stuffed the envelope in his coat pocket and pushed the elevator button. There were half a dozen people waiting for the elevator. Out of patience, he bolted for the stairs. By the time he reached his suite on the eighth floor, he was panting and had broken out into a sweat, more from speculating about all the possibilities of what the letter could contain than from the physical exertion. The blackmailer had found him and was following up as he had promised.

He rushed into his suite and tore open the envelope. Ryan's hands were shaking so much he had to put the letter down on the desk.

Welcome to Boston, Ryan Monti! Now that you've seen your two children, I am writing to collect the money. You are to leave two million dollars cash inside the Boston Public Library in a white sack, on the third floor of the Boston Public Library, in the Sargent Gallery, behind the third light fixture. I will follow up with you very soon on the day and time... No cops or you'll be very, very sorry. So sorry nobody would want to be you.

* * *

Across the street, sitting at a table at McDonald's facing the modeling agency, Ozzy spotted a car pulling out of the parking garage as he was munching on French fries. Ryan's car was driving out of the agency's parking lot. Ozzy had stopped and given the letter to the receptionist at the Mandarin Oriental while Ryan was in there. Fortunately, that didn't take him long, and he was even able to get lunch. He licked his lips and smiled, wishing he could see Monti's face when he read the letter.

He contemplated how he could get into the modeling agency to find out what was going on in there.

I could say I have to go to the bathroom! he thought, then frowned; after all, he could go into the McDonald's. Why would he take the trouble of trying to get into the modeling agency?

He felt like kicking himself. They wouldn't let him in to go to the bathroom. If only he was employed again and called, saying his paper wanted to cover them in a story. Then he'd have an opportunity.

Frustrated, he ordered another lunch. Before he took a bite of his sandwich, his cell phone rang. Ozzy mulled over ignoring it but, thinking it might be important, he put down his sandwich and picked it up.

"Ozzy!" Buddy snarled into the phone.

"What? Is this important? I'm taking care of some urgent business right now," Ozzy said as he was chewing fries.

"Monti wants me to find out who his blackmailer is. If I can't come up with anything in a day or two, he's going to the police."

Ozzy sat still, his mouth open in an O shape.

"Get lost now! He's accepted the kids, and he's going to deal with it."

Ozzy recovered from his shock and asked, "Well, what does he think about the media descending on his kids? Disrupting their lives? Scaring them?"

"Monti wants to handle it in his own way, at his own pace."

Ozzy gritted his teeth. "Oh, well, is that what he wants to do? If he doesn't pay me the two million, it's not going to happen that way. I'll take pictures of them and their mother and send them around. I'll hound them and make up my own version of what happened. That'll circulate rumors, and everyone will think he is a cold, uncaring monster for abandoning them."

"Ozzy, the game's up. I'll find you something, I promise. Just drop this. You have to," Buddy pleaded with him.

"No! It's time I deal with him on my own, and if you get involved, you'll regret it. My ship's coming in, and now it's time for me to collect." Ozzy hung up.

He stared at his meal. It no longer looked appetizing. He fought feelings of discouragement and became determined to turn this around in his favor. Monti wouldn't dare get the police involved. That would get rumors circulating. The media always loved the sordid secrets of a reputable actor who had fallen from grace. Ozzy wouldn't threaten the woman and kids directly, much less kidnap them, but he knew how to hound and harass.

Abandoning his meal at the table without throwing it away in the trash, Ozzy got up and headed for Ryan's hotel. He would have to continue watching his movements, confronting him at the right time.

CHAPTER THIRTY-THREE

Buddy felt like flinging the phone, but he didn't want to put a hole in his office wall.

He covered his face, thinking about what would happen to his reputation and his business if Ryan ever found out he knew Ozzy. He was in such a panic he couldn't even come up with a plan to stop him. For a fleeting moment, he thought about hiring a hit man but dismissed it. Too risky.

Thanks to Ryan's business, Buddy was now only two months late on his Tribeca condo payments instead of six. Sweat poured from his head, and he squeezed his eyes tight. Inside his head he hurled every invective he could think of at Ozzy, but he knew that would do him no good.

There was a knock at his door.

"What is it?'

Shana walked in. "Here's the packet you wanted me to copy." She stopped when she looked at him. "Boss, what's wrong? You look awful. What happened?"

Buddy eyed his assistant with hooded eyes. Shana was

twenty-seven but looked seventeen. Her black curly hair was pulled back into a braid, and she wore her usual modest attire – three-quarter-sleeved blouse and long skirt. But looks could be deceiving. Shana was no innocent and was sharp beyond her years. She had gotten him out of perilous situations with clients in the past due to her uncanny ability to see the whole picture. Might she provide him with some help now?

"Shana, have a seat," he told her, motioning for her to sit down across the desk from him.

When she sat, he asked, "How's it going with your condominium? Everything OK?"

"Fine," she said, with a grin. "I just bought a new couch."

"You still dating that guy? What's his name?"

"Robert." Shana blushed.

"Am I going hear wedding bells soon?"

"We're talking about it. I'll let you know if and when."

Buddy nodded. "Good, good. It's great when a man finds a woman who has a secure job and a nice place to live." He frowned. "Shana, I need you to know someone is trying to ruin me. It's to do with that Ryan Monti case."

Shana's smile disappeared. Her leg began shaking. "What do you mean, Buddy? Why does someone want to ruin you?"

"Someone sent him a threatening letter, so he came to me. His blackmailer is now blackmailing me. If I don't do what he wants, he'll lie to Monti that I helped initiate this whole case."

"Mmm." Shana sat back, deep in thought. "And I know that didn't happen."

Buddy narrowed his eyes at her, as if to say, *What do you think?*

"So he's blackmailing you, and now he wants to ruin you."

"If I interfere with his plans for Monti. The guy's in

Boston right now, where Monti is, and wants to take over and do things his way."

She sighed and leaned her elbow on the armrest of the chair. "We've certainly encountered a lot of characters in this business."

Buddy sighed as well. "Isn't that the truth, Shana? I need your insights for this one. I know I earned your everlasting gratitude when I helped you put the down payment on that condo you live in."

Shana sat up. "I know that, Buddy. You don't have to remind me. I paid you back with interest."

He continued, ignoring her last comment. "That last apartment you were living in was a dump. It was in such a dangerous area you told me you feared for your life, but I made sure to pull some strings to find you a nice condo in a good area."

Shana glanced over at him and smiled. "Do you have any dirt on this guy who's blackmailing you?"

"Nooo, but—"

"But I bet you could find out how to get some." She put her elbows on his desk. "A scumbag like him would have to have some dirt on him."

"Yesss… I would think so." Buddy was nodding. Then he narrowed his eyes and said, "Yeah! Of course he would!"

"Buddy, this guy has to be threatened himself in order to be neutralized. He'll only understand if you give him a taste of his own medicine. If need be, you may have to go to Boston yourself and tell Ryan Monti everything, the whole story, to save your own shirt… and mine. I still have twenty-seven years left to pay off that condominium."

Cupping his chin with a faraway stare, Buddy mulled over what she'd said. "You might be right. First, I've got to find out some dirt on this guy. I'm still a few months behind on the payments to my Tribeca condo."

"And, Buddy?"

He looked over at her.

"I've been thinking. You must know someone who could help me to possibly refinance my mortgage so I'll have twenty years of payments left instead of twenty-seven. I heard the rates have gone down."

Buddy steepled his fingers. He was no longer sweating, and the pounding in his head had stopped. "Shana, I'll see what I can do."

"Wonderful," she said. Rising from her chair, Shana told him, "I'll leave you alone now. I have a feeling you have some important calls to make."

Buddy's mouth formed a Cheshire Cat grin. "Darling, you read my mind." He watched her leave, thinking how lucky he was to have hired Shana. She always got the wheels moving in his brain when he was in a jam. She had once again given him an inspiration. He picked up his phone to call his crooked attorney friend who owed him favors.

CHAPTER THIRTY-FOUR

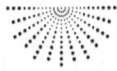

BRIGHTON

Christine stumbled into the front door of her house in a daze. She had to drive around a bit before coming home, trying to process Ryan Monti coming back into her life. Part of her felt like she was nearing a breakdown. The last thing she needed was more pressure and complications in her life. The other part of her felt relief at the possibility her twins would be provided for in case of an emergency. But Christine reminded herself that she was no longer the innocent and naïve young woman she had been eighteen years ago. She was confident she and Daniel would find a way to get through this crisis. All was not lost. She had a decent job, and Daniel would recover and begin working again. Christine pictured Tim and Trudy making it on their own, she and Daniel attending their weddings, enjoying grandchildren, and spending more romantic times together in the future.

Her relationship with Ryan was in the past, and she didn't need to be rescued again. She had managed to make a good life for herself and her family without him, and she would continue to do so. She conceded there might have been a misunderstanding with the actress on the film set, but there was no reason to rehash the past now.

Except that she had to tell Tim and Trudy the truth. They had wanted to know for years, and they had the right to know.

"Mom?"

Trudy was coming down the stairs. "Grandpa and Grandma were here. They left when I came home. I was just sitting with Dad to keep him company."

She hesitated. "How's Dad?"

Trudy shook her head. "He's not feeling so strong now, but I think when he sees you, he'll feel better. He keeps asking about you."

Christine feared her legs weren't going to hold her up. *How can I tell them about this now? It's too much for me to handle.*

She gave herself a mental shake. *No, it's not,* Christine told herself. *You're strong, and you* can *handle it.*

She didn't need to call Tim. He was coming down the steps. Christine told them, "I'm going to check in on Dad, and then I'm going to make a quick dinner. After that, I need to have a talk with you two."

She didn't elaborate, and Tim and Trudy stared at each other as she ascended the stairs.

Christine approached the bedroom, squeezing her eyes tight and taking a deep breath before entering the bedroom. "How's my honey?" Christine said as she walked in, determined to act natural and not shocked by her husband's weakened state.

"Christine." Daniel's eyes brightened upon seeing his wife. He tried to lift his limp hand, but it barely rose an inch. She tried not to wince when she saw how much of his hair had fallen out. "I feel so weak."

"Now, Daniel" – Christine stood straighter in an attempt to stay strong – "Dr. Sherman told us this would happen after chemo. This is the worst part before you'll feel better. You'll see."

Christine lay down gently next to her husband in bed. She didn't feel like talking – she wanted to lie next to him. She was blessed to have Daniel by her side. For that she was eternally grateful. She smiled as she closed her eyes pondering this, hoping and praying he would pull through.

It's a miracle I found such a wonderful man. I was on my own with twin toddlers, and he still married me and even adopted them – it was a miracle. Maybe, just maybe, a miracle could happen again. Daniel will get well, Christine prayed.

She longed to lie near her husband longer, but she had to make dinner. Daniel had begun to doze off, so she kissed him lightly on the forehead and left their bedroom.

Christine prepared a light dinner of baked salmon, reheated mashed potatoes from last night, and a green salad.

Then she led her kids to the kitchen. They gathered around the table in silence.

Christine took in a long breath. "It's about your biological father," Christine said slowly, shutting her eyes. Despite the extreme discomfort, she found her voice. The secret burden she carried inside her lightened as she began. The words practically rolled off her tongue now.

"I was in college at the time," she began. "I was dating Ryan Monti – yes, the actor," she said when she noticed their eyes widen. "He was just getting started in the acting business. As you know, Grandma and Grandpa raised me as a strict Catholic. We were very active in the church and I- I had no intention of going all the way with a boyfriend before marriage…"

"What?" Tim looked at his mother incredulously, as if he were seeing a new side of her for the first time.

Christine took a breath. "You have to understand, this is very hard to talk about…"

"Ryan Monti!" Trudy stared at her mother with her eyes sharp and wide. She whispered, "I saw him the other day."

Now Christine's eyes widened as she stared at her daughter. "Where?"

"At the Whitestone Creamery. I was working. A customer was giving me a hard time. He walked in with dark glasses, but he took them off when he stood up for me."

Christine's mouth opened, and she closed her eyes. Ryan hadn't told her about this.

"I'm sorry, Mom. Please, continue."

She took a few seconds, clearing her throat before resuming. "We went out for drinks and dancing," she continued, trying to steer herself to be strong and tell the kids what she dreaded them knowing all these years. "I guess we were a little drunk. When we went back into his car, we went all the way. It just happened."

When she opened her eyes, Christine noticed Tim shaking his head and commenting, "So that's why you've been such a prude all these years, Mom. You're not perfect either."

"No, Tim. Apparently, I'm not."

"So you can't expect the same from us."

"What do you mean? I don't want either of you to get into a difficult situation where you have to make life-changing choices! I want your lives to go ahead as you planned."

"What did Grandpa and Grandma say?" Trudy asked, putting her elbow on the table and her hand under her chin, intrigued.

"Grandma and Grandpa had a tough time dealing with it – living in a small town and being so active in the church! But I never regretted having you two, and your father marrying me with twins that were not his, biologically, at least, was like a miracle. The whole incident was such a shock... so unexpected, so surreal... I've never been comfortable with what happened, but I feel very lucky – we have been very lucky – that everything fell into place."

She continued, staring down at the table. "At the time I felt like I let everyone down and I was irresponsible. It took me a long time to come to terms with what happened. It's certainly not how I would want either of you to end up. Life was tenuous and uncertain for the first few years. I thought for sure we were going to have to live on welfare at a shelter. While I was expecting, I went to live with Aunt Ann in Boston, who didn't have room in her small apartment for the three of us. She wouldn't have been able to afford to feed all of us, and I had no means to send you two to a day care so I could work. Grandma and Grandpa also had to keep working. Neither one could have stayed home to watch you."

"And their church friends would have talked," Trudy interjected.

"Well, yes. It was an uncomfortable situation all around," Christine conceded.

"And did Ryan Monti know you had us?' Tim asked quietly.

"No," his mother said, shaking her head. "We both had already moved on, and I had doubts whether he'd make an acceptable father."

"Why not?" Trudy asked, looking at her mother with a pained expression. "Why didn't you tell him about us?"

"All I'll say is that there was a misunderstanding," Christine said.

"What kind of misunderstanding?" Trudy asked. "Mom, please. We have to know."

Tim sat there watching the exchange, comfortable with his sister doing all the talking.

Both her children's eyes bored into hers.

"I was in Los Angeles visiting him," Christine began. She took another breath and closed her eyes. "An actress was trying to be alone with him to seduce him. I thought he was being unfaithful, but I didn't realize she practically threw herself on him. I, umm, only found out the truth of what happened today."

"You mean, he came to see you?" Tim asked.

She opened her eyes. Both her children's faces were filled with the childlike wonder they used to show when they were little and thought she had all the answers. Indeed, she'd kept all this from them, and they needed her to reveal what had happened so many years ago – a major part of their lives that she had kept from them.

"Yes, he came to see me at the office today. He saw both of you earlier."

"One minute," Trudy said and ran up the stairs. Christine watched her, thinking her daughter would go into her bedroom to take time to process this revelation. But she came right down. Christine and Tim were still sitting in silence at the kitchen table.

Trudy's eyes were moist as she showed her mother and brother the photo of her and Ryan on her phone. Tim stared at the picture with a start. He faced his sister, waiting for an explanation, but none came. Christine could see from his shocked expression that the photo had further unnerved him. He sat paralyzed at the kitchen table with only his eyes moving in all directions. After a while, he put his hands on his head and stared down, trying to make sense of all this. Seeing his distress, Trudy reached out to him. He jerked his head as if he were coming out of a trance and asked her, "Did he tell you anything when you met him?"

"No, but he looked uncomfortable. He looked at me very intensely, almost like he was studying me, but he was careful not to come too close. When he helped me with that rude customer, I held out my hand to shake his, but I could tell he was pretending he didn't see it. It looked like he was actually afraid to touch me," she said quietly. "I couldn't understand why."

"I saw a man watching me behind the high school fence while I was playing basketball yesterday. He was tall and had on dark sunglasses. I had the feeling he was watching me. My friends thought so too." Tim reflected. "I thought he was watching me for a while, but then he went into his car and sped away. I didn't think anything more about it after that."

Christine and Trudy turned to him.

"He didn't try to talk to you?" Trudy asked.

Tim shook his head.

Christine witnessed their exchange.

"So what's going to happen, Mom? Are we going to meet him?" Tim asked. "Maybe he can help us."

"He doesn't seem to be the ogre I imagined. So that's why you've always been so protective. Because you went all the way. You didn't mean to have us," Trudy said as she and Tim stared at their mother.

"I didn't plan on getting pregnant, and I had to drop out of school, but you two have been the biggest blessings of my life," she said, smiling. "I do admit it was very challenging in the beginning. But everything worked out."

Christine forgot about putting dinner on the table and slid out of her chair, overwhelmed by all this news. "I'm going to rest."

"Mom, wait. Can you tell us more?" Trudy asked.

"How did he find us? Why now? Does he know Dad is sick?" Tim wanted to know.

Despite their pleas for more information, she shook her head and murmured, "Later," as she made her way up the stairs.

* * *

Christine didn't feel like eating and went to bed. She decided the twins could warm up the dinner themselves if they were hungry. She could not add anything more tonight. She had to preserve her strength for Daniel.

At four o'clock in the morning, Christine got up and walked to the bathroom mirror. She saw her face was pale, her hair was disheveled, and her eye makeup was smudged. Although always conscious of her posture, Christine was stooping, feeling too defeated to make the effort.

When she returned to bed, Daniel's eyes were open. He looked alarmed. He tried to get up but couldn't. He lay there in bed with his expression full of concern. "Christine, what's wrong? What happened?"

Christine approached the bed, lay down beside Daniel, and gently put her head on her husband's chest and sobbed.

"Shhh, don't cry, honey. I'm trying so hard to keep fighting. I have so much to live for." He laid his hands on her back and smoothed her hair. By now Christine's eyes were awash in tears. Her body shook, and strands of her hair became damp once it made contact with her face. She was wrapped in the fetal position and must have appeared like an adult baby to him.

"Shhh, it's all right. Everything's going to be all right," he tried to soothe her. "We're going to get through this. You'll see."

But a small voice in the back of Christine's head whispered that they were going to get through this, but he would no longer be with them. Her whole body shook, and she tried to ignore that voice. But Christine knew she had to tell Daniel the truth as well.

Finally, she lifted her tear-stained face and reached for tissues to wipe her face. "Daniel, we've got to talk. T- there are certain th- things I've never told you that we need to discuss."

He continued patting her. "Whatever it is, it can't be so bad to make you cry like that."

She blew her nose and tried to speak. "When I told you that the twins' natural father deserted me, it really wasn't the whole truth. I caught him cheating, but the woman was seducing him. He never even knew I was pregnant."

Daniel was studying her. "And?"

"He's Ryan Monti."

Daniel tried to lift his head. "Not the Hollywood actor?"

Christine nodded.

"Are you serious?"

Christine closed her teary eyes and nodded again.

She went on to relate to Daniel the whole story of dating Ryan while still in college, what she saw when she arrived at the movie set, and the pregnancy.

She slowly faced him and said, "You're probably angry with me for keeping this from you."

Daniel's expression remained unchanged. She wished she knew what he was thinking.

"You know, I had planned on staying a virgin until I got married, but I lost my virginity in his car after drinking and dancing in a club one night. It was very irresponsible of me. And I've kept Tim and Trudy from knowing who their father is all these years."

Daniel smiled supportively. "Christine, they had to find out at some point. It wouldn't have been fair to keep this from them. I'll do everything I can to comfort and support all three of you. I'll do everything I can."

"I've made a mess of all our lives!" she wailed. "I thought I was doing the best thing for them, but it was actually the best thing for myself! I never wanted them to know what a screw-up I am! How I'd been so naïve and foolish!"

Reluctantly, she met Daniel's gaze, and he said, "I figured it was something like that. You got carried away one night and didn't use protection. You never meant for it to happen. But it did, and you've been an excellent mother. And wife."

Resting her hands on his chest, she added, "You've been incredible. I couldn't have asked for a better husband... now, don't look away. It's true! All this time, you never asked me who the biological father was. Daniel, you've been totally selfless!"

Daniel stared at the floor as she marveled over his virtues. He sighed, and his shoulders drooped.

"What? What is it?" Christine asked, her smile fading, confused.

It took him a while to answer. He said, without facing her, "I made a decent enough living but never enough for us to live in comfort. We barely managed to save enough to buy this house."

"But you still respected the fact that I didn't want to discuss the twins' father," she insisted, cupping his face in her hands. "I continued my career, hoping to go up the ladder and help build a better life for our family. I was promoted once and got a salary increase, enough to start 508 plans for the twins' college."

He stroked her hair and said, "Yes, we've done the best we could under the circumstances. Now we've got to make sure they'll be able to go to college in the fall."

"And you regain your health," she added.

"We hope."

"I'm actually very proud of Tim and Trudy, especially Tim," Christine remarked. "How funny it is that the girl is usually the more mature one, but I see Tim as more practical and realistic. Oh well, but Trudy is coming around, realizing that her college plans will probably not go as she expected them to." She gave a humorless laugh and said, "Lord knows,

I hope their college plans go a whole lot better than mine did." She shook her head and said bitterly, "Mine just went up in smoke."

"But you did considerably well anyway." Daniel touched her cheek. "A college graduate would be proud to hold your position at the modeling agency."

She put her head on his chest, not noticing the look of consternation on Daniel's face.

Daniel tried to put his arm on her back to comfort her, but he was too weak to make the effort. Christine inched closer to him to make it easier for him to comfort her.

He moved her hair away from her face and stroked her cheek. He didn't say anything more. They stayed together like that for a long time.

CHAPTER THIRTY-FIVE

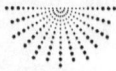

BOSTON

R yan had a long conversation with his agent. They agreed to a meeting the following week. By the time they finished, he did not call his parents because he knew his voice would betray his anguish, and he did not want to alarm them.

Ryan paced around the living room of his penthouse suite. His mind was in turmoil. His stomach was too tense to eat or even have a drink. He kept going over in his mind the encounter at Christine's office. Was he being fair to her, especially considering all that she was dealing with? Maybe he shouldn't have demanded a meeting with the children. But he was never given an opportunity to meet his children, and they were almost adults. There was so much time to make up. He feared Christine and her husband would feel threatened, like he was trying to take them out of their lives. Would the twins feel this was not the right time, given the father they had known all their lives was sick?

Ryan wished Christine would have let him know how

sick her husband was. She was determined to keep him out of their lives, as least for now. He knew he caught her completely by surprise, and she had even more to worry about now that he showed up in her life again. But once he found out about them, how was he supposed to ignore the fact that he was now a father?

Ryan's mind drifted to the question that had been bothering him since Christine brought it up. Who sent the letter? Did Christine's husband find out and decide the family needed the money?

No, Christine would never have married and stayed with a man who would be a greedy blackmailer. She had indeed changed, matured, since he'd known her, but she was the same woman he had fallen in love with all those years ago.

So who was it?

And what has Buddy Catalano found out?

Ryan was shaken out of his reverie by the ringing of the hotel phone.

"Good evening, Mr. Monti?" the receptionist said.

"Yes?"

"A Buddy Catalano is here to see you. Should I send him up?"

Ryan's head jerked up, speechless.

"Mr. Monti?"

"Y- yes. Yes, send him up. Thank you."

Why has Buddy come here all the way from Los Angeles? he thought. *What kind of news does he have to give me? My God! It must be serious if he traveled all the way here.*

He nearly jumped at the knocking of the door.

Ryan opened it and stared at the private investigator. Buddy was wearing a raincoat, a red wig, and dark glasses. When he took off the glasses and wig, Buddy looked like he had aged ten years. He had dark wrinkles under his red eyes, and it appeared he had stopped coloring his hair. It was almost all grey. He also looked like he had gained twenty pounds.

"What have you found out?" Ryan demanded. Ryan ignored Buddy's elaborate disguise, too focused on his fear that the blackmailer was now threatening his children.

"Mr. Monti, can I come in first?" Buddy whispered.

Ryan nodded and held the door wide open. As soon as Buddy came in, he shut it and asked, "Is there news from the blackmailer? Is he threatening my kids?"

Buddy glanced at the couch, ready to sit down, but Ryan couldn't wait to hear the latest developments.

"Mr. Monti, to sum it all up, I know who the blackmailer is – I hired him to do a job for me in Boston a few years ago. He knew as soon as you got that letter, you would come to me. So now he's blackmailing me, threatening that he'll tell you I concocted this whole plan if I don't give him half of your payments to me. This guy's a weasel. He's reckless and he can get information, which is why an investigator friend referred me to him for a job in the first place. But I've also come to see he becomes out of control, which is the reason he can't hang on to a job. He wants to make it big, so he goes too far, gets reckless. He wants to get ahead so badly he takes chances and ends up shooting himself in the foot."

Ryan found himself staggering. "Let's sit down."

Buddy appeared relieved and sat heavily on the couch. Ryan noticed he no longer had that easygoing spring in his step but trudged over to the couch like an old man.

When they both sat down, Ryan asked, "So who is this guy?"

"His name is Ozzy Dick." Buddy's mouth turned into a slight smile. "He lives up to the name. Ozzy lives here in Boston and has written for lots of different papers. He exaggerates on a story or does something illegal to get a story and loses jobs. But those newspaper jobs are drying up now, so he wants to get into private investigation. He's actually quite good at it. He's done jobs for people I know when they get desperate for information, but no one's willing to give him steady work because he's a loose cannon, unpredictable.

"Unfortunately, I needed his help on a job and used him. Ever since then, he has been hounding me to hire him or find him a job. I found out the hard way that Ozzy does that to everyone who uses him. I understand he's been out of work for some time and is getting desperate, but he needs to be stopped. Today, before I came here, I asked another investigator in Boston, a stable, reliable one, if he can find any dirt on this guy to get him off our backs."

Ryan listened. He studied Buddy and figured he must be telling him the truth. Why else would he fly all the way to Boston and expose his vulnerabilities? He was the premier private investigator to the stars in Los Angeles.

Buddy continued. "Ozzy doesn't want to use me anymore. He wants to take over and get the money all for himself. He told me he would tell you I worked with him to blackmail you if I tried to stop him."

Ryan studied the carpet as he spoke. Buddy looked bad, and he had to believe him – this Ozzy Dick character had put him in an untenable situation. If Buddy interfered, Ozzy would ruin him.

Ryan looked up and told him, "He's been following me."

"That's why I came here in disguise. He's probably outside this hotel now."

Ryan got up and strode to the terrace. He scanned the cars he saw parked in the street. He must have spotted dozens parked and riding along the street, but he was sure one of them belonged to Ozzy.

Ryan turned to Buddy. "Did you find out any more about Christine's family?"

Buddy nodded and said in a grave voice, "Her husband's

got leukemia. I understand he's got the worst kind, and it could go either way."

Startled, Ryan returned to the living room and stood behind the lounge chair he had been sitting on. "Then I guess I'll have to back off. Head to Los Angeles if the film isn't going to begin. They don't need me here putting more pressure on them. I'll give it a few months and wait and see what happens." He sagged in defeat. He dreaded the prospect of waiting even longer to meet his children, but what choice did he have? What would they think of him if he pushed himself into their lives while the father they had known all their lives was fighting for his life?

"And what about Ozzy and his threats?" Buddy asked.

"I'll do an interview with a highly respected publication, saying I just found out I was a father and ask for privacy at this time. I know it may backfire, but until you get something on Ozzy, and it would have to be real soon, what choice do I have?" He shrugged his shoulders.

"But I know it won't be enough for Ozzy," Buddy said. "Like I said, I've already called my contact in Boston three times to hopefully get some dirt on him. Dirt to scare him off. But so far, nothing criminal enough to land him in enough trouble that he'll go away."

Ryan breathed in. "So keep digging. If worse comes to worse, I'll have to pay him off. After the media finds out about the twins, they will likely respect my request not to have them photographed or put their names in print. That should be the end of Ozzy's threats."

But both men stared at each other, knowing that would not happen.

Buddy got up. "In the meantime, I'm going to keep digging." He walked over to the mirror and put his dark glasses and wig back on. "I won't stop until I find something. And it will be free of charge."

Fully convinced Buddy was telling the truth, he thanked him and shook his hand.

As soon as Buddy left, Ryan called his agent and then the director and producer of his upcoming film. He was returning to Los Angeles for a while. Once he hung up from those calls, he considered calling his parents and Megan to let them know he was coming home, but he was too demoralized to follow through. Ryan felt so useless in Boston – his children were better off if he was out of the way, and he wondered if they really needed or wanted him at all. At least his parents always welcomed him. His thoughts grew morbid – they were the only ones who really needed him. Once they were gone, he would be all alone in the world.

He pulled out his suitcase and proceeded to pack. Ryan would book a flight out tomorrow but see Christine in her office first to let her know his plans. He imagined she would be relieved to see him go. He assumed the twins would feel the same way. After all, they already had a father. A damned good one. He was another complication in their lives.

To cheer himself up, he contemplated taking Megan away for a romantic weekend. Unfortunately, this thought failed to lift his spirits, but this was all he had to look forward to in his personal life, so he might as well try to enjoy and make the best of it.

* * *

"Damn!" Ozzy said as he watched Buddy leave the hotel. *That guy looks awfully familiar. I know him. I recognize that gait! I've got to find out who he is!*

Ozzy got out of his car and walked over to him. When the man spotted Ozzy, he quickened his pace, but not before Ozzy caught up with him.

"Do I know you?" Ozzy said to the man's back.

Buddy just shook his head and kept walking.

"I bet you don't normally have red hair, my friend!" And with that he yanked off the wig and forced the man to turn around.

Ozzy was taken aback. He threw down the wig in the street and snarled, "Buddy, you warned him." He pushed Buddy against the hotel building.

"Hey, what are you doing?" A hotel guard ran in their direction.

"You left me no choice, Ozzy. He's accepted the kids, and there's nothing you can do about it," Buddy told him, speaking fast before the quickly approaching guard reached them.

By the time guard caught up with Ozzy and pulled him off of Buddy, Buddy told him, "It's over, Ozzy!"

"You'll have to leave the premises or I'm calling the police," the guard informed Ozzy as two more guards rushed over, one talking into his phone.

"Get off me, I'm going!" he told them. Then he turned to Buddy. "Now I'm going to bring both you and Monti down! You won't get away with this. I'll make sure you'll never be able to work again, and I'll be the next big private investigator to the stars. You wait and see."

"Give it up, Ozzy. You were never a good enough writer or investigator. You're only going to get in so much trouble, you'll never get out of it. Your overinflated ego is your downfall."

Ozzy opened his mouth to reply, but a young woman's voice called out, "Ozzy! Ozzy! What's going on?"

Everyone turned to the young woman hurrying over. She had on an oversized blond wig with the mane falling over her shoulders. Her lipstick was a bold red, too dark for her fair complexion. That, her dark blue eyeshadow, and hot pink blush made her resemble a clown.

"Zoe! What the hell are you doing here?" Ozzy barked at her. He clutched her arm and led her into the opposite direction.

"We had a dinner date, Ozzy. Don't you remember?" she whined.

"It was for tomorrow! Don't you remember? I told you I was working today," he fumed.

Zoe shook her head, her loose wig nearly falling off her head. "No, it was for today. I told you I had stuff to do tomorrow."

Buddy observed them walking away. The woman had skinny arms and legs. He wondered what she looked like underneath all that ridiculous-looking makeup.

He had a hunch. Assuring the guards he was all right, he took out his phone and punched in numbers.

* * *

Still clutching his girlfriend, Ozzy returned to his car with his shirt torn and the zipper ripped from his jacket. When he caught Zoe staring at his clothes, he said, "That man was dangerous. Those guards don't realize I was doing them a favor. I'll bet those security guys will be red-faced when they find out who I caught for them. But, honey, you can't interrupt my work. I don't want you to get hurt."

"I'm sorry, Ozzy. I keep forgetting you have important work to do." She looked up at him in admiration.

"Now tell me the truth. You know we made the date for tomorrow, not today."

Zoe turned away and reluctantly nodded. "I've got stuff to do tomorrow, Ozzy, and I couldn't wait another few days to see you. I wanted to be with you now."

"I can understand that, doll," Ozzy said while straightening his clothes to hide the rips. "But you've got to understand I have serious work to do. And this work will give us a better life."

Zoe's eyes lit up, and she said in a girlish high tone, "Do you mean that, Ozzy?"

He nodded in earnest.

"Do you think we can run away together soon?"

Ozzy rubbed the dirt off his pants. "Honey, I'm working toward that all the time."

Zoe reached for him and planted a long kiss on his mouth. "Oh, Ozzy! It makes me so happy to hear you say that! I can't wait to run away with you. I want to get out of this place. Please, please, make it soon!"

He smiled and touched her blond wig. "Don't you worry, I'm doing all I can to make that happen." He kissed her and even walked over to the passenger side to open the door for her. Zoe took delicate steps to hurry in. While he was walking over to the driver's side, his smile disappeared.

He would deal with Monti and Buddy later. He steamed, realizing this encounter dashed all hopes of impressing Buddy and his hopes he would find him a decent private investigating job. Ozzy couldn't wait to orchestrate the demise of the long-hailed "private investigator to the stars." But first he had to carry out his threats to Monti.

They drove to a fast food eatery. He gave Zoe a ten-dollar bill out of his tattered brown wallet and said, "You go get yourself something to eat, and I'm going to stay in the car and make a phone call. All right?"

"All right, Ozzy. Sounds good." She gave him a wide smile while lifting her shoulders in excitement. Zoe skipped into the restaurant to order her meal.

He grinned as he dialed Monti's cell phone number. He'd had to pay out the whole amount of money Buddy sent him last time to obtain the star's private cell phone number.

When Ryan answered, Ozzy said, "You've been spending

quite a few days in the Boston area. You got my second letter, I take it." It was a statement more than a question.

"Who is this?" Ryan demanded.

Ozzy continued. "Are you also scouting the town for a movie role? Or is your trip just for personal business? Such as seeing a son and daughter you hope to keep from the media? Tsk, tsk. If you are in the limelight, the public has a right to know you got kids. You can't pick and choose what you want people to know. You're public property, man! Secrets come out." He added in a low tone, "I hope you're not going to underestimate me. It will end up being to your detriment."

Ozzy heard a gasp on the other end of the phone.

When Ryan recovered, he sputtered, "Y- you've been spying on me? Who the hell are you?"

"Ah, so you're going to leave me the money?" To his delight, he heard Ryan gnashing his teeth. However, he was caught off guard when Ryan declared, "Your name's Ozzy Dick, isn't it?"

Ozzy gritted his teeth and swallowed the invectives he yearned to hurl.

Ryan continued, "Actually, I owe you a debt of gratitude. I am happy I found out about the children I never knew I had. I would never have known without your pathetic blackmail letter. I plan to fully acknowledge them, and you can go rot in hell with your threats."

This jolted Ozzy, who'd expected he would want to protect his children's privacy. It took him a moment to recover, and when he did he asked, "So you won't mind the all the glaring publicity they'll be exposed to? Followed and photographed wherever they go? Including their mother?"

"I am going to make sure they are never bothered. The rest is none of your business. You can disappear for all I care."

Ozzy knew he had to get back in control. He snarled, "I know you think this is none of my business, but I am a journalist, Mr. Monti. My work is to make this information my business. That blond woman is a knockout, by the way. I'd like to approach her and the kids." He chuckled. "It will be hard to keep my hands off the woman and her daughter. I've got a thing for blondes."

There was silence. Ozzy allowed Ryan to take in his threat.

Ozzy's mouth curled in glee. He was relishing this moment. His moment. "Now I need to decide exactly how to leak this information. I have contacts that would love to expose this information in ways you would not believe. They could plant all kinds of stories. I guarantee all of you will be humiliated – you, the mother, and the kids. They won't even want to look at themselves in the mirror by the time all these stories fill the press. In other words, how important is it to you to keep this private?"

Finally Ryan said, "You're bluffing. You don't know anyone. Who would be willing to help an inept journalist like you?"

Ozzy jumped in his seat at the insult, almost banging his head on the car roof. Clenching his teeth, he spoke in a low voice. "I saw you with your daughter in the Whitestone Creamery. Very pretty girl. Looks just like you. You knew her, but I don't think she knew you. I wonder what her reaction would be if she found out?" Ozzy grinned, his sharp, beady eyes revealing his evil intent. "She's a young girl. Girls that age are usually sensitive. Boys, too, can get easily rattled at this age."

"You would go so low to hurt kids just starting to make their way into the world? You're a fiend."

"I do what I have to do. That's my job," Ozzy said in a

more confident, detached voice. "Now we have to decide how we're going to proceed, huh?"

"You would be willing to devastate a young girl? You really think that's what's going to get you what you want in the end? I really don't think so. Mark my words, it's going to blow up in your face. And who are your contacts? What paper do you work for that's going to believe you and allow you to get all this media coverage? You can decide to be rational, and we'll end it right here... I won't report you to the police, and we'll all be better off."

Ozzy's smile vanished. His eyes lost their beady smugness. He didn't seem to know what to do with his hands, and his eyes shifted in different directions, struggling to find steady ground once again.

"Well, you'll find that out as soon as the news hits the media," he said, straightening his shoulders and sitting taller. Regaining his ground, Ozzy said, "I don't work for any one paper, but I have connections to many, including the *Boston Herald*." Ozzy paused to allow Ryan to digest those implications.

Ozzy could tell by the tone in Monti's voice that he was defeated when he asked in a flat tone, "So, you want me to leave the money at the Boston Public Library?"

"Ahh, I see we're finally getting somewhere." Ozzy relaxed in his seat. But he saw Zoe come out of the restaurant. He had to think fast. "I'll call you back with specific directions on the day and time. Be ready."

Ozzy hung up as Zoe entered the car. She was licking an ice cream cone. "Where to now, boyfriend?"

Ozzy touched her cheek. "Afraid I'm going to have to drive you home. Now wait," he said when he saw her pouting, "I promise in a few days, in only a few days, we'll spend more time together. This time in style."

His words failed to placate her. She made a sour face and ripped at the ice cream cone with her teeth.

"Zoe," Ozzy said, "believe me, I'm a man of my word."

Zoe gave in to a sideways glance before she consumed all the chocolate ice cream with sprinkles that was oozing out of her broken cone.

Zoe isn't the only one who will see I am a man of my word, he thought as he started his creaking car engine and pulled out of the restaurant parking lot.

CHAPTER THIRTY-SIX

BOSTON

Christine spotted a snag in her panty hose. It was on the back of her right leg. She was so demoralized she almost didn't bother changing. She felt like a heavy, intractable lump of mass and had to force herself to get ready for work.

She hadn't slept the whole night. She thought about Daniel looking so frail in bed, now burdened with a new worry. Before going to bed, Christine heard her children whisper her name from the hallway, but she ignored them, her mind and body too depleted to answer more questions or discuss Ryan any further. She even slept in her work clothes, which was a first. Organized, conscientious Christine did not bother with her nightly routine of flossing and brushing her teeth, removing her makeup, and cleaning her face with her four-step beauty routine, but instead collapsed into bed. In the morning, she felt no better but tiptoed around the house so she wouldn't wake anyone. She didn't have the emotional energy to face her children.

She wondered if their relationship would ever be the same again or if a cloud of doubt about her would forever hang above them.

It was a Saturday and she had volunteered to work today in case she had to take off during the week. No one would be there, but she wanted to get in early and finish as much work as she could. She dragged herself out of the house without even bothering to drink coffee – every action took such an arduous effort that she performed only the very minimum of activity. Her briefcase swung aimlessly by her side, and she slouched, abandoning her usual purposeful posture. Christine looked down the street and was relieved the gardener wasn't out. Her hair was disheveled, and she'd chosen her clothes without her usual care and attention; Christine had stuck her arm into the closet for a jacket, not even bothering to notice the color. Once seated in her car, she glanced at it for the first time – it was a casual beige jacket, not one she would wear for the office. Instead of going back inside and changing, she tore it off and threw it on the passenger seat. She didn't care if she was cold. She felt indifferent to everything. As Christine sat, she glanced at her clothes and was surprised she was wearing one of her newer suits; she was so oblivious when she dressed she could have put on a cocktail dress.

As she drove to work, she wondered for the first time if all this misfortune had descended on her because she was not a practicing Catholic. Was God only biding his time before all the ramifications of leaving the church fell upon her? Christine shook her head, dismissing that thought. She was a decent person, she did her best to raise her children, and she'd married a caring husband and father. She worked hard to help support her family. So she didn't reveal to the twins their biological father's identity. She did what she thought was best. And she did feel it was best for them not to know that he had cheated on her right before she found out she was pregnant. She was convinced he wouldn't have been a good role model and they were better off without him. But Christine did acknowledge she'd misjudged the compromising situation she witnessed all those years ago.

Another driver honked his horn because she was driving too slowly.

Time to stop thinking and concentrate on the road, she told herself.

When she arrived at work, Christine parked in the parking garage and put a comb through her hair. Looking in the rearview mirror, she saw yesterday's makeup still smeared on her face, but fortunately, she found a makeup remover towelette in her pocketbook. She wouldn't be wearing makeup but at least she would look more fresh-faced. Examining her navy-blue skirt, she remembered how flattering it looked on her when she had purchased it.

Well, at least I won't scare anyone with my appearance.

Telling herself that the chips would fall where they might regarding her children, Christine took a deep breath and made her way out of the car. She was going over yesterday's events in her head: encountering Ryan, meeting with him in her office, finding out the truth about his supposed dalliance with the actress, and her boss and assistant lingering in the background, waiting to find out the results of their "business meeting."

One thing she was relieved about: there was ample parking in the garage. Only a few people worked on a Saturday morning. Her head bowed, Christine tried to prep herself, determined to make it through the day. She opened the car door, feeling languid but putting her head up high.

"Christine! Christine!" a voice whispered.

She stopped and stood rigid, afraid to move or think.

"Christine! Christine! Over here!"

She turned around and saw Ryan Monti hiding behind a pole.

"I need to talk to you! Don't be afraid! It's urgent!"

When she spotted him, she saw the worry creases on his forehead and his pleading eyes that welled with tears. When they had dated eighteen years ago, she had never seen him look so upset. She had an ominous feeling in the pit of her stomach. They both looked around. No one was in sight, so he hurried over and clutched her arm.

"Can we talk privately in my car?" he asked her. "I know it's a Saturday, but someone else could be working in your office. I don't have a lot of time, and I'm guessing you don't either."

She would have protested, but seeing the desperation in his eyes, she nodded and then followed Ryan to his car and sat in the passenger seat.

"The twins know you're their father," she told him, and then bit her lip so she wouldn't cry.

His eyes grew large, and she saw a combination of joy and fear.

"What did they say?"

"It's not what they said, it's how they feel about me because I didn't tell them. I thought you cheated on me." She stared into his eyes. "I didn't want them to know their father cheated on me." She glanced down and shook her head. When she faced him again, her eyes were filled with tears.

He studied her. "I guess you told them everything. Everything that happened."

Christine nodded.

"Christine," he said gently, "they're almost adults now. They can handle the truth."

She looked away but said nothing.

"Unfortunately, a seedy journalist found out I'm their father, so we have to plan what to do."

Christine's jaw dropped. "What journalist? Is this the person who sent you the letter?"

Ryan closed his eyes and nodded wearily. "He's here in Boston."

"Oh no! Oh my God!" Christine sank down and clutched her hair. "What's going to happen now? They're not ready for that! I'm not ready for that!"

"I know," he said. "That's why we have to talk now."

"B- but you don't understand," she wailed quietly. "There's so much going on in our lives now. My husband is sick! He couldn't handle this now either!" She burst into tears, feeling herself sinking into this quagmire of doom once again. She fell back in her seat but soon felt herself enfolded in Ryan's arm.

He was trying to speak to her, but she was crying too loudly to hear him.

He shook her gently and said, "Christine! You've got to get ahold of yourself!" She stopped crying and listened.

"You survived the ordeal of leaving college to have the twins, and you'll survive this too. You try to be strong, but when you feel overwhelmed, you get into a helpless mode. You can't do that now. You've got to stay strong."

Christine was wiping away her tears when she looked up and saw Ryan's eyes shut tight and his mouth trying to form words.

He said, "And now we have the children to worry about." Upon saying this, he turned away, as if trying to grasp this implication himself.

"You're right. You're right," Christine said, sniffling. She took another deep breath in an effort to strengthen her resolve. She disengaged from him and said, "I bet my kids hate me now." She was too ashamed to look him in the eye.

"No, I'm sure they don't hate you. This is a lot for them to digest... especially now when the man they've always known as their father is sick."

"What will they think? How foolish and naïve we were."

"What do you think they're thinking?"

"They're thinking, 'Mom, you're so strict about dating and look what you did! Do you think we would do something as stupid as that?'"

"Yes, we were dead drunk, Christine, but we were kids. Very foolish, naïve kids."

Christine stared at him intently. "God, it was awful telling them how foolish and naïve I was." Christine stopped as a thought occurred to her. She turned to Ryan and said, "Are you trying to tell me I was your first one?"

Ryan was silent and stared down at her. He finally cleared his throat and said, "No, you weren't the first one, but I wanted to do things your way. I was willing to be patient to make you happy... you wouldn't have dated me if I had suggested we sleep together."

She looked at him, confused. "But why were you willing to go out with me if you knew I wouldn't go all the way?"

"Because I was in love with you."

Christine tossed her head back and studied him as if she were seeing him for the first time.

Ryan reached out to touch her but withdrew. He glanced at his watch.

"It's already 9:45. Why don't you wash up and get ready to go into the office? Just believe that everything will work out, and it will. You're strong, Christine. Stronger than you think."

Christine didn't move. She must have realized she was simply gawking open-mouthed at him and finally nodded.

She was about to open the passenger door but then turned to him, her eyes wide with fear.

"Y- you said a journalist knows about Tim and Trudy?

What are you going to do about that? Is there anything you can do?"

He checked his watch again and looked around. "I bet that bastard is spying on us right now. I'm going to do something. Don't worry. He's my problem."

"Don't worry? Is he blackmailing you? Threatening to tell the media? I don't want the twins to be forced to deal with that!" Christine had trouble breathing as that thought harassed her.

"I'm not going to let him. I have resources to keep him quiet, and I'm going to figure something out. Now don't you worry," he said. "I'll keep you abreast of all that's happening. You have my number, right?"

Christine forced herself to nod. She was already imagining worst-case scenarios.

"If I have to pay him off, I will."

"But for how long?"

"That's entirely for me to worry about." He patted her hand. "Try to go in and pretend the problem is solved. That's what I do when I'm uptight and need to face the public."

Christine closed her eyes and nodded. Touching his hand, she took a deep breath. Drying her eyes and peeking around, she hurried into the building.

* * *

Putting on dark sunglasses and a hat, Ryan searched around, convinced that garbage journalist was somewhere nearby.

After ten minutes of staring down every corner of the parking garage, he quit. What was the point? The journalist could be spying on him from far away with binoculars. If that guy knew, he most likely had told others. The secret was out. His head bowed, he returned to his own car. He was glad

Christine was at work and didn't witness his own feelings of helplessness.

Damage control. That's it! I'll hire someone to do damage control!

He stopped.

But why would I need damage control? I didn't even know they existed, he told himself as he shot his head up.

I have to think of something. If nothing else, I don't want Christine to be embarrassed if the press zeroes in on how she never told me. If her personal life is exposed, she'll never get over it. I can't let that happen to her or the twins. They'll suffer if she suffers.

At this point, Ryan couldn't help reflecting that this was the first time he cared so much for two people he hadn't even met. Not only did he care, but he was willing to risk everything to protect them.

"I guess this is what being a parent's like," he said out loud. *Parent,* he thought to himself as he got back into his car and stared in the rearview mirror.

This is what being a parent is.

* * *

Ryan was right about Ozzy: he was not far away, watching Ryan with a pair of binoculars.

He felt like patting himself on the back. *I'm a genius!* he marveled. *I knew he'd come back here at some point. I should've gone into this business years ago! I'd be a multimillionaire by now!*

Passersby stared at him with furrowed brows. He parked his car on the street near the modeling agency, which was across the Boston Common. He had discovered his car's muffler was broken this morning, but he didn't care. When he got his money, he'd buy a new car. The gardens and monuments were behind Ozzy. No one who passed by could understand why he had his binoculars trained on an office building's parking garage.

"Whoa, is this guy a Peeping Tom or something?" a young man in a jogging outfit asked his companion.

Ozzy put down his binoculars and watched the two young men smirk at him as they jogged by. He glanced behind him and caught two mothers with baby carriages whispering and pointing in his direction.

The hell with them, he thought. *They have no idea what I'm doing.*

On second thought, he decided to pack up and stroll through the park a little to distract the people who were coming in for an early morning walk or jog and were watching him. He hoped they'd forget about him. He even trained his binoculars on some of the statues dotted along the Freedom Trail.

But he was far too excited to do that for long. Five minutes later, he held up his binoculars toward the parking garage. And lowered them. Ryan Monti was nowhere in sight. He scratched his head. He hadn't seen a car pull out of the parking garage. Ozzy saw the woman walk toward the building and figured Ryan must be in there.

He contemplated entering the building but dismissed that idea.

No, what I'll do now is find out more information about the woman and her kids. She's still a pretty woman, sexy even. Even after all this comes out, I can make even more money in years to come by doing an exposé on her, he reasoned.

A smile crept across his small mouth in victory, as he figured he couldn't lose. Even if Ryan left him the money, he'd be rich and he could keep blackmailing him for years. If he didn't, he'd get rich informing all the media sources he knew about Monti's secret.

It's a win-win situation, he told himself. He then surveyed the Commons, the shops, the restaurants.

Ozzy, it's time you start living! I'm looking forward to buying a nice place with Zoe, he thought with a smile of tremendous satisfaction.

CHAPTER THIRTY-SEVEN

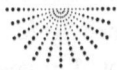

Boston

R yan was beside himself. He could think of nothing else to do but go back to his penthouse and think. He wished he could quell his rapidly beating heart. His head was swirling with worries and fears. *What if the money doesn't come in time? What if the machines go down at the bank?*

He had never felt this uptight, not even when preparing for a movie that was considered a box office risk. He tried pushing aside a creeping thought that he didn't know if it was a real or imaginary premonition: that evil little man was watching him everywhere he went. He paced around the parking garage, but no ideas came to him. Upon returning to his car, he drove down the street, but after a few miles, he parked his car on the side lot of a gas station. His cell rang. Ryan sped to answer it in hopes it was Buddy or someone who would give him a solution.

"Ryan?" a voice asked tentatively.

"Megan?" he asked. "Is that you?"

IDELLE KURSMAN

"Yes, we haven't spoken for ages, Ryan. How are you?" she asked with forced enthusiasm.

"I'm fine," he lied. "But right now I'm real busy. Can I call you back? Is everything all right?"

"Yes, yes, I'm fine. I didn't want to bother you in Boston, but I couldn't help thinking about you. I've been thinking about us and wondering where we stand."

Ryan stopped and rubbed his forehead.

Where we stand? he wanted to say out loud. *Where we stand! You're only a few years older than my daughter, for chrissakes!*

"Err, it's just been very hectic in Boston. I've been meaning to call you."

"It must be real important and a heavy movie role."

I wish! he thought. Searching for the right words to say, he finally managed to blurt out, "Listen, I've gotta go. I'll call you tonight. I promise."

And my parents too.

"Oh, of course. I hope all goes well."

Ryan closed his eyes and said, "Me too. Thank you," as if he had received a blessing he sorely needed.

She paused. "I saw your mother the other day. She's really worried about you. She's been leaving you messages."

"I'll get back to her too!" he promised.

"Oh, before we hang up, I want to thank you. Your friend Julio is going to interview me for the *Insurance Journal*. Hopefully, this will be a step up for me – my bosses are impressed!"

Ryan, who had tousled his hair in impatience to get off the phone, stopped. *Julio!* His friend from the old neighborhood where he grew up. He kept moving up in the publishing world. Would he be able to give him some advice about Ozzy?

"Ryan? Ryan? Hello? Are you still there?" Megan asked.

Ryan managed to return his focus to Megan. "Yes, I'm

fine. In fact, I think you just gave me an idea on how to solve a problem!"

"Oh, good, I'm glad. What's the problem?"

"Oh, I think a slimy reporter is trying to follow me in Boston. I think I'm going to call Julio and ask him for some advice." Ryan hoped his explanation was somewhat credible.

Apparently it was because Megan asked, "What? Do you think this reporter is a stalker? Is it a man or woman?"

"It's a man."

"Do you think he's dangerous? Does he just want a story, or do you think he's going to threaten you?"

Ryan couldn't believe how on target Megan was, but he just answered, "Oh, he's just a crazy guy desperately trying to get an interview, but I don't have time for interviews now. Nothing to worry about."

"Still, be careful, Ryan. Let me know when you get back to Los Angeles. How's the filming going?"

"Great," he answered, not feeling like going into specifics of filming being delayed. In truth, Ryan didn't feel the need to confide in Megan about anything. "I'll give you a call as soon as I get back."

There was silence on the phone. Finally, Megan said, "Aren't you going to wish me luck on the interview today?"

"Oh, I'm sorry! Good luck! I know you'll impress everyone in the industry."

More silence. Megan then said, "Thanks," in a low voice and hung up.

Ryan sat still in his car. There was too much going on for him to dwell on his relationship with Megan. So he picked up his phone again. He had heard about actors complaining about their children being photographed. Some threatened to sue. Ryan had never paid much attention to these discussions, but now he wondered if any of them had made any headway. Could a law have been passed that he never bothered reading about? Julio would probably know.

Ryan had no real relationships with other journalists or anyone else in the media. He considered them a nuisance and always tried to avoid them by wearing a hat, sunglasses, and nondescript clothing in public. When it came time to promote a movie, he left it to his agent Phil to seek them out for interviews.

Ryan looked up Julio's number, hoping he would reach him. Would he get lucky and be able to speak to his old friend now?

"Hi, Ryan. I'm interviewing your lady love today," Julio answered.

"Thanks, I appreciate it. How did you recognize my number?" Ryan sat up and grinned in relief.

Julio chuckled. "Megan gave me your cell phone number at least a hundred times to prove to me she was your girlfriend. She's persistent. I can see her moving up in the business world. Did she ask you to call me to verify she was your girlfriend?"

"No, Julio. I figured it would work out. I have a quick question for you if you have a moment."

"Of course! I always have time for my old friend, just like I did when we were in the tough old neighborhood."

"We helped each other all the time in those days," Ryan reflected. "I still remember all those gangs roaming around the streets."

"Oh boy, I remember! We both have strong mamas who warned us to stay away from them and the drugs. It was a good thing we were smart enough to listen to them."

"That's for sure, or we wouldn't be where we are today. Maybe not even alive... Julio, this is a stretch, I know, but since you're in the journalism world, would you happen to know anything about the media not being allowed to photograph celebrities' kids?"

"Not being allowed to photograph celebrities' kids? What happened, Ryan? Did you come across kids you never knew you had?"

Ryan's mouth went dry. He couldn't even answer.

"Hey, man. I'm just teasing you. Why would you need to know about something like this? Is it for a friend?"

"Sort of," was all he managed to say.

"Well, some actors and actresses – the moms, mostly – complain they don't want their kids followed by the paparazzi, saying it frightens the children and they need their privacy, stuff like that. But to my knowledge, there are no laws enforced. It depends on the journalist. Some will respect the children's privacy and back off. Others are so hungry for a story that they won't care what the parents say or threaten to do."

Ryan felt his heart drop. "S- so those parents, they can complain and threaten, but nothing ever comes of it."

"Nah, not that I know of. Those kinds of celebrities make it their business to live in some remote place so the chances of the paparazzi descending on them is greatly reduced. But if they live in places like Los Angeles or New York, hey, they're considered fair game and have to put up with it or move."

Ryan's mind was swirling. *Should I move out of California? Would that give me enough time. No, Ozzy has me marked. There is no escape.*

"Hey, Ryan?

Ryan forced himself to concentrate on the call. "Yeah?"

"If and when you decide to have kids, let me be one of the first to know. Not to hound you, of course, but to congratulate you. We go back a long way, man."

Ryan nodded his head. "Sure thing, Julio."

"You were one of the first to know when I had my first kid. I think I called you from the hospital."

"I remember. You let me know right after you told all your relatives. I'll keep that in mind, buddy. Stay good."

After he hung up, he stared at the phone, wondering if his old friend was a mind reader. He sank back in his seat in defeat. There were no laws to protect his kids. That bastard could do whatever he wanted. Ryan was powerless to stop him. He'd foiled his old girlfriend Kim's attempts to black-mail him, but he would have to capitulate to Ozzy. This was about his kids. And he would have to keep paying up because he knew blackmailers were just like anyone else: they were never content. They always wanted more. Ryan sighed and picked up the phone to make sure the two million dollars was in the process of being wired to him. He had no choice but to give in.

The phone fell from Ryan's hand. Sweat expanded from the back of his head to his forehead. He felt helpless. Protecting his children had become his top priority, and he had to placate this man rather than insult him. He sat in a daze of confusion, having no idea what he else he could do. He had forgotten about packing his suitcase. Instead, he thought about all the roles he'd played, even the bad guys. What would one of them do if they had a similar situation? After going over them in his mind for ten minutes, he was still stumped. Glancing around, Ryan saw the gas station employees staring at him. He knew he had to pull out.

Just then, the phone rang.

He scoured the car before finding it. When he retrieved it, all he heard was Ozzy restating his demand "to leave a white sack filled with two million dollars cash on the third floor of the Boston Public Library, in the Sargent Gallery, behind the third light fixture but also stipulating it be done by ten tomorrow" and then hanging up.

The loud click shook him. He was about to call his banker to confirm the money was being processed when his phone rang again. He heaved a sigh and dreaded taking it, fearing this nightmare would never end. Ryan turned and answered the call, his other hand over his face and his eyes closed. "Hello?"

He sat up upon hearing the excitement in Buddy's voice.

"Mr. Monti, I think your problem is solved," Buddy announced.

"What do you mean? How did you do it so fast?"

"I didn't do it exactly – Ozzy did. It was what I saw, and my contact was able to find the dirt real fast. Mr. Blackmailer is about to get blackmailed himself in a major way," Buddy said, chuckling. "And he still might end up in prison."

He told him all the details. Ryan was delighted. His salvation came so fast. However, when he hung up and sat pondering over the whole situation, an uneasy feeling crept over him. How could a young girl do that to herself?

He wondered if he could help.

Ryan had made donations to different charities over the years, more to get tax breaks than to actually think about helping those in need. He had concluded long ago that if he could lift himself up from modest circumstances, anyone could. But now for the first time, he wasn't so sure.

Should he care enough to do something?

Ryan wavered until the image of Trudy came into his mind. Who knew if she would do the same thing in a similar situation if she were desperate enough?

Propelled by thoughts of his daughter feeling she had no hope, Ryan called Buddy back to learn where he could find this young woman.

CHAPTER THIRTY-EIGHT

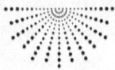

B uddy reached his contact, who told him where she hung out.

Ryan drove forty miles to Main South in Worcester. He passed Clark University and Tower Hill Botanic Garden, but his mind was filled with too much trepidation to notice the landmarks.

The morning was clear and crisp. He would much rather have strolled around Boston on a day like this. He continued to wonder if he was doing the right thing, questioning whether he should involve himself or not. Each time he thought of turning around, Ryan was reluctant to put on his turn signal. She wasn't his daughter. She was a perfect stranger, but he felt compelled to help her because he knew Ozzy was no good for her. Ryan had known women in different points of his life that had experienced heartbreak. It was inevitable that most people went through relationship woes at some point, but an inexperienced young woman who got involved with someone like Ozzy could suffer lasting damage.

He found her where the contact said she spent her time: a bench outside the Worcester Art Museum. The first thing he noticed was that her blond wig was knotty and hair was sticking out in all directions from the back of her head. She gazed downward as she twirled one of her feet. She wore dirty sneakers, a faded flowered top, and too-tight green pants.

As much as he wanted to, Ryan couldn't turn back now. He marveled over how suddenly becoming a father had given him a new perspective. Before, his parents were the only ones whose welfare occupied him. He always made sure they had everything they needed. Now, though, Ryan had double the number of people to worry about, but he couldn't understand why his shoulders already felt heavier with the responsibility, even extending to a young girl he had never even met.

With his sunglasses on and wearing jeans and a light coat, he slowed as he neared her bench. "Hey," he said.

She looked up, her hands over her eyes, shielding her squinting eyes from the sun. When she saw him, she put on a smile, got up, and swaggered over to him, trying to shake her hips suggestively. Her attempt to appear sexy saddened him more than anything.

"What do you need?" she asked him.

"What are you doing?" he couldn't help blurting out.

She stopped short, her mouth hanging open.

"Have a seat. I'd like to talk with you for a minute. Your name is Zoe, right?"

"How'd you know?" she asked, putting a hand on her hip.

"Just have a seat. I want to warn you about someone. That's all."

Zoe huffed and sat with her arms folded.

Ryan sat on the other side of the bench, as far away from her as he could.

"I want to warn you about Ozzy Dick," he said in a gentle tone.

Zoe looked aghast, her eyes bulging. "Now how do you know he's my boyfriend? Why do you know so much about me?"

"I want to warn you about him." Ryan turned away from her and continued, "I know Ozzy. He's a very bad man. No one should be hanging around with him. Especially a four-teen-year-old girl like you."

She stared at him for a long time with her eyes narrowed. Finally, she said, "What do you know? He's nice to me. He buys me things."

He faced her. "He wants to hurt my family. He's fifty-two. My daughter is only a few years older than you. He's using you, and he might be going to jail."

"What? I don't believe you! I should just walk away! He's the only person in the world who cares about me."

"You mean you have no family?"

"My parents both work two jobs," she pouted.

"They're never home for you?"

"Only late at night when they get home. Sometimes on the weekends when they don't have to work."

"Do you have enough to eat?"

"Of course!"

"Why do they work so much?"

"Oh, something about having to pay the mortgage and for my college," she said, rolling her eyes. "But I don't care about going to college."

"So what do you want to do?"

"Nothing. Ozzy said he's going to take care of me," Zoe said with a stuck-up grin.

"Ozzy's a liar. He can't even take care of himself. He loses jobs because he lies, and he once got arrested fifteen years ago for beating a woman up. Did you know that?"

Zoe put her hand on her head, dismayed. "God, I don't believe you. How do you know this? How do I know you're telling me the truth?"

"Go to his town hall. It's public record. He punched his boss in the face because she fired him. He broke her nose. You want to be with a man like that? Old enough to be your father? He's preying on you because he can't find a woman his age who will go out with him."

Her face a mask of shame, Zoe got up to leave.

"Wait, Zoe," he said, reaching out.

She had her back to him. "What else do you want to tell me to hurt me?"

"I'm not trying to hurt you – I'm trying to help you. Look at me, please, Zoe."

She turned around and eyed him.

"Your parents are working hard so they can give you a good future, but you've also got to be smart for yourself. Does your school have a counselor?"

Zoe shrugged her shoulders.

"Do you go to school?"

"Sometimes," she conceded.

Ryan said, "I'm going to do something for you, Zoe."

"Why?"

"Because Ozzy hurt me, my family, and you. I want to help you have hope for the future."

"Who are you?"

Ryan shook his head. "It doesn't matter. I know your name is Zoe Sawyer."

Zoe stiffened.

"Now don't worry. You probably will never see me again," he said while thinking, *unless you start going to the movies.* He continued, "My attorney contacted your parents to set up some money for your college. It may not seem like a lot of money, but it's going to stay in an account and build up interest, enough for your first year of college. Your parents agreed to quit one of their jobs, so they will work at their full-time jobs and give up their part-time positions. They were so happy to hear that. And they'll have more time for you."

Zoe's forehead wrinkled in disbelief.

He got up. "Just ask your parents," he said, looking at his watch. "Then you need to go to school. You can't get into college if you don't go to your classes."

Zoe was speechless.

"I have to leave now," he said. "But you're young, you've got your whole life ahead of you. Don't throw it away on someone like Ozzy. Take care of yourself."

Zoe found her voice. "B- but…"

Ryan raised his hand and walked back to his car. He wanted to see Christine before his plane flight, to reassure her that he would keep his distance until her husband was well and they were all ready to meet.

CHAPTER THIRTY-NINE

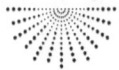

Boston

Ozzy made his way into the Boston Public Library. As he entered Sargent Hall, he considered making a sizeable donation to the library. *Would they then put a plaque in the library in my honor?* he mused. A possibility. He would soon be rich enough to be a big shot, he reasoned. Ozzy held his head high – he would now have to adopt the demeanor of someone respected. Of course, Zoe would also have to dress for the part. He calculated that in a few years he would be a multimillionaire from continuing to blackmail Monti together with all his journalism and private investigator jobs – people in those industries would be seeking him out. Ozzy touched his nearly bald head. *A hair transplant?* He grinned to himself. *Another good possibility.*

But upon reaching the third light fixture in Sargent Hall, he studied the back and saw no sack. Nothing. His mouth formed an O shape.

"Damn!" he heard himself mutter out loud. Nearby,

people glanced over at him with narrowed eyes. They soon resumed their activities, ignoring him.

What is this? Is he playing games with me? He gritted his teeth.

Ozzy looked again, hoping he just hadn't spotted it. But there was nothing there. He stuck out his forefinger and began counting the fixtures, making sure he had the right one.

He did.

"Ah, looking for something, Ozzy?" Buddy approached him. Ozzy did not even notice him walking over. No longer wearing a disguise, Buddy appeared more relaxed; his hair was smoothly combed, and he was wearing a brown suit.

Ozzy's lower jaw jutted out, exposing his uneven yellow teeth. "I think you know what I'm looking for. You and your client are finished, Buddy! And you!" He stuck his forefinger into Buddy's chest. "You are ruined for good. Say good-bye to your big investigation business!"

"Oh, I don't think so, Ozzy," Buddy replied, ignoring Ozzy's outstretched finger and maintaining a calm demeanor. He smiled and then grew serious. "It's you who's finished. Now you can crawl back into your hole, and if Monti or I ever hear from you again, you'll go to jail for dating an underage girl."

"Wh- what are you talking about? Underage girl, my ass!" he shrieked. He put his hand to his mouth when more people began staring at him. He saw a woman at a desk picking up a phone. Ozzy stared around, forgetting all about his name engraved on a plaque on the wall. His shoulders slumped, and he shot a menacing stare at Buddy.

"My girlfriend is not underage," he spat out. He was loud enough that his voice echoed.

Unruffled, Buddy put his hands in his pockets. "Then I think you'd better ask her. I'd say you must be blind if you haven't noticed that," he said, shaking his head and wagging his finger. "Ozzy, you're not observant or competent enough to be a private investigator." His expression grew hard. "So if we hear another word from you, you're headed for the slammer." He raised his hand. "Bye-bye for good!"

Two guards came and stood on either side of Ozzy and said, "Sir, you're causing a disturbance in the library. We're here to escort you out."

Ozzy struggled to free himself. "I don't need any help. I'm leaving!" He turned to Buddy. "And I'm going to find out the truth! Don't rest yet."

The guards watched as Ozzy stormed out, slamming the doors. Buddy shook his head and shrugged at the guards. "A real piece of work," he told them.

"We see these all the time," one guard said after Ozzy left.

"Not like this one," Buddy replied. "He's a real beaut!"

CHAPTER FORTY

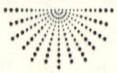

BOSTON

It was hard, but Christine began to get into the rhythm of concentrating on work. She was reviewing a new batch of model portfolios. Fortunately, young men and women continued sending their applications, and the Marie Cooper Modeling Agency was always busy. On Monday, Christine would be discussing them with her colleagues and then choosing a small percentage of the applications to arrange for interviews. Christine wished Linda were here. She appreciated their light conversations about family. Christine could use the distraction of hearing about other people's lives.

Then her mobile phone buzzed.

"Mom, I'm outside the building. Let me in!" Tim yelled in a panic when she answered.

"W- what's going on?" Christine jerked her head up, alarmed.

"Dad was taken to the hospital. Let me in!"

She put the phone down and raced to the entrance.

"Grandma, Grandpa, and Trudy were at the house. I went

to the city to meet a few friends for lunch and got the call. Was your phone turned off? Trudy couldn't get you. She went into the ambulance with Dad, and I drove over here to get you."

Before Christine could speak, they heard another knock at the door.

It was Ryan.

"Christine, I've got great news for you! The problem's solved—" Ryan stopped short when he spotted Tim.

* * *

Jolted, Tim stepped back and paled, looking scared, his hand still on the door handle as if he wanted to run away. Tim was glancing in all directions, but he finally settled his gaze on Ryan. Father's and son's eyes locked; neither of them knew what to say or how to react. Ryan's eyes grew moist, and he thought he saw his son's eyes also well up. Ryan stared at the living, breathing replica of himself when he was a kid. There was so much he wanted to say to Tim, so much he wanted to ask. But unfortunately, all that had to be put on hold.

His determination to help and protect his children and their mother was only fortified upon seeing his young son. Even though his son and daughter were still strangers, he knew he would pay any amount of money, even lay down his life, to protect them from any danger or harm.

Seeing they were both in a panic, he forced himself to tear his gaze away and ask Christine, "What's happening now?"

He had trouble hearing her, for she spoke in a weak, low tone. "Daniel had to be taken to the hospital."

The other news would have to wait.

"Drive your mother to the hospital," Ryan told Tim. He turned to Christine. "That other problem was straightened out. You have nothing more to worry about on that end. Just concentrate on your husband."

Christine didn't have the strength to respond. Her eyes were hollow and her face deathly white as she leaned on Tim for support. She appeared so fragile, as if she would shatter into pieces at the slightest pressure.

Ryan yearned to reach out to his son, to touch him to see if he was real or just an imaginary carbon copy of himself in his youth. He noticed with satisfaction how Tim took care of his mother; it was always his top priority to take care of his parents. He frowned as he realized for the first time that he hadn't spoken to them or answered their phone messages in a number of days – rarely had a day gone by that he hadn't spoken to at least one of them.

Christine stared ahead, allowing herself to be led by her son. Ryan was relieved no one else was present to notice them or ask questions. As they exited the building, he stayed at a distance behind Christine and Tim. Rain fell in the air, drenching everything in sight. Numerous umbrellas protected pedestrians walking along the sidewalk. Drivers weren't speeding and angling to get ahead of other cars but proceeding carefully in the deluge. Ryan headed for the parking garage once he saw Tim and his mother enter the car that was parked right beside the building door. As they were preparing to head out, what he saw directly in front of him stopped him dead in his tracks. He felt a fresh swell of anger rush up inside of him.

Standing before him in a worn raincoat and carrying an umbrella was Ozzy. He looked so enraged that steam could have been coming from his ears. He snarled, "Don't think for a minute this is over! I have my resources. I'm going to bring you down, Monti! You'll live to regret what you've done!"

Christine and Tim hesitated as they were getting in the

car. "Go on! Go on," he told them, waving for them to leave. "I can handle this."

"Are you sure?" Christine asked, her face a tight mask.

Ryan turned to her. "Oh yeah, I'm very sure. Go."

After watching Christine and Tim drive away, Ryan faced Ozzy. His eyes narrowed as he approached the man, whose hair was sticking out on all sides of his head. Ryan was glad it was raining – less visibility made it unlikely anyone would recognize him.

He headed to Ozzy and punched him in the mouth. Ozzy went flying backward into a puddle.

He caught a glimpse of Ozzy lifting his face with a bloodied mouth but didn't stay to listen to ramifications and threats Ozzy hurled. As he walked away, Ozzy's words were drowned out by the drenching rain.

Ryan got into his car and checked his watch. He had to pack and be at the airport in an hour. Now that Ozzy was neutralized, he had to give Christine and her family their space and return to his life in Los Angeles. But he knew they would be in the forefront of his thoughts.

CHAPTER FORTY-ONE

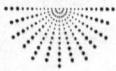

BOSTON

W hen Christine and Tim entered the hospital waiting room, Trudy was checking her watch and then the hall clock. Heather was sitting beside her, and Seth was comforting his parents. Harry had one arm around his wife while gazing downward, lost in his own thoughts.

Trudy was ready to fall apart crying when she saw her mother and brother.

"How's Dad?" Christine ran over to Trudy.

"We don't know yet. We're all waiting for the doctor to come out."

Trudy hugged her mother, allowing her tears to flow down at last.

Daniel's doctor appeared almost right away. The whole family quickly stood and gathered around him, waiting to hear every nuance of what he was about to utter.

"We're doing all we can," Dr. Sherman told them with a grim expression. "But he's weakening steadily. He's been fighting a brave battle considering he has the worst form of leukemia."

Daniel's mother let out a cry and covered her face with her hands. Daniel's father tried to comfort her, but his face crumbled as he took in the news.

Dr. Sherman turned to Christine. "He would like to see you alone."

Christine nodded and followed the doctor, trying hard not to cry, struggling to put on a brave face.

Fear gripped Christine as she entered her husband's hospital room. The strong antiseptic smell and the humming monitor raised her anxiety level even further. A glimpse of Daniel let her know that all the rallying and positive thinking that they were going to beat this would not be enough to overcome this terrible disease; his thin, frail body, the loss of most of his hair seemingly overnight, and his worn, haggard face made Daniel appear more dead than alive.

Christine couldn't control her shaking legs. She forced one leg to move in front of the other as she found herself walking into this waking nightmare. She wanted to cry out, *How could God do this? Whatever did he do to deserve this?* The man who was responsible for turning her life around and providing her and her children with a happy stable family was dying.

He is such a good man. Why, God, why?

Y is a crooked letter, she recalled her mother telling her as a child whenever she complained about how unfair life was.

She shook her head to dispel these thoughts – this was not the time to speculate about these unanswerable questions. Now she could only offer her husband comfort.

Sitting gently on the edge of his bed, she tried to smile while gently squeezing his frail, bony hand. "Hey."

It took a moment for Daniel's eyes to meet hers.

With great effort, his lips moved, struggling to get the words out.

"The money," he whispered. "The money for the kids… for the kids' coll…" He couldn't manage the last word.

"Shhh, don't, Daniel. Don't worry about that. You're the one who matters now," Christine whispered. She found it difficult to speak and not break down and cry. "The kids are in the waiting area, worrying about you. We all need you, Daniel." Despite her efforts, the tears threatened to stream down like clouds on an overcast day.

"I fought and I tried," Daniel said, shaking and coughing.

"Just rest, Daniel. Don't try to talk. You need your strength."

After he stopped coughing, he faced her and shook his head. "There's something I need to tell you, Christine. There's something you need to know."

She massaged his hand as gently as she would a baby's. "It can wait."

"No!" He tried to lift his head up, then sank back down on the pillow, his strength spent. He breathed heavily and clung to her hand. When he regained some energy, he gestured for her to come closer.

Christine put her head near his lips. He spoke in a tone so low she barely heard him. "I need to tell you…"

"Tell me what?" Christine faced him, her brow wrinkled. As much as she wanted him to preserve his strength, she had to know what was so urgent.

"T- Tim and Trudy," he said. "They're my children. T- thank you for l- letting me be their father."

She melted upon hearing her husband's words. "Of course you're their father. And I think you've done a damn good job." Tears resumed flowing down Christine's cheeks. "I love you, Daniel. Please don't leave us."

Daniel's smile disappeared, and he said, "How I don't

want to leave you! I want to live so badly and have the four of us stay together forever." His eyes turned down in sadness as he said, "There is one other thing I need you to know, Christine."

"What is it, honey?" Christine reached for some tissues to dry her eyes as she waited for her husband to speak, wanting to see him clearly when he spoke again.

After what seemed like hours but was in reality only minutes, Daniel faced her while giving her hand a slight squeeze.

Daniel said nothing for a few moments. When he finally spoke, he looked down, avoiding her face. "I already knew Ryan Monti was the father—"

Christine started to speak, but he stopped her with a slight gesture of his hand.

"Hear me out." He faced her. "I knew because when we were engaged, I came to your apartment one day. You had left the door open for me, and your parents were there. They were so engrossed in their conversation that they didn't hear me come in." He paused. "I overheard your father saying he would like to break every bone in Ryan Monti's body for getting you pregnant. They considered him scum and never wanted him anywhere near you again. When they turned their heads and saw me in the doorway, they froze. They begged me not to tell you I knew. Your relationship with them was strained at the time, and they were afraid you would never have anything to do with them if you knew they told me who the father was. They hated him and feared you and the twins would be dragged into the media and all your lives would be ruined." Daniel shook his head at the memory. "They thought of him as the devil! I guess it made me, a Jewish guy, look not so bad in comparison."

When he finished, Christine sat there, stunned.

She slowly said, "You're probably angry with me for keeping this from you."

"Actually, I was flattered that I was considered a better catch than a famous Hollywood actor." Daniel chuckled as he reached for her, and she lay on his chest. "I know how conscientious you are, Christine. You have principles, and you felt horrible for letting your parents down, for letting yourself down. I wasn't going to hold that against you. Besides, I'm proud and thrilled to be the twins' father."

Christine felt warm and heartened inside. Tears filling her eyes, she faced her husband and kissed his hand, saying, "Daniel, you're a man among men. You're worth more than all the gold in the world. The day I met you was the luckiest day of my life." She didn't care that the tears were flowing. Seeing the light in Daniel's eyes, Christine put her face gently next to his. She wanted to feel her husband's body for as long as she could.

CHAPTER FORTY-TWO

BOSTON

A nurse entered and gave Daniel methadone to ease the oncoming pain and induce him to sleep. Christine sat frozen at his bedside; she felt she should return to the waiting room and ask the rest of the family to come in, but she couldn't tear herself away.

Watching her husband sleeping as peacefully as an infant, Christine was shocked by the revelation that he knew the twins' paternity and never confronted her, honoring her wish not to discuss it.

Christine began reflecting on her own failings – wasting her parents' money on an unfinished college degree and then disappointing them by getting pregnant when she was not married. She covered her face with her hands in shame. Just when her gloomy thoughts were descending and threatening to overtake her, Christine thought about her job at the modeling agency.

I wasn't a total screwup. She thanked God, a guardian angel, fate, or whoever came to her rescue by reminding her that she wasn't a total failure. Then the image of her children came to mind, and she felt an overwhelming feeling of peace.

The job is great, but they're my crowning achievement.

Her eyes traveled back to her husband, most of his hair fallen out and not an ounce of fat left on his wasted body.

Christine didn't have the strength to think about the future but knew she would have to carry on somehow.

There was a soft rapping on the door. Dr. Sherman poked his head in.

"How are you, Mrs. Goldberg?" he asked in a low voice as he studied her intently.

Christine stared at her hands and then clutched her shoulders as if she felt chilled. "I- it doesn't look so good now, does it, Doctor?"

Dr. Sherman looked down. After a moment, he glanced her way and said, "What we want to do now is keep him as comfortable as possible."

Christine's face collapsed in tears. She knew this was the doctor's way of saying the end was near.

"Isn't there anything more you can do to save him?" Christine said as she broke down.

"I think now would be the time to bring in your children and the rest of the family," the doctor told her, pain etched on his face. He looked at Daniel and said, "Your husband is a good man. My brother worked in an office with him at Smith Marketing for twenty years. He told me he did many favors for my brother that helped him with his skills and his career. He would've given the shirt off his back to help someone." Dr. Sherman paused. "You have a very fine husband. A mensch."

Christine nodded as she grabbed tissues. "Y- yes, he is. He gave us a happy life. I wish he never got sick. It's so unfair."

"I agree. But we should all do what we can so he's

comfortable and pain-free. That's the best we can do for him now."

Christine nodded through her tears. Of course, the doctor was right. Now was the time to comfort the family and not sit here consumed with her desolate thoughts.

Christine waited until she heard the familiar footsteps of her children and Daniel's family approaching the room. She would rather have reflected in silence at the hospital chapel than deal with the family, but that wasn't an option; the family needed her, and she had to admit that being with them would take away the loneliness she was already feeling.

I need to take every minute as it comes, she told herself. Every second was precious, albeit torturous, and she needed to cherish every moment with Daniel, even if it was his last.

She heard her mother-in-law's wailing even before she entered the room.

Christine tried to stand and give them a moment next to Daniel's bedside, but her feet felt like bricks. She touched her mother-in-law's arm, her other hand covering her grief-stricken expression. The other family members filed in, somber-faced.

When Judy's sobbing ceased, her mother-in-law turned to face her.

"He's still with us," Christine said, trying to compose herself to get the words out. "He's sleeping, and they're giving him a lot of painkillers so he'll be comfortable. We want to make his final moments as peaceful as possible."

"She's right, Judy," Harry, said, his face ashen. He was an average-sized, broad man, but there in his son's hospital room he appeared weak and diminished.

Judy said nothing for a moment, staring at the ground. She then slowly lifted her head and faced Christine. "You know, I didn't want Daniel to marry you."

Christine gave a start. *Duh!* she wanted to say.

"Judy, for heaven's sake, why bring that up now?" Harry barked at his wife.

Judy ignored him. "But I'm glad he did. His marriage gave him the happiest days of his life."

Christine was so startled she wanted her mother-in-law to repeat those words to make sure she wasn't imagining her saying them.

"Thank you for coming into his life," Judy said. Her tears began flowing again as she embraced Christine for the first time. Both women cried. Tim rubbed his mother's back while Trudy leaned on him, sobbing.

Out of the corner of her eye, Christine saw her parents entering the room. Their expressions made her heart ache.

"They called yesterday, Mom," Tim whispered to her. "I told them what's going on. I didn't realize they were coming here right away."

By this point, Trudy had rushed over to them and was crying in her grandfather's arms.

Her parents seemed smaller since Christine had last seen them. Her father's hair was greyer, and his hairline had receded further. Her mother, who once had smooth skin so translucent and hair so thick and wavy that people often mistook them for sisters, apparently had stopped coloring her hair and now wore it in a grey bun. Her face was lined with wrinkles.

She wore a big silver cross on her chest and dressed so modestly that she could have passed for a nun. Christine, released from her mother-in-law, stood upon seeing her parents for the first time in five years.

She approached them.

"You've been so brave, my child," her mother whispered. "I wish we and life had treated you more kindly."

Christine's voice shook at first but grew more confident as she raised her head high with poise and said, "I have a wonderful husband and two great kids, food to eat, and a roof over our heads – what more could I ask for? I've been blessed."

"You're right," her father answered, "and we're so proud of you." He embraced her.

Tears came rushing to her eyes like a deluge. She felt unsteady on her feet. In the darkest hour of her life, everyone was reassuring her she was not a failure, a disappointment, a screwup. Her in-laws, her children, and now her parents. She always had this reassurance from Daniel, her rock. He was the one who made her life worth living, but now while his life ebbed away, those closet to her were rallying around her, making her feel like she actually had made some *right* decisions in her life, giving her the courage to go on.

While enclosed in her father's sheltering arms, she was still unsure whether her decision not to tell Ryan about the twins had been the right one. Perhaps her pride at being betrayed when she saw him in the actress's arms blindsided her, but now he knew, and they would have to live with those consequences. Christine clutched her father even tighter and sobbed.

"Baby, baby, we're here for you. You don't have to face this alone," he whispered, his voice cracking.

Christine felt overwhelmed by so many emotions that she couldn't respond. Events had played out, and what would come of it would have to be.

"I'm fine, Dad," she said, as she released herself from his embrace. "I'm just so happy to see you and Mom." She bit her lip to prevent herself from blurting out, *finally.*

"Why don't you sit down and make yourself comfortable. We want to stay near Daniel."

She again felt like she was in a waking nightmare. Christine felt dizzy as her father and Tim helped her sit down.

"Do you need some water, Christine?" Heather was beside her, but her voice sounded like she was miles away.

"There, there, child." Her mother stood in front of her, massaging her cheek.

Christine shook her head. "This is terribly hard, but I'm going to make it through."

CHAPTER FORTY-THREE

BEVERLY HILLS

R yan had never experienced this emotion before: laughing and crying at the same time. He rushed to the airport and sat quietly on the plane while he felt tremendous relief that Ozzy was finally neutralized. Buddy called him to say that if Ozzy breathed another word about him, they would call the police and he would be arrested. Ryan resolved to put himself together as he drove to his parents' house. Despite the calm he felt, his heart ached when his thoughts turned to what Christine and the twins were going through. Yet he was determined to collect himself as he parked in his parents' driveway.

"Ryan, why've you been hiding? It's been forever since we've heard from you," his father said before Ryan had even walked through the door. Waiting in the hallway, Jerry said, "Son, tell me, tell me, please, what the hell's been going on?"

Before Ryan could even open his mouth to answer, his mother ran out of the kitchen and practically fell on him.

"Ryan! What's been going on? I fought with Dad for days

about calling the police! I've been worried sick about you! It's taken years off my life!"

"It's OK, it's OK, really. It's just been a hectic time," he said between breaths while his mother clung to him.

"Sara! Sara! Let him talk! I want to know what's the hell's been going on!"

His mother released him. Clearing his throat, Ryan stared straight into the eyes of first his mother and then his father. With a taut, solemn expression, he said, "It's been so hectic and stressful. I've been running around like a madman. But I have news for you."

His mother asked. "Is it good news?"

His parents were silent, holding their breaths.

"I- I think so, although it didn't exactly happen the way you would have wanted it to."

Sara's eyes lit up, and she clapped her hands. "Did you and Megan elope?"

"No, I haven't seen Megan for a while."

Sara's shoulders sagged sulkily. "If you didn't get married, I don't know how this could be such good news."

"Do you mean you decided to star in a film where they want you to go nude so you can win an Academy Award?" Ryan's father winked as he asked the question. "Son, we've already discussed this. It's your decision, but I won't see the movie if you're in your birthday suit."

"No, it has nothing to do with a film," Ryan answered, shaking his head and chuckling.

Silence.

"Well, what is it then? Can't you see you're keeping your mother waiting?"

Ryan closed his eyes, at a loss where to begin. "It's a long story. A long, long story, but the long and short of it is I just found out I'm the father of seventeen-year-old twins. A boy and a girl."

His parents stared back at him, speechless.

"You see, when I was a kid and just started making movies, I had a girlfriend."

"Who?"

"Her name was Christine Zarzycki. We saw each other for a while."

"You mean that sweet Catholic girl I wanted you to marry?" His mother looked at him with her eyes narrowed. "You never did say why you two broke up."

"We only met her a few times. She was a looker. As beautiful as those girls you've seen since," his father exclaimed.

"Yeah," Ryan said, rolling his eyes. "We broke up because of a... a misunderstanding. I didn't know it, but she was pregnant with my kids." Ryan closed his eyes and turned his back on them.

"You mean you slept with her? That strict Catholic girl?" Jerry stared at his son, scratching his head.

"W- well, it happened when we both got really drunk one night." Ryan coughed into his hand to dodge any further explanation.

"Son, do you mean to tell me you got a girl pregnant and you didn't know anything about it? Why didn't she tell you, for crying out loud?" His father looked at him sideways as if he heard a riddle he couldn't figure out.

Ryan put his hands in his pockets. "Like I said, Dad, it was a misunderstanding. I'll tell you about it at some other time. The news is that I'm a father."

"And she just told you about them?" Jerry asked.

Ryan shook his head. "That's another story I would rather leave for another time. Trust me."

No one spoke. Each one tried to speak, but no words came out.

Finally, Sara got out the words, "Pictures? Do you have pictures of them?"

Ryan nodded; he turned around and showed them the pictures Christine managed to send to his phone after their first meeting. When he looked up at his parents, their eyes were moist.

"Jerry." Sara slowly turned to her husband, her lips curling upward and her eyes sparkling in a way neither man had seen since Ryan became a movie star. "Do you know what that means?"

"Yeah! We're grandparents."

"And I have grandchildren!" she shouted. "I'm a grandmother! And I don't even care how!" She fell on Ryan once again but released him. "When are we going to meet them?"

"As soon as possible, Mom," Ryan said, his head a muddle of conflicting emotions once again. "They're in Boston with Christine. You see, Christine got married, and her husband adopted them." He paused, and his features turned downward as he said, "Her husband's real sick now. He's dying."

Sara and Jerry stared at each other until Sara finally said, "Oh, those poor children."

"They're going through a rough time right now, Sara," Jerry said. "We've got to give them space."

"Yeah, we have to tread very carefully now. I don't think we should descend upon them immediately," Sara agreed.

"We'll have to think this through," Jerry said. He gazed upward and shook his head as he said aloud, "I can't get over it!" He turned to his wife. "All this time we've been grandparents. Imagine."

Sara opened her mouth to speak but was interrupted when they heard footsteps approaching along the walkway to the front door. They froze when they saw who it was.

Sara put her hand to her chest. "Oh my," she gasped. "Megan called me this morning, and I told her you were coming here. She said she wanted to drop by."

When Ryan recovered from his shock, he faced his

parents and said, "Mom, Dad, I need to talk with her privately."

Sara and Jerry glanced at one another. "Of course," his mother said. She took Jerry's elbow. "Come, let's go upstairs. I am feeling so excited I need a rest to take this news in."

Jerry nodded, but before he joined his wife on the stairs, he told Ryan, "Son, I have complete confidence you'll do the right thing."

Ryan watched them both go up the stairs as he turned around in the same moment the doorbell rang.

CHAPTER FORTY-FOUR

R yan opened the door at once. "It's good to see you, Megan."

Megan smiled tightly as she entered the house.

"Come in and sit down." Ryan ushered her into the living room.

She sat down. "Ryan, I don't think—"

Ryan held his hand up. "I understand," he said. "I completely understand. I've been very distracted lately, and I haven't let you in. Megan, the truth is you're a wonderful, patient person, and you deserve better than I can give you. Circumstances have come up that have forced me to grow up and do some serious reflection. I can't commit right now, but I should have treated you better. You need someone who can. I own up to my shortcomings, and this breakup is all my fault, but I want you to know that I'm here for you as your friend and wish you only the best. That's really what you deserve."

Megan stared at him with her mouth agape. Her gaze

turned downward, and she hung her head. But then it appeared she had reflected on his words, for she faced him again with a soft smile forming on her lips. "I realized I'm not your first priority, but I can respect that you can admit you were not fully committed to our relationship. I wondered if it was something I did."

"Absolutely not. It was all me."

Megan stood. "I wish you all the best, including an Academy Award."

Ryan smiled and got up. They embraced.

"Thank you for being honest with me. I have to admit that, even though we're breaking up, you've made me feel good."

"If anyone in the media asks why we broke up, I'll say you dumped me."

Megan laughed. "Oh, you don't need to do that, but Ryan – you don't have to answer this if you don't want to – is there someone else?"

He was silent for a moment before saying, "Actually, there are two people, but let's save that for another time." When Megan looked questioningly at him, he replied, "I don't mean to be all mysterious, but to tell you the truth, I'm still sorting it out. So much is happening right now that I don't know where to start, but once it's all clear, I'll let you know, I promise. I owe you that."

CHAPTER FORTY-FIVE

Christine had needed solitude, so for a few moments she sat in the hospital chapel for some peace and faith. When she felt better, she was anxious to return to her husband's bedside. Christine walked through the waiting area where the family sat. Her mother had sunken eyes and a wooden expression. Her father, his face grey and appearing stoic, sat next to her mother, clasping her arm; he nodded when he saw Christine. Judy was weeping fresh tears as she clung to Heather, and Seth held up his father, who looked crushed and downtrodden. A trembling Trudy had her arm around Tim, whose face was tear-stained. Trudy hugged her mother while Tim covered his face to hide his weeping. Christine reached out to them and was surprised that Trudy turned out to be the stronger one at this bleak hour.

She knew every passing second was crucial – she wanted Daniel to be comfortable and pass away in peace. Christine made her way to his room and saw her husband's emaciated, rail-thin body ensconced in blankets. His eyes were shut, but he wore a small smile. Christine guessed he was relieved the heart monitor and all the tubes had been removed; he was finally released from the apparatus that had held him down for the last few hours. It would not be long now.

"Hey, baby." She touched his thin, weightless hand and tried to smile.

Daniel opened his eyes. It took him some effort to turn his head, but when he saw her, he flashed a big smile that reached his heavy, sunken eyes.

She sat on the bed by his side, trying to take up as little room as possible. "I've been blessed – we've been blessed – to have you in our lives."

"I feel the same – you and the twins gave me a happy and complete life." His eyes dimmed and his smile disappeared. "If only I could have made a fortune so all of you could be taken care of…"

Christine tried to speak, but Daniel spoke again.

"I wish I could contact Monti myself. I am so worried about you having enough."

Christine took his bony hand and reassured him. "Ryan has offered to help."

"But will you let him?"

"Y- yes," she said uneasily, for she wanted her husband to pass away in peace. She hoped she sounded convincing.

Christine patted his hand and tried to change the subject. "Besides, you've always done your very best to provide for the family. And my career has given me satisfaction and fulfillment. I always had a reason to wake up in the morning. I need somewhere to go every day. We've had a balanced, happy life together." She added, "And I couldn't have asked for a better husband."

To her relief, Daniel's smile returned. Then he said, "But will Monti really help…" Daniel began coughing so he couldn't continue.

"Don't worry! Ryan told me he'll help us."

When he stopped coughing, he stared into her eyes. "Is that true? Will he do that, Christine?"

"Yes, he will," Christine said with conviction, trying to hide her uncertainty. More than anything, she wanted Daniel to be at peace.

Daniel reached for her arm. "Then I can truly die a happy man. With no worries."

"No worries, I promise," she told him, biting her lip.

Just then, there was a knock at the door. The nurse poked her head in. "Mrs. Goldberg, can the rest of the family come in now?"

Christine turned to her husband. He nodded. Despite his weakened condition, there was a brightness in his expression. He was ready.

Tears flooded their cheeks and their faces were ashen as the family all entered together in silence. Daniel's parents, Seth, Heather, Tim, and Trudy reached out to him but had to hold themselves back from crushing him with their bodies.

"Everything's going to be all right now," Daniel told them.

His mother stiffened as she stared at him, but his father touched his shoulder and said, "You've always been the strongest of all of us. I'm proud of you, son." Harry's lips quivered as he tried to prevent himself from breaking down, and he leaned on Seth.

Everyone was choking back sobs for Daniel's sake. When Christine faced her husband, she saw his whole body trembling. He was struggling to breathe. It looked like he wanted to speak but couldn't.

"Daniel, Daniel, what is it? What is it, honey?" Christine asked urgently, getting everyone's attention in the process.

Everyone rushed over to the bed, half assembling to one side and the other half to the other. Everyone was sniffling as they tried to dry their eyes so they could have a clear view of him. His mother clasped his hand, his father placed his on Daniel's shoulder, and then everyone ended up touching him. Christine placed her hand on his cheek. The only noise was the occasional footsteps in the hallway as they held their breaths, waiting for Daniel to speak.

With great effort, Daniel turned to his parents and then directed his stare at his wife. "I adore Tim and Trudy, and they'll always be my precious children. They've been the joy of my life." He began coughing and couldn't say any more.

"Well, of course, Daniel. We adore them too. They'll always be our grandchildren. Always," his mother whispered, heaving and breaking into a fresh round of tears.

"They'll always be a part of our lives, son. Don't you worry." Harry's voice broke as he spoke. He caught Christine's eyes and nodded to her in confirmation.

Christine's heart melted when she saw Trudy put her head on Daniel's chest.

"We love you, Daddy," she said before collapsing in tears. Tim just stood frozen, his jaw trembling as he tried not to break down.

Christine reached out to her son. "It's OK, Tim. It's OK to cry. It doesn't make you any less of a man." As she spoke, Tim sank down on the very edge of the bed, sobbing and shaking his head. Daniel tried to lift his arm to touch him but couldn't.

"I love you, Dad," Tim whispered. "I always will. You will always be my one and only father."

"I'm leaving a happy man. My family will be taken care of. I…" His voice trailed off and his eyes fluttered closed as the breath left his body for the last time.

"Good-bye, Daniel. I love you." Christine kissed his forehead and then covered her face. She sobbed and was surprised that she still had fresh tears to shed; she felt like she could spend the rest of her life crying. She ignored the wails and screams in the room; she couldn't comfort anyone now, not even her own children.

"Here, sit down. This is an awful lot to take," a nurse said, touching her shoulder. Even though she was right beside Christine, her voice sounded like it was coming from a distance. Christine heard a chair propped up behind her, and someone eased her into it.

"Mom."

Christine opened her eyes and spotted Trudy's light blond hair in her blurry vision. She wrapped her arms around her daughter's neck, and they wept their loss together.

Christine heard Seth comforting her son in a choking voice. "Tim, if there's anything you need, anything at all, you know I'm here for you. Oh God! I can't believe this is happening! Why, why, God, did you take my brother and leave us here without him? He's too young to die!" Seth sank to the floor. Judy hugged Tim in an effort to shield him from witnessing his uncle's grief. Harry reached out to his surviving son but was too immersed in his own grief to do or say anything more. Heather knelt down beside her husband, rubbing his back and whispering in his ear.

Christine felt a strong hand on her shoulder. It was her father as he held up her mother.

"It will be all right, Christine darling. You've been a very brave girl," he told her. He was sniffling, and she heard her mother break down.

"We've been so stubborn!" Fran said. "We haven't been a part of your life for years, and for what? What did we accomplish?"

"Fran, Fran, calm down." Her husband put his arm around his wife. "What's done is done. The only thing we can do now is to move forward." With that, his wife sank into his arms, and he had to let go of Christine.

Before she could react, she found Judy approaching her with determined eyes.

"You've been a wonderful daughter-in-law, beyond reproach. And I should have said this to you a long time ago, especially in Daniel's presence." She hesitated, holding back tears. "Christine, I love you! We all love you."

By this point, Christine felt totally depleted: all of her emotions were spent. She felt she was falling over, and Trudy needed to hold her up. Her throat began contracting when she tried to speak. She imagined she must look pale and bloodless. She allowed herself to be led away by her parents while Seth and Heather put their arms around the twins.

Christine's mind turned numb as they left the room. She was grateful for her parents' support as they held her arms, for she didn't have the strength to walk by herself.

CHAPTER FORTY-SIX

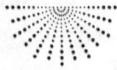

IN THE AIR FROM LOS ANGELES TO BOSTON

"Ryan, tell me again what they're like." His mother squeezed his arm in delight.

His parents were sitting across from him in first class on the plane. The flight attendants were fawning over them. While his parents were flattered, Ryan was annoyed. It took all his self-control not to tell them to get lost and to tell his mother to leave him alone. He felt anxious and wanted to stay in his own thoughts.

"Honey, can't you see he needs some time to himself? This is a tremendous shock and life change for him. The kids' adoptive father is dying, and when we get over there, things are gonna be rough."

"I'm aware of that!" She turned to her husband. "I feel very bad about that, I do. Those poor children." She shook her head and raised her eyes to him. "They're going to need us now more than ever."

"But we gotta approach this delicately. We can't over-whelm them with love and affection while they're grieving."

"Of course, I know that!" she said. "I just can't contain myself. I feel like I'm in a dream, and I'm going to wake up any second and find out I am not a grandma anymore." Her voice choked.

"Don't worry. You're not in a dream. We're in this plane 'cause we want to see our grandchildren. I wouldn't be doing this if this wasn't real. And my head is aching as usual when I fly."

"Jerry, get one of the stewardesses to give you some aspirins."

Ryan was grateful for his father's practical perceptiveness. He closed his eyes and put his head back. He felt nauseated, and his stomach was tied in knots. He actually feared he was going to have a heart attack. *That's all the kids need. Losing two fathers at once.* His eyes shot open as he realized he cared more about his children than he did about himself. It was a new feeling he had never experienced before, but somehow it felt appropriate, natural.

He was a father.

Despite his inner turmoil and physical pain, his eyes brightened, and he turned to stare out the window. He loved flying above the clouds. It made him feel anything was possible. Like he would be a father and finally give his parents grandchildren. He had never thought that was going to happen. He would've even bet his whole fortune on it. The idea put an unexpected smile on his face. He felt satisfied and fulfilled. Ecstatic. He had never experienced this before, not even after receiving Academy Award nominations.

Life is so strange. I'll never figure it out.

He spied his mother opening her mouth to speak to him, but he shut his eyes before she had the chance.

* * *

IDELLE KURSMAN

As soon as they got off the plane, Ryan and his parents found the town car waiting for them. The pain in the pit of his stomach sharpened as he took out his cell phone to call Christine to arrange the most nerve-wracking meeting of his life.

"Ryan, what's wrong? You almost dropped your phone," his mother said, sitting next to him in the back seat.

Her husband placed his hand over hers, and when she turned to him, he shushed her, making her realize the utter importance of this call.

The phone rang repeatedly. Ryan was about to hang up when he recognized his son's voice on the phone. His stomach lurched, and he found unexpected tears in his eyes.

"Tim," he said, "may I speak to your mother, please?"

Ryan heard his son's choking sobs as he said, "She's not here… my father passed away yesterday." He could hear his son breaking down over the phone.

"I'm so sorry." Ryan bit his lip, suppressing the unexpected urge to add "son." "This is probably the worst time," he stammered, "but I am in a car in Boston coming to see your mother. If this isn't a good time, I'll call later."

Tim continued weeping. In between sobs, he said, "Nothing matters anymore."

Ryan sat up. "Tim, where are you? Where's your mother?"

"She's at the funeral home making the arrangements."

"Is Trudy there with you?"

"She's here, but she's too upset to talk."

Ryan had to think. "Listen, Tim. I'm going to check into a hotel in Boston. I don't want to intrude on the family now. Can you take down my number in case you need me?"

"I don't know," he said, hesitating. There was silence. "Wait, Trudy, give me a pen and paper. What is it?"

Ryan recited it. "Tim, again, if any of you need anything, I'll have the phone near me at all times."

"OK." Tim hung up.

When Ryan hung up, he bowed his head, feeling useless and no better than an intrusion.

His father patted his arm. "You did good, son," he said. "I'm proud of you."

"Yes, you said all the right things. I can't believe how prepared you are to be a father. It's as if you've been doing this for years," Sara said.

His parents' support buoyed his spirits. They'd always said they were proud of him, but this time it was the most heartfelt he had ever heard them speak. It was as if they had given him a quick shot of hope to carry on.

He faced his parents with solemn eyes and said, "I've had training from the best."

His mother clutched his chin and gave him a kiss.

CHAPTER FORTY-SEVEN

BOSTON

Her head still groggy, Christine woke up and found herself in her own bedroom. When she'd returned from the funeral home, Christine took a sedative and went straight to bed. Her vision soon adjusted to see her children seated on chairs near her bed. Both looked like they needed sleep, and their eyes were red and sore from crying. They looked gaunt and weary, and Christine was about to tell them to have something to eat when she realized their new reality: Daniel was gone.

She sank her head back into the pillow and put her arm over her head.

"Mom, are you up? Are you OK?" Tim asked, getting ready to leave his chair.

She nodded. As shattered as she was, she had to think of her kids.

"How long have I slept?" she asked.

"About three hours," Trudy replied.

310

Christine lifted her arm and reluctantly faced them. "And have you two been sitting here the whole time?"

"No," said Trudy. "We slept a little, but we were mostly talking… and crying."

Christine nodded. "I understand. How are Grandma, Grandpa, and Uncle Seth holding up?"

"Uncle Seth drove them home. Uncle Seth mentioned that Jewish people bury relatives right away, so he said he's going to call their rabbi about funeral arrangements."

"Well, I'll have to let him know I already started that," Christine answered in a determined voice. "I may not understand all the Jewish burial rituals, but he was my husband."

"Relax, Mom," Tim said. "He just said he needed to get the ball rolling. He's going to consult you on all the major decisions about the burial."

A wave of nausea descended on Christine. Funeral arrangements weren't the only thing she had to take care of. There were hospital bills, insurance, funeral costs…

Would Ryan help?

No! I don't want to accept his charity. He had played no part in their lives until now.

Would he offer? Would he now want to be a part of their lives?

I bet he'll just return to his luxurious lifestyle, filled with women, parties, and travel. He'll soon forget all about us, she thought with bitterness.

As if reading her thoughts, Tim said, "Ryan Monti is in Boston, Mom."

The news jolted her. She didn't dare face her children when she said, "I suppose he has business here."

"Mom, he knows Dad died. He's here to help."

Tim's words made her feel awash in relief, but she eschewed those feelings of being rescued.

I will not accept his charity except for the children's needs. I'll take care of the children myself, she vowed. *I am no longer that twenty-year-old who couldn't do anything for herself.*

Just then, their doorbell rang.

Tim went downstairs. She overheard him talking with someone and then two sets of feet coming up the stairs. "My mom just woke up, Dr. Sherman."

Dr. Sherman came in, looking drained and solemn. He took Christine's hand. "I am so sorry."

She clasped his. "You did everything you could, and we're grateful."

"He fought a valiant battle. He had the worst form, and when it got bad, he lasted longer than we anticipated," the doctor whispered. Dr. Sherman put a hand on her shoulder. He turned to the twins. "How are the two of you holding up?"

"Fine," Trudy said in a meek, little-girl voice.

"Is there anything I can do?" he asked them.

Solemn-faced and cloudy-eyed, Tim shook his head.

"Well, let me know if there's anything. I'm sure you already know this, but your father was a good man. They don't come much better than him."

Trudy attempted to smile but gave up. She nodded her head in acknowledgement.

Dr. Sherman didn't know what to do with his hands and looked around, starting to speak but not knowing what to say.

"We'll be all right." Christine sat up and reached out to the doctor. "I'll let you know when we're having the funeral."

"Please do. And the shivah information." He stared at Christine. She nodded, and then he approached the twins, shaking Tim's and Trudy's hands. "All of you, take care. Look after your mother."

"Will do," Tim said, nodding and staring down.

When the doctor left, Christine moved her stiff limbs out

of bed. More than anything, she wanted to stay lying under the covers and fall back asleep into oblivion. But she swung her legs out of the bed, and her children rushed over to help her stand up. Christine felt like a frail old woman, but she accepted their help.

She dreaded looking in the bathroom mirror, afraid of what she was going to see. Her hair was tangled and matted, her eyes were red, and her face was pale and drawn.

I've got to put on some makeup or I'm going to scare people.

Christine, she immediately chided herself, *Daniel just died. Is this a time to worry about your looks?*

Better that than dwell on losing Daniel, she answered herself.

She splashed cold water on her face and attempted to push down her blond hair but gave up. It was a losing proposition.

As she left the bathroom and joined Tim and Trudy, Christine recalled Jewish rituals of mourning she had discussed with the director of the funeral home. Covering mirrors, sitting on a low seat, and shivah, which involved friends and family visiting and bringing over food. She was already making a mental count of whether she had enough chairs for guests.

"You OK, Mom?" Tim asked, breaking into her thoughts.

"Yes. I'm better. You don't have to help me," she told her kids when each one was reaching over to steady her.

She glanced up at her children. Both looked beside themselves.

What were they going to do?

Christine recalled the drive home from the hospital yesterday. Trudy did the driving. Christine marveled at her daughter's ability to cope. Tim, on the other hand, struggled not to break down again. Christine sat in the back seat and kept telling herself she had to take one second at a time. Literally, only one second. Heather had called and invited them to stay overnight at her house. Seth was sleeping at his parents'. When they declined, Heather even offered to sleep at their house with her kids. Everyone couldn't help chuckling at that offer.

There was a contemplative silence on the ride home – they were each lost in their own thoughts.

Before they opened the front door, Tim reached for the mail. Upon entering the house, he shoved a letter at Trudy, and they both ripped open envelopes embossed with Boston College's golden label. They both stared at each other open mouthed. They exchanged letters. Trudy let out a little laugh and then cried.

"Wh- what is it?" Christine asked.

"We both got into BC," a stony-faced Tim told her.

He turned around so his mother and sister couldn't see his expression.

CHAPTER FORTY-EIGHT

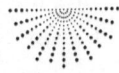

WEST ROXBURY, MASSACHUSETTS

Her whole body was rigid as Christine sat in the front row at the funeral home, a few feet from the casket. The twins, Daniel's parents, Seth, and Heather wept, but she only shed silent tears. She still nursed a small hope that this was only a nightmare; she would wake up, and Daniel would be lying right beside her – getting ready for another day. Her father planted his solid, comforting hand on her shoulder, and she heard her mother blowing her nose behind her. The rabbi was speaking about Daniel's life and virtues while the closed casket lay before the podium.

Before the funeral, the caretaker had asked Christine if she wanted to view the body, but she declined. She wanted to remember him as very much alive and vital, there for her and the children. Christine wished she could blot out the memory of his weak, gaunt body clinging to the last vestiges of life. She cherished his memory and their happy times together; she wished she could open the wooden casket and welcome him back into their lives.

Neither she nor the twins mentioned Ryan. She had not expected him to attend the funeral. Indeed, it would have been awkward for him to show up – she couldn't even begin to explain his presence there. Christine tried to shut him out of her mind. All she thought about was her happy marriage after all the stress, struggle, and uncertainty in her life. Meeting Daniel had been nothing short of a miracle after finding herself alone with twin babies. Sure, there were plenty of challenges, but she was able to meet them with Daniel by her side. After every setback, they always lifted each other up and smiled in the end. Until now.

Seth struggled to keep himself composed as he read a tribute to his brother. She felt Tim taking her arm and helping her stand up as the rabbi recited the mourner's kaddish, the traditional Jewish prayer for the departed. Daniel's mother cried softly into her tissue, and Seth took her in his arms. Daniel's father did not even turn toward his wife; he was too engrossed in his own pain. Out of the corner of her eye, she saw many of Daniel's friends and relatives crying. The funeral director began handing out dozens of tissue boxes.

Christine reflected that even though Daniel had a lot of hard luck in his life, he was beloved and cherished by family and friends.

Then Tim, Seth, and some of Daniel's male relatives and friends lifted the coffin, and the rest of the family escorted the casket out of the chapel. She felt the eyes of the attendees watching her rigid, tear-stained face as she followed the casket before they followed her out. When they opened the doors, the weather looked dark and cloudy as if the heavens were also mourning Daniel's passing. Trudy and her mother walked beside her.

By the time they arrived at the cemetery, the sky was releasing light rain.

Tim and Trudy kept their heads bowed, and one glance informed the other mourners that it would be better not to approach them. Christine held her head up. She had to be the one to accept peoples' condolences. She knew there would be plenty of days when she could be as uncommunicative as she would like, but today she had to give people the opportunity to reach out.

"Oh, Daniel! Daniel! Why did you have to go?" his mother wailed. Her husband and Seth reached for her, but their pained expressions revealed they were feeling the same. Christine's father put his hands on the twins' shoulders, and the mourners kept staring at the ground to avert their faces from the rain as they listened to the rabbi's explanation of why it was considered a mitzvah, a commandment, for people to take turns with the shovel and pile a mound of dirt on top of the grave. Christine kept rubbing her palms. Her hand went over her wedding ring, which she was still unable to relinquish, as if it would keep the reality of Daniel's passing at bay for as long as possible. Her mother leaned on her. She wished she could tell her mother that she needed her space. As Christine eyed her mother, she came to realize her mother was trying to offer support and affection in an effort to make up for the years of distance over Christine's marriage. Still, she wished her mother would lean on someone else. She turned and signaled her father; fortunately, he understood and eased her mother into his arms.

Mourners took turns now with the shovel as they dug into the earth and placed piles of dirt on the casket.

As each mound of dirt covered the box, the reality of losing her husband sank in further. Why did life have to take away loved ones so cruelly? How could she go on without Daniel by her side? One glance at the twins reminded her that she would have to find a way, if not for her own sake, then for theirs. She closed her eyes, strengthening her resolve that she would not only go on but thrive. Christine and the children would thrive in order to honor Daniel's memory. She was determined to make him proud and continue his legacy as a loving, caring parent.

Christine felt her legs give way as she contemplated the task she set before herself.

"Christine! Christine!" her father whispered. He rushed over, but fortunately, Heather came over to help her stand.

"It's OK. I've got you," Heather whispered in her ear in a quaking voice. "You're going to get through this."

Christine nodded her thanks while willing herself to stay strong and not fall apart.

By now, mourners had piled up enough dirt to bury the casket.

"Daniel! Don't go! Don't leave us, please!" his mother pleaded at the now unseen coffin.

The rabbi looked around, at a loss over what to do. His words of comfort and the unknowable divine plan could not console Daniel's mother. He leaned toward Mrs. Goldberg and said, "He is at peace now. His soul is going up to heaven now that he has left his physical body. He is no longer in any pain."

"But now all I feel is pain! I'll never know peace again." She lifted her face toward heaven. "God, you should've taken me instead! Take me instead of my son!" she cried and fell on her knees near the grave.

Daniel's father buried his face in his hands; Seth, with his face covered in tears and his body shaking, tried to lift his mother, but he could only clutch her shoulder. Thankfully, other people comforted her until she was ready to rise.

"Uncle Daniel didn't want to leave us, Grandma," Rachel said when her grandmother finally rose and stopped to catch her breath. "He'll always be here with us."

Christine found it difficult to breathe. She felt like she was choking and bent down to get air in her lungs. She feared she would get sick in front of everyone. The last thing she wanted to do at her husband's funeral was get sick and embarrass herself and the family.

Rumbling filled the air and dark clouds gathered as if hurrying to end this heartbreaking scene as quickly as possible. Christine and the rabbi glanced above in amazement, their desire for a speedy conclusion answered.

"Mom! Mom! We've got to leave. There's going to be a lightning storm," Seth pleaded with his mother, encouraging her to break from her despair and leave the grounds.

"If I get sick and die, it'll be a blessing! I'll be with Daniel again!"

"Don't do that, Grandma! We can't lose both of you!" little Charlie wailed.

Heather rushed over. "Grandma won't do that! She knows we can't handle any more sorrow."

"We need you, Grandma." Trudy reached out and clasped her hand. Judy's eyes were still a pool of tears and her face was ravaged with grief, but she took Trudy's hand, and in that moment, her eyes conveyed everything words couldn't: yes, she would go on for the sake of her family. Trudy and Tim were still her grandchildren. They placed an arm behind each other's backs as they slowly made their way out the cemetery grounds as more rumblings pierced the air.

"G- good-bye, son. For now," Harry said to the grave. Tim and Seth's children held on to him as they left.

"So long for now, brother. I love you," Seth declared to the temporary plaque on the burial site before departing.

Seth and Heather held each other, and Christine walked between her parents. For a moment she stopped, looked back at the grave, and said, "Bye, Daniel. I'll always love you."

Turning to her parents, she held her head high as she declared, "He was the best thing that ever happened to me."

"We know," her father said.

Her shoulders shook, and she burst into tears again.

CHAPTER FORTY-NINE

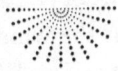

It would soon be sunset. The first day of shivah was drawing to a close. The last guest had left, and family members couldn't wait to go home and collapse into their beds.

Christine insisted they sit shivah in her Brighton house even though Daniel's parents and brother offered their own homes. She ripped a garment, sat on a low chair, and covered all the mirrors, as prescribed by Jewish law. Platters of food were heaped onto the kitchen and dining room tables. Family and friends kept bringing over food and asking if they needed anything else. Christine mused they had meals for at least two weeks. Dr. Sherman visited and left a catered meal. The retired neighbor came over, carrying the most beautiful tulips. Christine couldn't help smiling when she saw him walk in wearing his big, floppy straw hat. He was discreet enough not to give her his usual once-over with lovey-dovey eyes and wink. Flowers arrangements adorned

IDELLE KURSMAN

so many walls that Christine couldn't help worrying if Tim's allergies would act up.

Daniel's father rose. "Let's go, Judy." His face remained drawn, and he no longer had any hint of humor in his expression. Christine noticed his skin sagged more and his gait had slowed down.

Judy didn't stir – she looked like she was in another world. Upon glancing out the window, Harry's head jerked back and he turned to the others. "Who is that man standing in front of the house?" His eyes narrowed in further examination as he remarked, "Why does he look so familiar?"

Tim was jolted out of his trance and hurried to the window. His face held no emotion as he turned to his mother and said, "It's him."

"Who, Tim? Who is it?" Heather asked, and when her nephew didn't answer, she approached the window herself. "My God!" She jumped back.

"What? What's going on, Heather?" Seth got up, but not before Rachel rushed to the window. "My God!" she also said. "It's Ryan Monti! He's gorgeous!" Upon surveying the room, she blushed, shrugged her shoulders, and said, "All the girls love him. I wonder what he's doing here."

Christine's parents sat there, still and speechless. They had only tonight begun talking with Daniel's family in short, awkward conversations, but their expressions told the story: it was apparent they knew something the others didn't.

"Why would a famous Hollywood actor be over here?" Harry asked as he turned to them. "Did he know Daniel?" He attempted a weak chuckle.

Christine, Tim, and Trudy all looked at each other. Finally, Christine said, "It's a long story, but yes, Ryan and Daniel knew of each other. Distantly, of course."

Everyone stared at her, waiting for further explanation.

322

Finally, Seth cleared his throat and asked, "How did they know each other, Christine?"

Christine took a deep breath. "This is a tough subject to bring up, but you need to know that Ryan and I dated when we were kids. Even though it seemed like a mistake back then, it really wasn't."

Everyone stared at her, leaning their heads forward, nodding for her to continue.

"B- but it wasn't a mistake after all." She turned toward her kids. "What happened was the most wonderful thing that ever happened to me. They're my pride and joy, and they're the ones that connected Daniel to Ryan."

Christine's mother put her hand over her eyes, and tears ran down her cheeks. Her father's eyes were swimming with tears.

Without saying another word, Christine opened the front door and stepped out. Before leaving the room, she glanced back and saw Daniel's family turning their heads from her to each other.

Before she walked toward Ryan, she turned to her parents. Her father's grave face gave away a hint of a smile. He shrugged and said, "If there's one thing I've learned in my old age, it's that life isn't black and white. Sometimes the people you think are horrible can surprise you and are actually all right."

Her mother took her hand away from her face and did something her husband and daughter hadn't seen her do in years.

She laughed.

Feeling energized, Christine was ready to meet Ryan in front of her home.

CHAPTER FIFTY

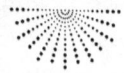

R yan paced and kept looking around the street. How he wished Christine would have answered her phone. He had lost count of the number of times he'd tried to reach her. As he eyed their front door, his shoulders tilted up, as if ready to take on the challenge of approaching the house, and then he turned away, the prospect far too daunting. He kept putting one foot toward the door but then lost his nerve and backed away. He carried flowers and was dressed in a dark formal suit, a sign of respect upon entering a mourner's home. Ryan was tempted to return to the car and drive around the block to revive his courage when Christine opened the front door. She wore a black dress with a torn white sweater. He then recalled from visiting his Jewish friends after a funeral that mourners wore a torn garment at the shivah sitting.

Christine had tired, haggard eyes and pale skin. She had lost too much weight, and she covered her trembling hands in an effort for him not to notice as she approached. He did, however, detect her signature scent: musk.

She must have put it on through habit, he thought. But he had the pleasure of taking in his favorite scent.

Even though she was clearly distressed, Ryan thought she still looked beautiful, as captivating as when he first came across her twenty years ago. She tried to appear strong, but he wished he could just take her in his arms and tell her everything was going to be all right.

But they were not the same people they were eighteen years ago. He took a deep breath and prayed his parents would adhere to his strict instructions of staying in the car in front of the house. He looked over at them. Their faces were tight and anguished as they realized, again, the family had experienced an unspeakable loss.

When Christine reached him, she moved her mouth but no words came out. He grasped her hand and said, "I'm so sorry, Christine. I really am."

She stared at the pavement and nodded.

"Whatever you and the twins need, I'll be here for you."

Tears welled up in her eyes. "There's a lot I have to do, a lot of adjustments that have to be made…"

"I'll do whatever I can to help."

She shook her head, still staring at the ground. "I've got to handle this by myself. I never told you about the kids, and I'm not asking to be rescued. I've got to figure things out on my own, but I know I can." There was a brief hint of a smile on her face that soon vanished. "I'm an older and a more confident person now."

"Jesus, Christine! We're not just talking about you here." Ryan stared at the sky, clearly exasperated. "We have the kids to think about."

Now Christine covered her face and sobbed.

Ryan attempted to console her. He touched her arm and

said, "Christine. Christine? Can you hear me? Let me know you're listening."

She nodded.

"Listen, I understand why you never told me about the twins. You were right, I wouldn't have wanted them because I was in no way, shape, or form ready to have kids back then." He paused and then said, "I am not quite sure if I'm ready now, but they're here, and you know what?"

Christine rubbed her eyes. "What?"

"You have to look at me before I tell you."

She reluctantly stared into his eyes, still sniffling.

"I'm glad they're here. You've done a great job raising them. I know I had nothing to do with it."

Christine hugged herself, unwilling to smile or acknowledge his praise. She whispered, "Daniel was a very devoted father too."

"I know that. I'll always be indebted to him. You got yourself a good man, Christine."

"You mean I did." Her tears came trailing down again. She breathed and put her fist to her mouth but was unable to stem the tears.

"I know that, but I'm going to help out now. They're almost grown, but I still can do something." Again he paused. "Where will they be in the fall?"

Christine shrugged her shoulders and hugged herself again. "They'll probably be working."

Ryan's forehead creased. "They had no plans to go to college?"

"They did," she said, shifting her eyes everywhere, refusing to steady them on his face. "But we have to use that money to pay for medical bills and to stay in this house as long as we're able."

"Christine. Christine, look at me." When she finally rested

her gaze on him, he said, "You're staying in this house. The kids are going to the college of their choice."

"Ryan, please…" she begged, shaking her head.

"Listen to me," he said. "You're staying in this house, and our kids are going to the college of their choice. Don't deny me the chance to provide for my own children."

"OK," she conceded. "If you want to pay for their college, we can work out a program where they can pay you back. I am the one responsible for maintaining the payments on this house."

"Where do they want to go to college?"

"Boston College."

"How far away is that?"

"Fifteen minutes."

"That's all?"

She nodded.

"So I'll help you pay for the house. It'll be good for the kids if you live nearby."

"And I'll pay you back whatever money you give me for the house."

Ryan bowed his head and then shook it. "Fine, but I'm paying for their college."

A small smile crept onto Christine's face as she stared into his. "We'll work something out. They don't have to know everything." She shrugged again. "The twins have been applying for scholarships like crazy. Something's bound to work out to decrease their loan."

"Christine, please! Save the scholarship money for kids who really need it. They're not going to!"

Realizing he was carrying flowers, Ryan was about to hand them to her when he spotted Tim and Trudy standing behind the front door. They didn't seem to know where to fix their gaze or what to do with their hands. When they saw him staring at them, Trudy stepped back, looking as if she were ready to flee back into the house.

"Let me offer my condolences to the children," he said. Christine nodded.

He handed her the flowers, but when he approached them, he was at a loss for words. He did not know whether to shake their hands or hug them, so he did neither. "I am sorry for your loss. I- I wish I could have met him. I am so glad you had a wonderful father to bring you up, but" – he looked down, searching for the right words – "I wish I could have met you a lot sooner. Been in your lives, watched you grow up. But since we found out about each other now, there is nothing I want more than to be a part of your lives. On your terms, of course."

Seeing their tear-stained faces, he knew they didn't know what to say. Finally Tim replied, "It's going to be kind of awkward at first..." He glanced at his sister and added, "We'll need some time."

"I understand completely," Ryan told them. "I'll give you your space. I know it will take time for you to adjust to having me in your lives..."

"And having us in your life." Trudy gave a mirthless chuckle.

"But I'll be here for you."

Tears ran down Trudy's face, and Tim looked like he was trying not to cry.

Trudy hugged herself, just as Christine did when she grew tense. "What do you want us to call you?"

"Call me Ryan," he said. "I promise I'll do my best for you, but I realize I'll never take the place of the man who raised you." In a halting voice, he added, "Not that I ever should. The man you just lost is the only one who should have the honor of the title 'dad.' But from now on, I'd love nothing better than to have you two in my life."

"OK," Tim said and looked to his sister for agreement. When she nodded, he said, "I think we can agree to those terms. It'll be weird at first. We've got a lot of catching up to do, but we'll try."

Ryan smiled. "That's all I ask."

* * *

Christine held her breath as she observed their encounter. Upon hearing a car door open, she turned. Although they wore solemn expressions, their eyes were shining and filled with hope and yearning. Ryan's parents emerged from the car. Wobbling a little as they approached her, Sara said, "I'm so sorry for your loss, Christine." She took her hand and held it. "I wish we were meeting under happier circumstances. I know your husband was a wonderful man."

"He adopted the twins and helped raise them," Christine told her.

Sara gave Christine's hand a little squeeze. "He was special."

"He was," Christine whispered. She smiled as she fought fresh tears.

Jerry put his hand on Christine's shoulder. "Let me add my sincerest condolences, dear. Your husband's parents are in there?"

She nodded.

"We don't want to interfere with your mourning, but would it be all right if we meet the children briefly? Or would another day be better?"

Christine couldn't help noticing their eyes staring longingly at the twins. They and Ryan were watching them, waiting. Christine took Sara's arm and brought her and Jerry over to meet them.

"This is my daughter, Trudy, and my son, Tim." Christine

rubbed her neck as she made the introductions. "And these are Ryan's parents."

"I'm sorry," Sara said quickly as if she didn't trust herself to say more.

"So sorry for your loss," Jerry said. He wavered a bit with his hand before extending it.

Tim stared as if he were inspecting it but soon reached out his own hand and shook his newly discovered grandfather's. Glancing at her brother, Trudy held out her hand. Christine noticed the older couples' eyes were gleaming as they took in the children. Sara embraced both twins at once, closing her eyes as she took them in. When it was Jerry's turn, he clutched them as if he were afraid to ever let go. When they finally separated, Jerry was rubbing away tears.

He turned to his wife. "Sara, this is a lot for them to take in. We should give them time and come back in a few days."

Sara slowly tore herself away, and she, her husband, and Ryan stepped back, returning in the direction of their car, when Trudy said, "Why don't you come in and meet the family?"

"Would that be all right?" Ryan turned to Christine.

"Of course," Christine said. As she looked toward the house, she saw the entire family staring out the window with questioning expressions on their faces. "Please come in."

A chill went through Christine as she saw her parents opening the front door. She closed her eyes and held her breath.

"Ryan," said her father, extending his hand. "It's good to see you again."

Her mother had the widest smile Christine had ever seen since the twins were born. All bad feelings vanished like a chipmunk disappearing into a hole.

Daniel's family stayed back and observed. Christine knew she would have to deal with this as delicately as possible.

Trudy put her arm around Judy's shoulder and said, "Grandma, Grandpa, Uncle Seth, and Aunt Heather, we want you to meet some new members of the family."

Ryan walked over to Daniel's parents and Seth and Heather. "Please accept my sincere condolences for your loss," he said with utmost seriousness. He offered his hand and each one shook it.

"Unfortunately, Daniel is not here for me to thank him personally, but I am forever indebted to him for bringing up and taking care of the children," Ryan continued, keeping his hands behind his back as if he didn't know what to do with them. "I'll never be able to fill his shoes or take his place for Tim and Trudy. We," he said, eyeing his parents, "just want to be a part of their lives. You'll always be their grandparents. You've earned that a thousandfold."

Jerry and Sara introduced themselves, shaking hands with the members of Daniel's family while keeping at a comfortable distance.

Everyone waited for Judy to speak. When she finally did, she glanced at Tim and Trudy and said, "We're willing to share them. It's going to be a little awkward at first, but they're yours too."

Harry added, "That's what we want. And it's what Daniel would have wanted."

Trudy walked over to her grandmother and put her arm around her. "Grandma, what should we call them?"

"How about the third set of grandparents?" Ryan's father smiled.

"Oy vey," Harry exclaimed. But he was smiling.

At that moment, Christine knew there would be an abundance of challenges ahead, but she was confident everything would eventually work out. Because they were doing what Daniel would have wanted.

ACKNOWLEDGMENTS

First of all, I want to thank my husband, Michael, and my sons, Benjamin and Kaleb, for being so supportive while I wrote this novel.

There were plenty of ups and downs while writing this book. Fortunately, my editors, Kristen Tate and Alida Winterheimer, were incredibly helpful. Kristen's guidance strengthened my manuscript, and even though I had to spend countless hours editing, it was well worth it. Alida initially pointed out the weaknesses in my characters and plot, and although I did not appreciate the criticism at the time, she was spot-on correct.

Of course, I could not end my acknowledgments without mentioning my parents, Stanley and Arlene Kaplan. They always imparted to me and my sisters, Melissa and Hillary, that family comes first. My main characters' outlook continually emphasizing this point came from my parents' values.

ENJOYED THIS BOOK? LEAVE A REVIEW!

Positive reviews make a big difference in the life of a self-published author. Will you please take a moment to leave a review on your platform of choice? Now matter where the review resides, they truly help authors like me gain more readers.

Thank you for your kindness!
—Idelle Kursman